She breathed in one of her favorite scent combinations, garlic and butter.

Dinner prep was well underway. Despite having eaten the sandwich, she was hungry, and eager to feast on whatever it was that Nicola was back there preparing. Her proximity was in the air.

“Table for one?” A voice came from behind her.

Her heart in her throat, Rosie swirled around, coming face to face with those same deep eyes that had locked with hers while she sat perched at the coat check at Persimmon years ago.

Nicola’s expression sparked with remembrance and something else. Surprise, maybe. But there was something more. It was the look of holding your breath for as long as you could and finally taking in a gasp of air.

Nicola remembered her.

Dear Reader,

Welcome back to Sunset County—where bucolic countryside meets new beginnings, and a parcel of the Walker family's land has blossomed into a gorgeous four-season retreat. At the heart of this transformation is the Inn at Sugar Maple Farms, home to a celebrated restaurant led by none other than celebrity chef Nicola Kim.

Nicola didn't just come here for a fresh start. She's carrying the weight of the past—grieving the loss of her mentor and determined to help his son succeed, even if it means stepping away from the spotlight.

For journalist Rosie Franklin-Smith, the inn is her last shot at saving her struggling magazine. But when the subject of her big story turns out to be the woman she once shared an unforgettable night with, things get complicated. Nicola isn't interested in interviews—or in revisiting the past—but the spark between them proves impossible to ignore.

This story is a feast for the senses—full of flavor, emotion and second chances. I absolutely loved writing about food, love and the healing power of a beautiful natural setting, and I hope you're transported by the beauty of the inn and its dining space.

As always, I love connecting with readers! You can find me online at elledouglas.com or on Instagram @elledouglaswriter.

Warmest wishes,

Elle Douglas

SERVING UP A SECOND CHANCE

ELLE DOUGLAS

Recycling programs for this product may not exist in your area.

ISBN-13: 978-1-335-18042-1

Serving Up a Second Chance

For questions and comments about the quality of this book, please contact us at CustomerService@Harlequin.com.

Harlequin Enterprises ULC
22 Adelaide St. West, 41st Floor
Toronto, Ontario M5H 4E3, Canada
www.Harlequin.com

HarperCollins Publishers
Macken House, 39/40 Mayor Street Upper,
Dublin 1, D01 C9W8, Ireland
www.HarperCollins.com

Printed in Lithuania

Elle Douglas is a lover of ’90s alternative music, a wannabe chef specializing in comfort food, and a sometimes reluctant but usually dedicated gym-goer who lives in Toronto with her wife and their cat, Lucy (or Lucifer, depending on the day). Between writing romance novels and working as a high school guidance counselor, Elle works exclusively in helping others find their happily-ever-afters. Visit her at elledouglas.com.

Books by Elle Douglas

Harlequin Special Edition

The Vet’s Shelter Surprise

Sugar Maple Farms

Serving Up a Second Chance
Autumn Nights, Holiday Lights
Her Fairy-Tale Farmer

Montana Mavericks: Behind Closed Doors

Snowed in with the Maverick

Visit the Author Profile page at Harlequin.com.

For Kaili Glennon, the ultimate savorist.

Chapter One

Rosie Franklin-Smith spotted the painted sign at the side of the country road alerting her that she was approaching the turnoff: The Inn at Sugar Maple Farms. Her nerves suddenly ratcheted up to a ten, and without thinking, she pulled her Toyota over onto the gravel shoulder and killed the engine.

The "Best of 1984" Spotify playlist she'd been blaring for the past ninety minutes continued over the car stereo. "Runaway" by Bon Jovi. Rosie took a deep breath before jabbing the power button on the audio console. No need for Jon to give her any ideas.

Moments earlier, she'd felt carefree, the clean, warm countryside air, with its faint scents of freshly cut grass, honeysuckle and topsoil whipping through her hair. The drive up Highway 400 and through the winding side-roads brought her right into the heart of Sunset County, through bucolic farmland, rolling vineyards, farm-to-table restaurants and bed-and-breakfasts and the sparkling waters of Lakes Shaughnessy, Hollyberry and Robescarres. It was a stark contrast to the smell of exhaust and hot-dog stands she'd left behind only hours earlier in the city.

"Damn you, Gertie," she muttered. Rosie's best friend, who she'd had been counting on to be the perfect distraction, had canceled on her not two hours before they were meant to leave Toronto. And while Rosie was at the inn for work purposes, Gertie was going to tag along. A stolen getaway with her best friend, a sacred seventy-two-or-so hours of making up for lost time in between research and writing; spa afternoons in plush terry-cloth robes, lingering over coffee, gossiping about their friends from college, laughing about nothing and talking about everything. Perfection.

And necessary, because this was no average work trip. The nerves in the pit of Rosie's stomach were churning, whipped into a full-blown butterfly storm. She wasn't ready.

She dialed Gertie's number. "Did you make it there okay?" Gertie's voice sounded through the car's speakers. "I'm so sorry I had to cancel. Just when I thought this deal was wrapped."

Rosie closed her eyes. "Gertie, I have to tell you something." She sat for a moment, trying to predict what Gertie's reaction would be to what was, quite possibly, the juiciest gossip she had ever, *would* ever, share with her best friend since they'd been sat next to one another in Mr. Floyd's ninth grade science class.

And the gossip was about her. Which she'd held on to...why? Because when it happened, it seemed too surreal to be true? Because, despite how desperately Rosie had tried to convince herself over the past seven years that it had meant nothing, deep down she knew she was utterly, tragically wrong? It was perfection, and keeping it to herself meant the memory would never be tarnished.

She cleared her throat as a couple on Dutch cruisers coasted by, a little wobbly, big grins suggesting an afternoon spent visiting one of the local vineyards. "I have something to tell you." Rosie took a deep breath and heard herself blurting out her secret. "I slept with Nicola Kim. Seven years ago. And I didn't tell you because you'd just broken up with Kai, and I wanted to spare you all the details of what was a crazy perfect weekend. So I'm telling you now."

There. She'd said it.

There was a long pause, and Rosie checked her phone to see if she'd lost reception. "You *what*?" Gertie exclaimed. Rosie winced and turned down the volume on the stereo console. "Nicola Kim. As in Top Chef Nicola Kim. As in *At Home with Nicola* Nicola Kim. As in—"

"Yes. As in Michelin-starred, James Beard–winning, multimillion-dollar culinary and lifestyle empire Nicola Kim." There was silence, punctuated only by the call of a nearby sparrow. "Yeppers. That's the one."

If it weren't for the creased black-and-white photobooth strip that was tucked into the billfold of her wallet, picturing her and Nicola with wide grins on their faces, she might have trouble believing it herself. While packing for the trip to the inn where Nicola's new restaurant was housed, she'd dug it out of the shoebox in her closet where she kept warranties, receipts, replacement buttons and other items she didn't quite know where to keep. It seemed fitting, that un-fileable moment with Nicola, which she'd never quite been able to process.

"So, you mean to tell me that you're there. At the Inn at Sugar Maple Farms. The only journalist *in the world* invited to interview Nicola since her disappearance. And you *slept with her*?" There was a moment of silence. "Well now it makes more sense that she—"

"Don't say it," Rosie said. "I called you to make me feel better, not worse. Come on, it's not a big deal. It was years ago! And I'm sure it's a total fluke. She's traveled the world, met the most interesting people and done amazing things with her life. There's no way she remembers me."

Gertie scoffed, and Rosie could almost hear the wide, satisfied grin on her face. "Wait, does your editor know?"

Rosie cleared her throat. "Of course."

"So, he knows you had a thing with Nicola Kim. Your boss. But you only chose to drop this bombshell on your best friend *now*?"

To be fair, Rosie hadn't intended on telling Jeremy Krause, her sixty-some-odd-years-old editor who was kind of like an uncle to her, anything related to her dating life, but she knew that it was proper journalistic procedure to reveal any connection to the subject.

To his credit, Jeremy hadn't made a big deal out of the fact that Rosie, nowhere near a household name, with no clout in the industry, had been chosen from a bevy of seasoned journalists who would have killed for this opportunity. Nor had he flinched when funding the trip with the rapidly diminishing coffers of *Savorist* magazine.

The magazine was facing a certain end unless it was able to put out some content that would put the publication on the radar of the foodie community. And an unforgettable interview, delivered by Rosie, would be just the ticket.

"Anyway, it doesn't matter because it was a long time ago and I'm here to write this article. A very important article. And your job was to keep me company and prevent me from sleeping through the morning forest-bathing session. Why aren't you here?"

She knew exactly the face that Gertie was making. "I'm mad at you for keeping this from me. And I'm sorry I'm not there. But you've got this. Gotta go."

"Thanks. I'll keep you posted. Bye." She ended the call and tossed her phone onto the passenger seat.

Just as she'd predicted, her best friend's voice gave her the jolt of confidence she needed. The last thing she could afford this weekend was to take her eyes off the prize. Seeing Nicola again after all these years, after that sublime night she'd played in her mind so many times since, well. It would be...interesting.

Here we go, she thought and turned on the ignition. *Savorist* was footing the bill for a three-night stay for her to be very, *very* interesting.

Moments later, Rosie passed the farm bearing the inn's name—she'd read there was a local family, the Walkers, who'd run the farm for decades and had sold a parcel of their land to developers for the inn—then made the right turn into the Inn at Sugar Maple Farms's acreage. She took a deep breath as she passed the stone walls of the entrance, and the expanse of the sweeping grounds revealed itself to her. The website hadn't done it justice.

She slowly navigated the winding road toward the main building, taking in the inn's grounds. The three-acre lakefront estate in its lush, saturated late-spring bloom was remarkable.

In the distance, the main estate sat perched on a hill, overlooking a forested area to the east and a pasture to the west adjacent to a red farmhouse and a small sugar shack. The gentle waves of Lake Shaughnessy lapped onto the inn's south shore. As she continued the path to the main building, Rosie saw smaller cottages nestled into the forest, the swaying sycamores and cedars offering privacy to their occupants.

It wasn't pristine per se. And she wouldn't go as far as describing it as rustic. But there was something homey, something earthy and something that made you feel that you'd stumbled into a little piece of perfection that hadn't yet been touched by the corporate luxury-hotel industry or been broadcast to the world by social media influencers. That even though you might have never set foot on the grounds of Sugar Maple Farms, it was somehow *yours*.

And somewhere, on this property, among the buxom crimson peonies and whisper song of the blue jays, was Nicola Kim. Would Nicola be surprised to see her? Would she even remember her? Rosie had to think yes. And all she could hope for was that their little fling so long ago gave her some kind of in.

Rosie parked, then pulled her suitcase out of the trunk. Just as she started to wheel it to reception, a voice called from across the parking lot. "Welcome!"

Rosie looked up to find a young man in a bellhop uniform, with close-cropped brown hair and an eager smile and a nametag reading *Ethan*. "Let me help you with your things. You are?"

"Rosie," she said, standing back as Ethan deftly organized her few bags and motioned toward reception.

"Rosie, I'll make sure these get to your room while you're checking in. Please, follow me to reception."

A good start, to be sure. She'd already read about the top-notch service, which was described as "attentive yet discreet," as well as about Sugar Maple Farms's sustainability practices, local sourcing of bespoke furniture and luxury linens and, of course, the restaurant.

Before entering the reception area, Rosie surveyed the grounds once more, trying to guess where Nicola was at that very moment. And when she'd see her. And what she would do, and what she would say, and if she would be as awkward as she was picturing in her mind.

A drink felt like a good idea. And the other half of the sandwich she'd picked up from the roadside stand to tide her over until dinner.

After checking into her room, a second-floor suite with a king-sized bed, a wood-burning fireplace and a stone terrace that was the size of a Toronto bachelor apartment, Rosie changed out of her traveling clothes into a cream-colored tank dress, grabbed her notebook, her sandwich and a mini bottle of Sancerre from the bar fridge—no additional charge, a classy touch—and plopped down on the shaded balcony overlooking an expansive vegetable garden. While Jeremy's directive was to focus as much as possible on the restaurant and its elusive chef, it would be important to include some context about the inn, and the overall experience, since the dining room was available to overnight guests only.

She'd have no problem writing about the property—that was becoming obvious. The interview with Nicola and ingratiating herself to her as someone she could trust with her story was Rosie's number-one priority. And that started with her eight-o'clock dinner reservation.

The butterflies from earlier made themselves known again for a moment, until Rosie bit into her sandwich, closed her eyes and willed herself to enjoy the moment.

It was her long mane of dark waves that caught Nicola's eye. Her tanned skin against her white dress that held her gaze for a moment longer.

From the vegetable garden, Nicola Kim squinted in the afternoon sun, until she saw it. The expression on Rosie's face as she bit into whatever it was she was eating transported Nicola immediately back to the tiny kitchen of her Queen West apartment seven summers ago.

It had been a sun-drenched morning with a blissful break in the August humidity. Nicola wasn't due at the airport until later that afternoon, giving her just enough time to pack away her last few items to drop off at the storage unit before her subletter arrived: some kitchen equipment, sheets, towels, her record player and an assortment of records. But first, there had been breakfast.

A refreshing breeze had floated into the kitchen as Nicola tipped two grilled cheeses onto plates and passed one to the beautiful woman whom she'd just spent an unbelievable night with. Rosie Franklin-Smith was looking at Nicola expectantly after she'd been promised the best grilled cheese of her life. Fresh challah from Harbord Bakery, Gruyère from St. Lawrence Market and a juicy beefsteak tomato from the Dufferin Grove farmers' market. No holding back on the butter. Nicola's secret was the perfection of her cast-iron pan, which she'd seasoned attentively over the past several years. She'd have packed it in her suitcase if it didn't put her already heavy luggage into overweight territory.

It was a simple meal, yes, but in all of her years as a chef at some of the finest restaurants in the world, where she had access to the best ingredients, the most technically proficient colleagues and her own ever-increasing experience, she'd never again seen the same completely blissed-out expression that she'd seen on Rosie's face the moment she bit into that grilled cheese. Even during the events of the previous night, which had extended well into the early morning.

Rosie was a woman, Nicola knew, who didn't just love and appreciate food. She reveled in it and seemed to disappear into another dimension, as if under a spell of flavor and texture. It was totally gratifying and unbelievably sensual. Even seven years and two Michelin stars later, Nicola was still chasing that same look.

So when out of nowhere, she found Rosie's bio among the journalists who had been presented to her by Gabriel Callais, the proprietor of the inn, Nicola figured that if she was bound by contract to do one interview per year, she would choose the woman who had been so memorable to cook for. And if somehow Rosie was able to inspire her to get out of her current rut, even better.

And there she was. Sitting by herself on the balcony overlooking the garden of the Inn at Sugar Maple Farms, where Nicola was crouched down inspecting the radicchio for that evening's service. Soon enough they'd sit down together and Rosie would be probing into places Nicola had no intention of going. But in the meantime, she was clearly enjoying her sandwich, and Nicola was doing her best not to stare.

She turned to Shane, the resident gardener, who was busy tilling some mulch near the pattypan squash. "These look good," she said, motioning toward the bulbous, garnet heads of radicchio dotting the ground. "Can you get some to the kitchen in an hour?"

"You got it, Chef," Shane said, plucking one from the ground and brushing its roots with a practiced hand then inspecting it proudly. He was one of her best hires for the restaurant. A former pastry chef from her time at Persimmon, who'd traded sugar and butter for soil and seed and whose easy humor often lured her out to the garden when tension bubbled up in the kitchen. "I'll have it there in twenty."

So easy. So peaceful. How she hadn't set herself up in a situation like this until now was beyond her.

Nicola glanced up at the balcony again, but the woman she was sure was Rosie had slid down in her chair, feet up on the balcony rail, her face no longer visible.

She left Shane in the garden and returned to the dining room of her restaurant, where Leo, the maître d', stood briefing the team on the evening service.

It was four hours until showtime, and the kitchen would soon be buzzing with prep for dinner. Lunch had gone off without a hitch, and the same diners who'd lingered over their meal earlier in the day would be back, ravenous after an afternoon of horseback riding, tennis, hiking, fly fishing, stand-up paddleboarding or any of the other activities offered by the inn.

Nicola always preferred dinner over lunch. The dim lights, the mystery, the expanded number of courses and sensual flavors.

The kitchen was her orchestra, and she was the conductor. And the Barn at Sugar Maple Farms would be her masterpiece.

As soon as she got over her...whatever this thing was. Something akin to writer's block. Ever since they'd opened the restaurant, after her self-imposed exile from the industry, delighted guests departed every evening, compliments to the chef pouring in. Excellent feedback on top-notch service.

But there was something missing, and Nicola wondered how long it would be before things went south. She wasn't moving forward the way she'd been used to all her life. She was good. She was damn good. But she no longer felt *great*.

She pushed open the doors to the kitchen, which

was alive with movement, color and, of course, glorious aromas.

Her team was in the final hour of preservice prep, almost ready to break down and clean the kitchen. The staff meal would be going up soon after, and then it was right into service. *Showtime.*

She strode through the kitchen, inspecting the different stations and murmuring a few notes to the various members of the team.

"Bonjour, Chef," said Richard, the new pastry chef who'd recently arrived from l'école Lenôtre Paris, with a nod. Quiet, diminutive and graceful, he'd gained immediate respect by taking down two of her sous chefs hard in poker the night after his first shift, or so Nicola had overheard the next morning.

"Richard," she said. "I'm still dreaming about that strawberry rhubarb tarte from last night."

Richard blushed, then gestured toward a rack of springform pans. "Wait until you try tonight's cheesecake. *C'est bon.*"

Nicola knew that if Richard said it was "good," then it would be nothing short of stupendous. And she'd have to stay away from it. Of course, cooking involved eating, but she knew the line between quality control and overindulgence.

"Chef!" she heard a voice call from the back office. "A moment?"

Nicola moved to the source of the voice, Gabriel Callais, the proprietor of the inn, and the son of her former mentor, Alexi. Even though they'd been working together for months now, every time she saw Gabriel in his immaculate suit, perfectly pressed dress shirt and well-coiffed hair, she couldn't help but smile and remember the skinny little gap-toothed kid who hung out at the dishwashing station with Nicola, trading sports stats and bad jokes. Gabriel had looked up to Nicola like a big sister, and now he was Nicola's boss.

She was thrilled to be working for him. Helping Gabriel find success was high on her list of priorities. She owed it to Alexi, and while being with Gabriel every day was a cruel reminder of just how much she was indebted to his father, working to ensure Gabriel's success gave Nicola a strong sense of purpose.

"Hey, boss," Nicola said, sinking into a deep club chair opposite Gabriel's desk. The chance to get off her feet for even a moment was welcome; she'd be moving for the rest of the night. "What's shakin'?"

Gabriel poured them both a glass of water from the crystal decanter on his desk. "Just wanted to remind you that there's press here tonight."

Nicola's least favorite word. While she knew that her presence in a kitchen again, after what *The New Yorker* had called her "disappearing act," was newsworthy, part of her deal with Gabriel and the inn's shareholders was that she'd do press only once per year, with the publication of her choice. The food would speak for itself, and Gabriel's charm with reviewers and bloggers was more than enough for the property, as was evident in any press clipping Nicola had read since the opening. "All right," she said. "Want me to send anything special to the table?"

"No, not necessarily," Gabriel said, but Nicola could sense there was something else he wanted. "I just..."

"Come on, out with it. Complete honesty between us, right?" It would be disappointing if Gabriel went back on their agreement and asked for anything more than what they'd agreed upon in her contract. Being in the public eye—the attention, the fanfare, the way so many people wanted a connection just to advance their own interests—it was everything that brought her down the wrong road in the first place. If Gabriel was about to ask her to go back into the lion's den, he had another thing coming.

Gabriel scratched his neck. "It was that sole last week. It was—"

Nicola grimaced. "Lackluster, right? I know. I overdid the puntarelle—"

"No, no. It's not that it wasn't amazing. It was. It's just that you had the exact same dish on the menu at Avra."

Nicola paused, flipping through the mental catalog of all her menus from over the years. Her brief stint at Avra was at the height of her fame, when her home product line had just launched and she'd just shot a campaign with Rolex. She was dating Jessica. Or was it Tatum? Didn't matter. They had both taken advantage of her, and she'd let it happen. "Sorry. You're totally right."

"I just want to make sure that what we're putting out—"

"Is fully original. I agree. Won't happen again." She gazed out at the late-afternoon sunlight peeking through the swaying trees and blanketing the grounds in a honeycomb glow. "Remind me about the details of this magazine."

"*Savorist.* A smaller publication, mostly digital, not a huge reach but has decent downloads in Ontario and Quebec and the Northeastern states."

"I've read it a few times. They put out good stuff." Not that she'd ever had time to read, until recently.

"There's one more thing," Gabriel said, hesitating.

"Don't tell me there's going to be a restaurant critic in the house too," Nicola joked. Gabriel's expression was unchanged. "Wait, you're kidding, right?"

"I just found out today," Gabriel said. "Or I would have told you sooner. The reviewer posted a photo of himself in his car with a hashtag—*SunsetCountyBound*."

Nicola's stomach dropped. There was only one reviewer she knew of who publicized the next restaurant he planned to review that way. "Marcellin?" she said. "Don't tell me it's Mark Marcellin."

"He's…coming here tonight," Gabriel said, trying and failing to hide the annoyance in his voice. "Apparently, he was supposed to be dining at Dasha, but they had a fire in the kitchen yesterday, so he's making the trek up to Sunset County. Leo took the call, and we had one room and a free table tonight, so…"

"Ugh," Nicola muttered under her breath. Mark Marcellin was the famed restaurant critic for the *Toronto Tribune* who had a huge online following and was notorious for his hot-and-cold reviews. He was witty and acerbic, not to mention cocky as hell, and his legions of fans took his every word as fine dining gospel.

He was also well known in the industry as a reviewer who expected the red carpet to be rolled out for him when he did a restaurant the honor of gracing them with his presence. The best tables, off-the-menu treats—even if they were supposed to be playing the game of *I know who you are, but I'm pretending not to know*—if Mark didn't feel like royalty by the time he walked out of an establishment, there was a not-so-insignificant chance that the perceived slight would make its way into the review.

He also held grudges like an old lady clutching her purse in a dark alley—ready to swing it at the first sign of trouble. Because of his unpredictable nature, most restaurateurs made a point of keeping him happy, even when their establishment was already doing well and less reliant on his seal of approval, if only to protect their next venture.

In the past, Nicola had loved when reviewers visited her restaurants. She relished the challenge, the chance to showcase her inventive menus and finely tuned dishes. But she was also committed to treating critics like any other guest, refusing to bend over backward or fawn for a glowing write-up.

Ruth Reichl had taught her that. In her famous *New York Times* review of Le Cirque back in the late nineties, Reichl published two versions of the review side by side: one as herself, where she arrived at the restaurant to find the proverbial red carpet rolled out for her, even displacing the king of Spain for the best table in the house. She was fawned over and presented with an exquisite meal, delivered with the finest service.

She visited again, solo, in disguise pretending to be

a schoolteacher from Long Island. This time, she was seated in the back of the restaurant, was spoken to disparagingly by waitstaff and had an altogether forgettable experience.

The reviews had served as a warning to the industry: Treat every one of your customers like VIPs. Not just because any one of them might be a critic in disguise, but because people have chosen your establishment to spend their valuable time and hard-earned money. They deserve the respect of your full attention and hospitality.

At Persimmon, Nicola had done just that, and Mark had given a decent review but not the glowing one they deserved, and Nicola hadn't been shy about sharing her criticism about him with other chefs in the industry.

So now, the idea of having him invade her space, given her recent whatever it was with Rosie in the mix as well, it all just felt a little bit…claustrophophic.

"Can you call back and say we had a flood?" she suggested.

Gabriel gave her a tight smile. "He's going to love it here."

"And here I thought that coming out to the middle of nowhere I could escape the fray," Nicola said wryly. "Now I have a journalist *and* a reviewer to contend with."

"And you'll charm them both," Gabriel said. "I'll put his party at the tree-side table."

"Seriously?" Nicola asked. "So not only do I have to cook for him, I have to perform for him too?"

"You know he'll say something about it if he thinks

you're hidden back in the kitchen. Let him see you. You have nothing to worry about."

Except for my abject fear of disappointing you, Nicola thought. "All right," she said. She'd been looking forward to this evening, to cooking for Rosie again. Now she just felt a nagging undercurrent of dread. She stood up. "Let me know when he arrives," she said. "I'll come out and say hello, play nice."

Gabriel nodded, satisfied. "I'd expect nothing less."

It was time to knock the socks off Mark Marcellin and keep Rosie Franklin-Smith at bay while she was at it.

Screw Mark. All she wanted to focus on was the shiver of delight she felt at the thought of having Rosie back in her kitchen.

"All right, boss. Thanks for checking in."

"Stop calling me boss. I should be calling you boss."

Nicola stood up, finished her water and deposited the glass on Gabriel's desk. "You got it, boss." She winked, then made her way back to the conductor's podium.

Chapter Two

After a short nap and a shower, Rosie descended the wide staircase leading to the lobby of the building, where she found the concierge busy helping another guest. She was eager to locate the restaurant, but she could find it herself.

Her dress fluttered in the warm early-summer breeze as she exited the main building, looking left and right and trying to decide which way to stroll. Every direction promised charming, idyllic scenery. But she was looking for one place only. She tucked a loose strand of dark hair back behind her ear as she tried to visualize the property map she'd seen on the front desk.

"Forest path begins just over there," a voice behind her called, and she turned to see a young man in a crisp navy suit, clean cut with chestnut-brown hair, emerging from the front entrance. He was pointing to a white gazebo beside a clearing of forest, with a path leading into the woods.

Rosie recognized him right away: Gabriel Callais, the young proprietor of the Inn at Sugar Maple Farms, who was well-known in the industry for turning around struggling properties. Sugar Maple Farms was his first solo venture, and Rosie remembered reading somewhere that Nicola's first restaurant gig had been in his father's kitchen.

"Thank you," Rosie said. "Actually, I'm looking for the restaurant." *And the woman at the helm.* Running into Gabriel this early in her visit was not just convenient but might be a win. Maybe he could take her to Nicola early.

"It doesn't open for a few hours," Gabriel said. "But there's a selection of fresh fruit and charcuterie in the hospitality room, if you're hungry."

"I just wanted to see the building," Rosie said.

"I'm headed in that direction. Please," he said, gesturing toward the path to the right. "Right this way."

Rosie nodded and began walking down the path, Gabriel at her side. "I'm Rosie. Rosie Franklin-Smith. I'm from—"

"Ah, from *Savorist*! Well, welcome." His expression didn't betray any anxiety that he was in the presence of a reviewer. "We're thrilled to have you here. Thank you for making the trip up north."

"My pleasure," said Rosie. "We're so excited to be able to showcase your beautiful property. And, of course, Nicola."

She wasn't sucking up. It really was nothing short of spectacular. The path to the restaurant was lined with bushes, gushing with ballet-slipper-pink peonies and, behind them, stately swaying willows. With the early-afternoon sun peeking through, creating a kaleidoscope of shimming light on the path, for the second time since they'd arrived, Rosie felt like she was in her own little private heaven, with every detail orchestrated just for her.

The inn had only been open for four months, but there was no doubt it was on its way to join the ranks of Relais & Châteaux and Small Luxury Hotels of the World properties. And with Nicola involved, a Michelin star wouldn't be far behind.

"I can't wait for dinner tonight," Rosie continued. "Any recommendations?"

"Definitely go with the tasting menu," Gabriel said, grinning. "Chef will take good care of you."

There it was. Her in. "Speaking of Chef Kim," she said. "Would it be at all possible to arrange some time to speak with her before dinner? Just a short sit-down. Since I only have three nights here." She flashed her most winning smile.

Gabriel returned the smile, albeit an apologetic one. "I'm very sorry, but unfortunately, Chef Kim's schedule is very busy. I have an hour booked for you both tomorrow after the cooking demo. And I will confirm, but Chef has suggested that the following afternoon, between lunch and dinner service, will likely work for your second session. But," he said, checking his watch, "I'd be more than happy to give you a tour of the property. And you chose a good day to arrive. You were likely informed at check-in about Afternoon in the Grove, our weekly manager's cocktail reception. I hope you can make it."

Rosie strained to keep the smile on her face. Not two hours in and she'd already been shut down. But she was in no position to turn down Gabriel's invitation for a tour. She would do her best to ingratiate herself to him, then ask again. "I would love that. Thank you. And definitely, I'll be at the reception."

"Wonderful. Right this way..." Gabriel motioned.

He led her down the forested path, pointing out the native species of trees and flowers. He shared some history about the land where Sugar Maple Farms was built, situated on Anishinaabeg Territory, a people known for their rich cultural traditions, strong governance systems and deep connection to the land and water. He took her by the recreation hut, the pool and the fitness studio, where a yoga class had just let out, and several zen-looking guests wandered out of the building, blinking in the sun.

"And this," Gabriel said, stopping and motioning toward a red barn, "this is the building you're looking for." Rosie surveyed the building, which looked like its original purpose had been indeed as a working barn. Now it had a large stone walkway that led to a cedar-shingled entrance flanked by cast-iron urns filled with ivory hydrangeas, deep burgundy dahlias and soft apricot zinnias. "Our restaurant. The Barn at Sugar Maple Farms."

Suddenly Rosie felt self-conscious, as though at any moment she might come face-to-face with Nicola. "It's stunning," she said. "I read somewhere that Nicola used to work for your father. Is he still in the business?"

For a moment, Gabriel's professional sheen showed a small crack, his lips pursing quickly before he smiled again. "No, my father passed away not long ago. But yes, Nicola used to wash dishes and help with prep in my father's kitchen."

"And now she's working for you."

"*With* me," Gabriel said. "I would never pretend to have any authority over Nicola. Having her in the kitchen here is a true honor." He looked at his watch once again, and suddenly it seemed as though he'd rather be anywhere than standing with Rosie. "It's been a pleasure to meet you, Rosie. If there's anything we can do to make your stay more comfortable, please don't hesitate to reach out." He reached into his pocket, pulled out a business-card holder and passed a card to her.

Rosie accepted the card. "Thank you," she said.

She watched as Gabriel strode purposefully down the path toward the main building, then turned back to look at the restaurant.

The restaurant technically wasn't open for another hour, but the front door was propped open slightly, so Rosie pulled the door back a bit further and entered.

As she stepped into the restaurant, she took a deep breath, taking in the quiet and empty dining area. The whole room was surrounded by barn board siding, with a crystal chandelier casting a twinkling of light across the dining tables.

The din from the kitchen floated through the space, but other than that, it was quiet and still.

Rosie slowly walked through, taking in the imposing fireplace and the full-wall glassed-in wine racks. There was even a live dogwood tree growing in the center of the dining space that brought the beauty of the outdoors inside.

Breathing in, she noted one of her favorite scents, garlic and butter. Dinner prep was well underway. Despite having eaten the sandwich, she was hungry—and eager to feast on whatever it was that Nicola was back there preparing. Her proximity was in the air.

"Table for one?" A voice came from behind her.

Her heart in her throat, Rosie swirled around, coming face-to-face with those same deep eyes that had locked with hers while she sat perched at the coat check at Persimmon years ago.

Nicola's expression sparked with remembrance…and something else. Surprise, maybe. But there was something more. It was the look of holding your breath for as long as you could, then finally taking in a gasp of air.

Nicola remembered her.

"Nicola. Hey. Hi," Rosie stammered, willing herself to keep her cool. So what if Nicola looked even better than the last time she'd seen her, her hair cropped in a neat bob and what looked like a new tattoo peeking out of the collar of her chef's whites? Rosie had a job to do. And that job started with making a winning second impression.

"I thought that was you. On your balcony earlier," Nicola said. In her chef's whites, she looked exactly like the press photos Rosie had seen in her cooking-show ads. Nicola tucked a strand of dark hair behind her ear, and Rosie tried to quiet the memory of that same hand holding hers. Gentle but purposeful. *Focus.* "I didn't realize anyone could see—"

"I'm sorry—that sounds creepy," Nicola said. "I was down in the vegetable garden. Below your room." Rosie blushed, thinking of how she'd inhaled her sandwich, unaware that anyone was watching her.

She steadied herself, smiled and looked around. "Beautiful place you have here," she said.

"It's amazing, isn't it?" Nicola said. "I lucked out."

"Well, according to Gabriel, he's the lucky one."

"You know Gabriel?"

"We just met. He took me on a tour of the property." *And told me I had no chance of talking to you today.* It was incredibly strange, standing in the company of someone she barely knew but who had made such an indelible impression on her.

"He's a terrific host. Are you joining us tonight for dinner?"

"Absolutely," Rosie said. "I can't wait."

"Are you here with…" Nicola paused. "Anyone?"

"Solo," Rosie said, noting a flicker of curiosity in her eyes. She was about to ask Nicola about the article. Maybe having Nicola right in front of her, with this undeniable current of energy flowing between them, might tilt the balance and get her to start talking earlier than expected.

As soon as Rosie opened her mouth, a statuesque woman with a stern expression strode into the dining room. "Chef?" she said. "I'm sorry to interrupt, but when you have a sec I have some questions about the tasting notes before service begins."

Nicola nodded to the woman, then turned back to Rosie. "This is Ynez, our sommelier. Ynez, this is Rosie. An old friend from Toronto."

Old friend?

“Welcome,” said Ynez. “And sorry again. But it’s a thin line between Vouvray and Viognier depending on the saffron concentration.”

“Of course,” Rosie said. “Don’t let me get in the way. Looking forward to dinner.” Ynez nodded, then left them standing alone again in the dining room.

Rosie turned back to Nicola. “I guess I’ll see you later. Unless you’ll be at the reception?”

“I’ll be tied up in there for the rest of the day,” Nicola said, nodding toward the kitchen. “But I hope you enjoy it.”

“Thanks,” Rosie said. “I’ll see you later on.”

“I’ll see you then,” Nicola said, flashing her a quick but knee-weakening smile before Rosie saw herself out the door.

As she stepped out into the dappled light of the Barn’s garden path, Rosie let the grin spread across her face.

The interview hadn’t begun.

But the ice was most definitely broken. And now this job felt real.

Rosie felt a touch of glee, and something else—elation?—as she continued to walk the inn’s grounds, eventually ending up at the waterfront where she took some photos of the shoreline and the sailboats coasting by.

Back toward the inn, she spotted what she guessed was the manager’s party in a courtyard off the main building. She passed through an archway that was covered in pale pink climbing roses, the kinds she saw on the covers of books set on Nantucket. Through the arc was a collection of people holding drinks and plucking canapés off trays offered by circulating waiters.

The courtyard felt like a secret garden. There were stone walls lined with vine-covered trellises, and on each side of the entrance back into the inn's lobby, flickering oil lamps added an elegant touch.

A number of guests had already assembled, most standing at white-tableclothed round tables, sipping cocktails and keeping to their couples. A jazz trio played in the corner.

Rosie approached the bar. "Beer, wine, Champagne?" asked the bartender with a friendly smile. "I'm also making our feature cocktails. I have a French 75 with elderflower liqueur, a white negroni with a grapefruit twist or a peach-and-basil bellini." He dipped his chin knowingly. "Personally, I'd go with that one. The peaches and basil were just picked an hour ago. You'll feel like you're wrapped up in summer."

Rosie very much liked the sounds of that. The others sounded equally delicious. Could she have one of each? What would Nicola think if Rosie rolled into the restaurant three sheets to the wind?

Or would she even see her again tonight?

"That—the peach and basil—sounds perfect," Rosie said, eyeing another reception guest's perspiring cocktail coupe, which looked like the perfect cool treat in the hot late-afternoon sun. She turned her attention back to the bartender in his crisp white shirt as he muddled the basil syrup with peach puree, then topped it with a splash from a bottle of Pol Roger Brut Réserve and set a small purple pansy to float in the delicate blush-pink drink. "There you are," he said, then moved the glass across the bar with a smile.

"Thank you," said Rosie. Where *was* she? The hospitality at this place really was above and beyond. The staff, so far, had a way of making her feel like they weren't really working. They seemed happy to have her there and like it really was their pleasure to serve.

Lately, in the city, it seemed like the servers felt above their jobs and that she was putting someone out by making an order and spending her hard-earned money to be there.

Here it felt like everyone was just celebrating life, all guests at the same picture-perfect Instagrammable party, but it wasn't just for show.

This was the real deal.

Rosie stood alone at a table. She wasn't a stranger to attending events solo; while she often invited Gertie to accompany her to restaurant openings or tasting events, she was equally comfortable going alone. She slipped her phone out of her pocket and was about to take a picture of her drink.

"Cheers!" a voice came from beside her. A forty-something woman in a purple tank dress and a wicker handbag held out her glass. She had a cute blond bob and diamond earrings as big as peas. "Solo traveler too?"

Rosie nodded. "Yes," she said. "I'm here for work. I'm Rosie."

The woman held out her glass, her gold bangles tinkling. Rosie clinked her glass against the woman's.

"Nice to meet you," the woman said. "I'm Kerry. Here on my own, but just for tonight. My friend's coming tomorrow for the night. She's on a budget, so that's all she could swing, but one night didn't feel like enough for me to make the trip from Vancouver. So I decided a couple of days ago to come out early for a few extra nights."

With her designer handbag and expensive jewelry, Rosie could tell that Kerry didn't have the same financial constraints as the friend she was meeting. She imagined what it would be like to have the means to take a solo trip to a place like Sugar Maple Farms on a whim.

"So you've been here a couple of days now," Rosie said. "How's it been? I just got in this afternoon."

"Have you tried your drink yet?" Kerry asked. "That'll tell you all you need to know."

Rosie tipped the coupe into her mouth and took a small sip, the silky peach puree coating her palate, followed by the fine mousse bubbling on her tongue. "Mmm," she said, closing her eyes and swallowing. "That good, huh?"

"It's fabulous," Kerry said. "Make sure you check out the spa. The morning yoga is amazing. And I took a kayak out yesterday. The lake is gorgeous."

"And the restaurant?" Rosie asked. "Does it live up to the hype?"

Kerry blinked, then paused for a moment. "It's good!" she said, as though she were trying to convince herself. "Yeah, it's good." She leaned in a bit and lowered her voice. "I'll be honest, though. I was expecting better. Something about it felt… I don't know. Muted?"

Rosie blinked. "Really?" she asked. "Was Nicola Kim in the kitchen when you went?" She knew that as a seven-day-a-week operation, there were meals that Nicola wouldn't be presiding over. Maybe Kerry had picked the wrong days for extending her trip.

"She was there," Kerry said, nodding, her voice still low and conspiratorial. "Maybe it's just that I've been to a couple of her restaurants before. Madrid and Toronto, but that was years ago. Who knows, that could have been her peak." She took another sip of her cocktail. "Don't get me wrong. The food was *good...*" She shrugged and took a sip of her cocktail. "I won't go as far as saying 'meh,' but..."

Just as Rosie was about to prod further, a clinking sounded near the bar, and they turned to see Gabriel holding up a glass of Champagne and beaming at the group that had assembled.

"Good afternoon, everyone," he said. "It's my distinct pleasure to welcome you to our property and to this small gathering to celebrate the most exquisite time of day."

He wasn't kidding. In the last fifteen or so minutes since Rosie had arrived, it was like a blanket of the more ethereal golden sunshine had settled over the whole patio. Every last person looked a better version of themselves.

The jazz trio was taking a quick break for Gabriel's speech, so a nearby hermit thrush's call was audible through the warm air. As if the moment couldn't get any more picturesque, out of the corner of her eye, Rosie spotted a monarch butterfly landing on the rose of Sharon bushes that framed one side of the patio. Was this real life or a movie set?

“My name is Gabriel Callais,” he continued. “I’m the proprietor of the Inn at Sugar Maple Farms. If you encounter any issues during your stay, although I can assure you that we do our utmost to ensure you won’t, I invite you to speak with me directly, and I will be more than happy to assist. Please enjoy your day, the grounds and, of course, our wonderful restaurant. Cheers to you all—thank you for making the trip to our treasured home.”

Glasses clinked and a soft chorus of voices sounded in approval.

“I’d better go. I’ve got the early seating,” Kerry said, taking the final sip of her drink. “Maybe tonight will be the night. I smelled something amazing on the way here.” She deposited her glass on the table. “Enjoy your time here, Rosie.”

Wait, Rosie thought. She had more questions than she did answers. What did Kerry mean, that “something felt muted”? It was clear the woman was no stranger to fine dining, so she had enough comparison points.

Rosie glanced across the field to where a few guests were already assembled outside of the restaurant waiting to be let in for the first service. That would be her soon.

She’d find out for herself.

Chapter Three

Nicola poured herself a small splash of the Laphroaig Quarter Cask she kept in the back pantry and sat in Gabriel's empty office for a moment before the doors to the restaurant were due to open. She wasn't in the practice of drinking before (and definitely not during) work; over the years she'd seen enough of what substances could do to otherwise talented people's work in the kitchen. Sure, they gave some chefs the energy and bravado they needed to make it in the high-stress, high-stakes environment, but for Nicola, being one hundred percent in control of her faculties was the state of mind she liked to work in.

Or maybe that was her problem of late. Overthinking.

She took a long sip, the amber liquid burning her throat as it went down. But the sting offered a brief escape from the nerves that had crept in since she'd run into Rosie. Having her here at Sugar Maple Farms was… unsettling, sure. But also kind of exciting. Nicola was dreading the interview but oddly looking forward to cooking for her. Was there still a spark between them? She felt it. Sharp and sudden. Like it had never really gone out.

And it was the best-possible scenario. Rosie was a guest, which meant that she'd be leaving soon. Hopefully she'd take a hint and stick to surface stuff.

The best thing about working at a place like Sugar Maple Farms was that there was no possibility of getting involved in a messy romance. Her fellow staff were, of course, off-limits (even more so because of her rank). Visitors were, by definition, temporary, and for the most part, it wasn't really a place frequented by singles.

Nicola stuck to the kitchen, the walking trails and, on the rare day she felt like leaving the property, a few select spots in downtown Sunset County on the less busy and less touristy days, where she could go into town for a coffee at Rise and Grind, sit by the water or visit with one of her providers. The locals seemed content to offer her the anonymity she required.

It suited her perfectly. Coming out of "hiding," which was fourteen months of living with her sister and her niece and nephew in a small seaside community just outside of Peggy's Cove where either no one seemed to know who she was or just didn't care, she needed somewhere she could continue to fly under the radar and evade the messy trappings of fame that had led her down the wrong path.

So Rosie being here? No problem. She'd be gone the same way she came, which was fine with Nicola.

There was no denying she looked incredible. Seven years later and somehow even better than when they'd first met. That same wild, dark hair tumbling past her shoulders. The constellation of freckles across her nose. And the gap between her front teeth, the one that showed when she smiled, really smiled, with her whole face. Time had given her a few more curves, and a scattering of fine lines around her eyes that hinted at years spent laughing.

And then there was the unfortunate matter of Mark Marcellin, which Nicola had done well to push out of her mind for the best part of the day. How was it possible that the two were converging on the same evening?

A light rapping on the door of the office took Nicola out of her reverie. It would likely be Danielle Morales, her sous chef, reminding her that it was go time.

She took the last sip of her drink and stood up, looking out at the vista from Gabriel's office. Her favorite time of day.

She whistled as she stepped back into the kitchen, where the engine of dinner service was already roaring at full speed. Danielle looked up from her station and nodded at Nicola. "We're ten out."

"Got it," Nicola said.

Danielle hesitated. "You missed lineup."

"I'll catch them tomorrow."

Danielle nodded again—not pushing back, just acknowledging.

"No substitutions tonight, okay?" Nicola asked, tying her apron behind her back.

"Understood." Danielle stood waiting a half a beat longer, but when nothing came, she returned to the line without comment.

Nicola set about arranging her station. She didn't need to look up to see that the rest of the staff were now aware that she'd arrived in the kitchen and whatever they'd been doing before her arrival required a subtle adjustment.

She straightened her shoulders, doing her best to summon the confidence that had carried her this far in her career, a hard-won self-assuredness, even if it felt more elusive these days.

It was time to make some magic happen.

The menu for the evening, as always, reflected the bounty of the season: An amuse bouche of strawberry-basil sorbet. Tuna tartare with chili-plum dressing. Rabbit with porcini mushroom and rhubarb and a sage reduction. Beef tenderloin on a bed of morels and asparagus. And then, of course, Richard's cheesecake, which Eloise was pairing with an orange muscat.

And, as always, Nicola had a small off-menu surprise that she liked to send to the tables as a way to delight her diners.

From her station, where she had a view of the dining room, she surveyed the guests who had already been shown to their tables. She didn't see Rosie yet; she must have booked the second seating.

She did, however, notice when Leo seated Mark Marcellin and his dining partner, a mousy-haired woman with pursed lips and an expression of distrust. Mark sank into his seat like it was a throne, letting Leo pull it out for him without so much as a nod of acknowledgment.

Gross, thought Nicola as she moved to another counter and did her best to focus on the plates that Karlos was adorning with a selection of the small edible flowers that Shane had painstakingly removed from the garden that afternoon with an almost religious focus. At least someone was thriving in their element.

"Take these to the two top," Nicola muttered, unable to believe she was stooping to feed into Mark's ego with the first-out dishes. *It's not about you*, she reminded herself. This review mattered. A lot.

The servers were moving purposefully through the dining room, filling water goblets, providing the tasting notes on the evening's menu and gracefully sidestepping one another while delivering dishes to tables with the precision of a Swiss watchmaker.

Timing is second only to taste, she could hear her mentor Alexi's voice as though he were standing over her, inspecting her work. What would Alexi advise Nicola, in this strange stalemate of hers?

She took a sharp breath in and shook off the guilt that shrouded her whenever Alexi came to mind, which was often. While Nicola had achieved more in her career than Alexi ever had in his small French bistro, Nicola had learned the foundation of everything she knew about the kitchen from him and would forever be grateful. She would give anything to repay the man and hoped that by helping his son find success with his business, it would be a shade of the debt she owed.

Her reverie was interrupted with a clatter from the back corner of the kitchen.

"What's going on back here?" she barked as she rushed over to the source of the noise which had interrupted the perfect cadence she worked so hard to orchestrate, like a cacophonous off-beat skipping of a record.

She found one of the line cooks, Tim, who was steady, dry-witted and normally meticulous with his hand under rushing water, the skin red and a pained look on his face. "I'm sorry, Chef. I was blanching the asparagus, and—"

"Karlos," Nicola ordered the other line cook. "Get an ice pack from the back freezer." She surveyed the scene. "Take the ice pack, and go to the break room. I'll take over."

"I'm sorry, Chef. Thank you, Chef," Tim said, his face redder with embarrassment than his burn. Nicola knew she was being harsh, but the show had to go on, and every moment tending to a grown man who could more than take care of himself would compromise the flow of the service.

She washed her hands, picked up a colander and picked up where Tim had left off. She might've been a head chef, but she wasn't above doing menial jobs when it was needed.

As always, time flew as Nicola issued commands and moved deftly through her kitchen, tasting, scolding, tweaking and admonishing—not in a demoralizing way, but in a way that told her staff that nothing could ever be quite good enough until it was perfect. And when they got there, she would let them know.

She could feel the tension, though. It was like the rest of the kitchen was walking on eggshells. Nicola did her best to keep an eye on Mark and his reaction to the dishes being delivered to his table, but now that they were shorthanded, it was nearly impossible to step off the line.

Damn it, she thought. It wasn't that she was expected to be nice all the time, even though she was certain as a female there was a thin line between commanding and palatable, but she also knew that bluntness landed best when there was trust behind it.

Her team respected her—of that, she was certain. But she hadn't yet broken through that wall, the one where colleagues became something more. Where they weren't just employees but family. The way Alexi had once made her feel.

Were they intimidated by her? Afraid of her? Maybe.

She had to do better.

Excellence didn't come from training alone. It came when a team moved as one, reading each other, anticipating, trusting. That was the real magic. And they weren't quite there yet.

The dining room thinned slightly as tables turned over before the second seating.

Nicola gritted her teeth and took a moment to visit Mark's table, but through his slick superlatives, it was impossible to tell what he'd really thought about the meal. His dining companion had all the personality of a Pet Rock, so she was no help either. All Nicola could do was hope her mismanagement of the kitchen hadn't been noticed by the dining room.

The slower pace between the two seatings felt like a reset. Tim returned with his hand bandaged, and they all set to work again on the second service.

And then she spotted Rosie, being ushered to her

table by Sebastien. Good. Seb was the best server of the bunch and especially good at keeping single diners company in a way that made them feel comfortable, not over attended to in the way that might make them self-conscious for dining solo. His quiet Scandinavian elegance made him discreet. No ego, just excellence. Rosie would be more than well taken care of.

Nicola watched as Rosie graciously accepted the chair that Seb pulled out for her, flashing him her magnetic smile and smoothing her dark hair that appeared to have been straightened. She wore a form-fitting sleeveless navy dress and high-heeled sandals that accentuated her long, shapely legs.

Desire stirring deep in the pit of her stomach, Nicola shook her head. Time to concentrate.

Before turning back to her task, seasoning the tenderloin just so before passing it off to Danielle, she turned to the bar back, who was passing through the kitchen with a clean rack of cocktail coupes.

"Hey, Adam," she said, nodding at the young man.

"Yes, Chef," said Adam, pausing at Nicola's station.

"Champ table four for me, will you?"

"Right away, Chef."

I'll know I'm successful when I can drink Champagne every day for breakfast, she remembered Rosie saying as they lounged in Nicola's bed, talking about everything under the sun and amazingly wide awake even in the early hours of the morning before they'd fallen asleep.

It wasn't breakfast, but hopefully it would bring a smile to her face. Hey, it was hospitality, wasn't it?

She grinned to herself as she peered out from the

kitchen, watching Rosie accept the drink from Adam with another wide smile. Gosh, she was gorgeous. Nicola couldn't wait to see Rosie taste her first course, see that look on her face that she remembered all too well.

They were no longer shorthanded, but it was a full house, so Nicola wasn't able to get out to see Rosie.

Instead, she pictured her at her table, surveying the plating of the sorbet. Taking her first taste from her spoon and sitting back in her chair, savoring the layered flavors.

As Nicola sliced the asparagus into even coins, she felt a calm come over her as she started thinking about different flavors that Rosie might like. Lime leaf. Cardamom. Fenugreek. Lavender.

Images of different dishes were starting to flash in her mind. She paused for a moment, unable to believe what was happening.

"You okay, Chef?" Karlos asked, and Nicola straightened her shoulders.

"Yeah, yeah. Hey, grab me a notepad from Gabriel's desk, will you?" she said. Karlos nodded and disappeared, seemingly unfazed by the unusually timed request.

Could it be that her culinary muse was sitting in the other room? And this slump she was in—Rosie's presence might be the cure?

According to Gabriel, Rosie was staying at the inn for three nights. She had three nights to see what Rosie could do for her and her return to force in the kitchen. For Gabriel. For Alexi.

"Well, that was…" Rosie paused as Sebastien stood by her table, waiting for the verdict on the meal. "Lovely," she said. And it was. The rabbit was probably the highlight. Perfectly tender, inventively seasoned with a melt-in-your-mouth texture. Was it the best she'd ever had? It was up there. But to Rosie's surprise, she couldn't state it decisively.

The whole meal was very, very good. The service was excellent.

So where was the…je ne sais quoi that she had expected from a meal by Nicola Kim? Or had she just been influenced by Kerry from the cocktail reception?

"Is there anything else I can get for you this evening?"

"No, thank you. Looking forward to tomorrow," Rosie said, truthfully. Maybe this was just an off evening and tomorrow she was in for a tour de force befitting of Nicola's reputation.

Once Sebastien had wished her a good evening, she took one last look at the kitchen, hoping to catch a glimpse of Nicola in her element before returning to her room for the evening. No luck.

An hour later, after wrapping herself in the thick plush robe from her closet, Rosie grabbed her notebook and let herself onto her balcony. The combination of her meal, the deep soaker tub in her room and the lavender-and-peppermint-infused salts had put her in a state of hypnotic relaxation, and she was ready to jot down some notes about her experience at the restaurant and her initial observations about the operation of Sugar Maple Farms.

Jeremy would be asking for some early copy by the

following afternoon, and while Rosie did her best writing in the early mornings, drafting her first impressions would give her something to go off when she woke up.

The onyx night sky was punctuated by a streak of faint dotted lights. Rosie took a deep breath in, marveling at the still quiet of the evening and the absence of cars honking, sirens and the other noises that made up the soundtrack of city life.

As much as she appreciated the beauty of country life, it was almost too quiet for comfort, and her mind wandered back to the cottage in Sauble Beach where her parents brought her and her brother every summer, where they'd spend their days at the waterfront, riding their bikes into town for ice cream and catching tadpoles in the creek in sand buckets. She could vividly remember the last summer they'd spent there together as a family before her brother, Ashton, left for Stanford.

Not only did he find out at the beginning of the trip that he'd won a prestigious scholarship for the community service program he'd spearheaded at their high school, but he was the area's most sought-after sailing instructor, and he looked the part with his perfect tan, hair in an easy wave and wide smile. Their parents' friends were all lining up to introduce him to their daughters, and he was well-known at the tennis club for his incomparable slice.

All Rosie got that summer was a wicked sunburn and two massive horsefly bites smack in the middle of her forehead...and an email from the boy she'd been dating back in the city informing her he'd met someone else at his overnight camp and he was done with her. She'd never felt so ugly, unloved and altogether mediocre in her life.

At least during the school year, she'd get a break from existing in her brother's shadow. At the beach house, she'd endured it twenty-four seven.

From the balcony of her hotel room, the crickets were taunting her, so she returned to her room and retrieved her AirPods, streamed a vocals-free playlist, then settled back in her chair and picked up her notebook.

The first few pages were full of notes she'd taken so far, facts, dates and other points she could refer to during the interview if necessary.

She reviewed the timeline of Nicola's trajectory leading up to her disappearance, beginning with her departure from Persimmon seven years earlier. There was a year and a half of staging in various restaurants in Europe. Then two years starting her first solo endeavor in Spain before relocating to California, where she'd started up a buzzy LA restaurant. Then the first TV show, the cookbooks, and the awards and endorsements had come flowing in.

Then, abruptly, three years earlier, she'd simply vanished.

While a celebrity retreating from the spotlight wasn't unusual, what made Nicola's disappearance so strange was the number of high-profile commitments she left behind. There was the Times Square billboard promoting her guest judge appearance on *Top Chef*, quietly taken down three weeks after going up. A twelve-city book tour, canceled with no explanation. A prestigious

James Beard–award ceremony where her name was called and no one appeared on stage.

One day, she was on every screen, every shelf. The next, she was gone.

Rumors had swirled ever since. A kitchen accident that had left her disfigured. A drug overdose followed by a secret stint in rehab. Even whispers that she'd died and her family was covering it up while the money kept rolling in from her product line.

And now, for the past four months, helming a kitchen at a resort in the middle of nowhere, the only sightings from those fortunate enough to be able to afford a stay at the bucolic retreat.

What *had* happened?

Rosie tapped her pen against her notebook. If she could uncover the real story behind Nicola's disappearance, *Savorist* would have a fighting chance. At least for the foreseeable future.

For now, all she had to go on was what was here right in front of her.

After jotting down some initial ideas, Rosie sat staring out onto the inn's grounds, thinking about how to get more time with Nicola than her two measly half-hour sit-downs. Was Gabriel just protecting his star chef's time?

She took a long sip from her water bottle. If only it were that easy. Word on the street was that even *Oprah's* people had tried to get an interview with Nicola and been denied.

The fact that Rosie was even getting an hour was unbelievable.

No pressure.

The sight of a figure waving exaggeratedly shocked her out of her reverie. She sat up and took out her headphones.

The person standing below her balcony laughed. "Did I put you in a food coma or something?" her voice called.

It was Nicola. Turned out Rosie didn't need to go that far to find her.

Heart pounding, she secured the belt on her robe and approached the edge of her balcony. Nicola stood on the path bordering the vegetable garden, directly under Rosie's balcony. She had changed out of her chef's whites and was wearing a pair of jeans and a slim fitting black T-shirt, looking like an average person off the street and not a world-renowned celebrity chef. In the dim light coming off her building, Rosie noted the slim definition of Nicola's upper arms and how her shirt hugged her shoulders perfectly.

"Sorry to bother you," Nicola called up. "Just wanted to make sure the mini bar is stocked. And that you've got fresh towels."

Rosie smiled. "The service here is remarkable."

"Anything for our guests," Nicola said. "If you need a lint brush, I can..." She motioned toward the front lobby.

Rosie couldn't help but laugh. "I should be okay for now. Are you checking in on all your guests this evening?"

"Just the ones who seem in danger of falling asleep

on their balconies. You never know who's a sleepwalker."

"Well, I appreciate that. No, not sleeping. Just daydreaming, I guess." They were alone. They were flirting. It was a total Romeo-and-Juliet scenario. Now was the time to ask Nicola up for a nightcap. She didn't need to frame it as an interview. It could just be a conversation. Yes. A conversation. Two "old friends" (or whatever they were) catching up. She could throw in the interview part later.

"The dinner was unbelievable," Rosie said. She wondered if there was even a hint of insincerity in her words, and she grasped for a follow-up. "Honestly, I could have been happy with even just the bread basket. That stuff was heavenly. What a treat."

Bread? She went for the *bread*? Should she follow up with another compliment, or would that be laying it on too thick?

"Well, I'll leave you to it," Nicola said. "Good night, Rosie."

Damn it.

"Wait," Rosie said, now desperate not to let her get away without making something out of this encounter. "Do—do you have time to get together tomorrow? Before we talk? For a walk or something? I'd love to...see the inn's grounds through your eyes."

Nicola paused, and Rosie couldn't quite make out her expression in the dim light. "How's coffee? Eight o'clock? I know it's early, but I'll need to be in the kitchen by nine."

"Eight is perfect. Where should I meet you?" Rosie's

heart skipped a beat at the idea that in less than twelve hours, she'd be doing exactly what she came here to do. It would be a short conversation, but if she played her cards right, she could prime Nicola to open up before their official interview time. Show her that she was on her side and could be trusted.

"Why don't I bring us some coffees here, and we can walk," Nicola said. "I don't make it a habit to be in the inn's public spaces too often."

"Of course," Rosie said. She wouldn't be able to whip out her notepad, but she'd always been decent with mental notes.

"Now, don't be dozing off on this balcony," Nicola said, starting to walk away. "It would be a shame for you to miss sleeping in one of the inn's beds. They're the Cadillac of mattresses."

"Got it," said Rosie, at once trying not to jump for joy at the opportunity that had fallen right into her lap.

She waved, then flopped back into her chair, grinning ear to ear.

For the first time in weeks, Rosie felt something that looked a lot like hope.

Chapter Four

The following morning, Nicola hummed to herself as she extracted two take-out cups from a cupboard behind the bar. The restaurant was dark and quiet. She deftly measured two scoops of coffee grounds into the basket of the portafilter, then pressed the button on the machine and checked her email as the amber liquid poured into the two cups.

After the dripping stopped, she pulled the hot-water tap, steam hissing gently as boiled water filled the cup almost to the top, the dried-cherry and hazelnut notes wafting up from the cup. Perfection.

The coffee that the inn provided for guests was good. Nespresso machines were available in guest rooms, and there were carafes of a nice Costa Rican medium roast scattered at different convenient locations around the property, reception, the spa, the lounge near the activities desk.

But the restaurant staff, who were a finicky bunch about their caffeine, and understandably so, knew that the best brew on the property could be made behind the bar with the Victoria Arduino Black Eagle espresso machine.

Nicola poured a splash of cream into both cups, fitted lids over top, carried them out the door, stepping out into what was shaping up to be a stunner of a morning: the air slightly crisp, the sun making its way up into a cloudless cerulean sky.

In a ball cap and sunglasses, she could usually move through the grounds of the inn undetected. The public was used to seeing her in her chef's whites, so she rarely turned heads while going about her business in civilian garb.

Ever since she moved to Sugar Maple Farms, she walked every morning before service, to clear her head and simply enjoy the scenery. It had become another part of her daily ritual, a forty-five-minute outing before returning to her cottage for a light breakfast and a shower prior to heading into the kitchen.

Her cottage (the word suggested a more rustic establishment than it truly was: Gabriel had seen to it that her living space was every bit as luxurious as the rest of the accommodations on the premises) was set at the far edge of the property, in an area well removed from the rest of the resort. It offered her the peace and privacy she so desperately needed, but the proximity to her kitchen that made life easy.

While she owed her sister big time for taking her in when everything happened and she could no longer manage the life she'd created for herself, the solitude suited her better. She also loved her niece and nephew and was thrilled to be there for the day-to-day minutiae of their lives and see them growing up, but there was something so incredible about having a space of your own that was the same when you returned.

She'd learned a lot over the past few years, and one of the biggest and most important lessons was that she didn't need a lot to make her happy. Her small, four-season cottage in a forest in rural Ontario definitely made her happy.

Nicola crunched along the gravel path toward the inn's main building, where a bellhop was helping a guest with her luggage. Today's walk would be a bit less reflective than she was used to. She would be lying if she'd said she wasn't hoping to see Rosie on her balcony on her way back the night before. She'd decided, after bidding her staff good-night for the evening, that she needed to see Rosie again before the demo and interview the next day, to see if this spark she gave her the day before did anything to combat her "chef's block." And she hadn't even had to go to the trouble of asking her.

After returning to her cottage, she cataloged some ideas for some new dishes for later in the summer, based on the bounty of what the Sunset County would be offering. How long had it been since she'd felt this kind of inspiration? Gabriel was going to be thrilled, and probably relieved, to hear that the creative juices were starting to flow again.

Then there was the matter of managing expectations. A brief walk before their interview later would give Nicola the chance to let Rosie know, subtly, where she was willing to go with the discussion. She needed Rosie to understand that there were boundaries.

She glanced up at Rosie's balcony. Rosie wasn't there…until she was.

Nicola's pulse started to beat more quickly as Rosie placed her hands on the balcony's railing, her eyes closed. The morning sunlight made her smooth, lightly tanned skin glow. Her hair was pulled back out of her face into a long ponytail, revealing the delicate skin of her collarbone. Something stirred in Nicola, a kind of ache she hadn't felt in a very long time.

Just as she was about to call up, Rosie opened her eyes, grinning when she saw Nicola. "Well, thank goodness," Rosie said. "I was starting to think that a fresh coffee delivery had been a figment of my imagination."

Nicola raised the cups in mock cheers. "World-class service, remember?"

"I'll be right down," Rosie called, disappearing through her balcony door. A small current of energy coursed through Nicola. It had been a while since she'd gone for a walk with a beautiful woman. Done anything, really, with a beautiful woman. The thought made her senses sharpen and her mind race with possibility. Could Rosie be the one to snap her out of her rut? And if so, what would happen when she left?

It wasn't the time to worry about that yet. Rosie would be here for two more nights. Four more meals, if she had both lunches and dinners at the barn, although most guests usually went into town at least once or twice to have something casual and, fair enough, less expensive. She made a mental note to check the reservation system. She could ask Rosie but didn't want to seem…overly interested.

Something that could prove to be a tall order. Just then, Rosie emerged from the building looking effortlessly gorgeous in a way Nicola wasn't used to. Her last two girlfriends would have gotten up early just to apply a full face of makeup. Rosie's natural, radiant complexion was more beautiful than any red-carpet model Nicola had ever encountered. And she'd seen many.

She surveyed Rosie's outfit—a simple red sundress, belted at the waist, and a neckline that was at once classy and suggestive. If she was wearing makeup, she was doing a good job at keeping things subtle. Everything about Rosie was pleasing to the eye.

"I took a leap of faith and brought you a dark roast, splash of cream," Nicola said, passing her the coffee.

"Good guess," Rosie said, accepting the cup Nicola passed her. Nicola took in a slow draw of breath, that same strawberry scent filling the air between them. "Where are we walking?"

"This way," Nicola said, gesturing to the path toward the Walkers' farm. "We can check in on my friends, then continue on through the forest path."

Rosie nodded. Several quiet seconds passed as Nicola racked her brain for what to ask her. It was a strange scenario: They'd spent not even twenty-four hours together, many years ago. Yet somehow, Nicola felt like she knew Rosie. And there was something about her that really affected her. Something that she needed.

Luckily, Rosie wasn't as tongue tied. "So last time I saw you, you were on your way to somewhere exotic. Maldives, was it?"

"Seychelles," Nicola said, the image of the powder-white beaches and sparkling turquoise waters as her connecting flight from Nairobi made its descent flashed in her mind. The resort where she was working had only nine rooms, so the kitchen's output was small but extremely specialized. She was able to spend her months there learning precisely how to cook seafood to the highest standard: giraffe crab, swordfish, fish aiguillettes, jobfish.

It was also where she'd met Travis O'Keefe, another talented chef who had convinced her to forego the next leg of her trip, which was meant to be traveling through parts of Southern Africa, and go with him to the Peloponnese Peninsula, where her adeptness with seafood earned her a stellar reputation in the Greek culinary scene and was the beginning of her upward trajectory as a chef to watch.

Nicola glanced over as Rosie slid a pair of sunglasses over her eyes. They were big and black with a hint of understated glamor—they suited Rosie, effortlessly stylish. "You ever been?"

"No, I wish," Rosie said. "My job keeps me pretty tied to the city. The fact that I'm here is a real fluke." Nicola noted the inflection. Something about the way Rosie said *fluke* made it sound like she didn't entirely believe she belonged here. But to Nicola, she looked like she fit into the sunlight and quiet as if it had been designed for her.

"Tell me more about your writing," Nicola said. "Last time we saw each other, you were just finishing your master's, right?"

"Good memory," said Rosie.

Nicola dipped her head a bit as a couple walked by hand in hand, but they were deep in conversation and didn't seem to notice Nicola. There was something about their ease that hit her in the chest. On the surface, her conversation with Rosie was casual. But Nicola was on edge.

"I worked for a few months at a digital news publication, which I hated," Rosie continued.

"Too much bad news?" Nicola asked.

Rosie sipped her coffee. "I guess," she said. "There wasn't a whole lot of creativity involved either."

Nicola motioned to the turn-off, which would take them along the perimeter of the property to what she wanted to show Rosie. "So then what?"

"I started daydreaming about writing a novel someday, but that wasn't going to pay the bills," she said.

"What kind of book?"

Rosie was quiet for a moment. "It might sound kind of stupid, but I wanted to write a novel that was a kind of fictionalized account of my grandmother's life. A woman who suffers a major loss, then packs up and starts over somewhere new. I know—it reeks of *Eat, Pray, Love*." She laughed, but Nicola could hear the self-conscious edge behind it.

"It doesn't sound stupid to me," Nicola said. In fact, it sounded a lot like her own life story. Just that one simple premise—suffering loss, starting over somewhere new—it was like Rosie had reached into her chest and taken out her life story, about to make it into fiction. It stirred something inside her, a longing to know what Rosie was keeping deep inside her behind her easy smile and quick wit.

"I'll write it one day," Rosie said. "Anyway, like I said, it wasn't going to pay the bills, but I liked thinking about my grandmother in her kitchen in Lyon. Going to the market and picking up fresh ingredients. Trying new recipes. Cooking for herself and then eventually, when she got to know people, new friends and more-than-friends. I'm sure you'll understand this part—I just wanted to spend time thinking about food."

Nicola nodded. "All of that, I can understand." *More than you know*, she thought.

"So then I saw a job posting for *Savorist*. The woman who wrote short features had just had a baby, so it was a maternity leave. But she didn't come back, and eventually Jeremy, my editor, offered me a full-time gig. And here we are."

"Do you like it?" asked Nicola.

"I mean, it's allowed me to visit some interesting places. Meet some interesting people."

Nicola felt Rosie look sideways at her. "Is that right?" she asked. She looked over to find Rosie smiling knowingly.

"Interesting…and hopefully cooperative."

Before Nicola could respond, Rosie gasped, and Nicola watched her face light up with joy. "Is that…" She stopped in her tracks, then started ahead full speed to the edge of the horses' pen. "Is that an Akhal-Teke?"

Nicola quickened her pace and joined Rosie at the fence, watching as she held out her hand to Ayla, a golden-furred mare that lived on the Walkers' property. The horse approached with cautious curiosity and moved her head toward Rosie's outstretched hand. She ran her fingers underneath the horse's jaw, then sighed happily and looked back at Nicola.

"I rode one of these when I was younger," she said. "I haven't seen one in ages. They're so incredibly beautiful."

Not as beautiful as you, Nicola thought, admiring how the straps of Rosie's red dress met the collar at a point that showed just enough to see the shadowy beginning of the place between her breasts, her gold necklace set off next to her olive skin.

It was a miracle she'd ever let her leave her apartment all those years ago.

Nicola's breath caught. She hadn't meant to think it, not now. But something about Rosie, how she seemed to glow in the sunshine, was beckoning her away from the place of safety Nicola had vowed to stay in during Rosie's stay at the inn.

She steadied herself, then reached her own hand out to stroke the horse's soft mane. "This is Ayla. She's my favorite. A bit of a 'tude, but sweet as pie the next minute." She watched as Rosie stroked Ayla's cheek, seemingly lost in a daydream. "Let me know if you want to ride while you're here. I'll text Knox. I'm sure he or one of his stable hands will take you out on the trails."

Nicola silently congratulated herself for bringing Rosie here. Maybe she'd be distracted enough by the horses to cut their interview short later. She made a mental note to contact Knox.

But then, a flash of what that might look like intruded in her mind. Instead of spending the rest of the day in the kitchen, a day out on the trails with Rosie, maybe a stop for a picnic at the far end near the creek, was starting to seem very appealing. She imagined Rosie riding through the sun-splashed forest trails beside her, her dark hair flowing in the breeze.

It was ridiculous. She had a kitchen to run. But for the first time in as long as she could remember, she felt an inkling that there might be more to life than executing a menu to the highest standard.

Rosie's eyes lit up. "Really?" she said. "Thank you. I'd love that." She reached her hand back through the fence and allowed Ayla to nuzzle her nose against it. "You're just like a big piece of golden caramel, aren't you?"

Nicola pointed to the other side of the paddock, where a miniature horse was grazing. "Close, actually. Her name's Taffy. She's a little therapy horse. Works with some of the local kids, I think."

"I love that," cooed Rosie. "Thank you for taking me here."

What Rosie didn't realize was that this was a tactical move on Nicola's part. A move designed to charm and distract before the real questions started to come her way. Now it felt fraught, like she was dipping her toe into something dangerous, something that had nothing to do with journalism.

"My pleasure," said Nicola. "These guys are always a crowd pleaser."

"No doubt," Rosie said, still running her hand along Ayla's fur. Nicola watched as Rosie's fingers traced the fur, slow and gentle. There was something magnetic about it, like she was soaking up the moment with every movement.

Watching Rosie with the horses was almost as enjoyable as seeing the woman enjoy her cooking. Was Rosie just someone who savored life in general?

"Any other plans for the day?" Nicola said. "Spa appointments or anything?"

"No, no other plans. Well, of course, I'm looking forward to our sit-down." Rosie grinned. "And the cooking demo before it."

"Ah yes. The petting zoo," Nicola said, rolling her eyes at one of her least favorite parts of the week, but secretly, she was glad that Rosie would be there. She chose to ignore the first part of Rosie's comment.

"What?" Rosie said, laughing. "The petting zoo? What do you mean?"

"I mean exactly that. It's a petting zoo. No one's really there to learn how to cook."

"So what you're saying is the risotto isn't the star attraction."

"What I'm saying is that I could do without the part of my job that involves people paying attention to me instead of my cooking." Nicola looked at Rosie pointedly.

"Shots fired," Rosie said, narrowing her eyes, but the amused smile creeping across her lips softened the blow. "Now explain to me how that fits with you signing on to have your own television show."

Her words unsettled Nicola almost as much as the brightness of her smile. *That was a different me. The wrong me*, she wanted to say.

Nicola flashed back to the moment when she'd gleefully scrawled her signature on the contract with the production company in their office in Burbank, California, unable to believe how much money they were going to pay her to do what she did but on camera with some scripted banter and a makeup artist who fussed with her hair and face powder between each take.

The episodes were shot over long days, with retake after retake under the hot bright lights, but in the end, not only did it catapult her to a household name, which for some unknown reason was important to her at the time, it was also helpful in her media training.

Something that was going to come in handy over the next couple of days.

"That sounds like an interview question," Nicola said coolly.

"Well then, I guess I'm doing my job," said Rosie. Her voice was light, but Nicola could see the flicker of caution in her eyes.

"Ah. And here I was thinking we were just two old friends catching up," Nicola said. She knew she was getting under Rosie's skin and was enjoying watching it.

"Old friends, eh? Is that what we are? If that's the case you did a lousy job staying in touch."

Nicola imagined the agony of being simply *friends* with Rosie Franklin-Smith. But what was she supposed to call it? "I seem to recall us both agreeing that morning that it was a great night. And wishing each other well with our next adventures."

What neither of them were mentioning was the airline gift card Nicola had received as a gift at her going-away party, in a small box that she'd slipped into Rosie's purse before she'd left that morning along with a note suggesting Rosie visit her at some point during Nicola's travels.

Nicola could still recall every word from the email Rosie had sent a few months later, tentatively feeling around to see if the invitation was still open.

From her small on-resort accommodation overlooking the ocean in Anse Royale, late at night after service and after a few too many drinks at the Rhum Shack with the rest of the kitchen staff, Nicola had drafted a response dozens of times but could never seem to hit Send.

Between the long hours in the kitchen and the afterwork parties she'd had a hard time saying no to—who would, with Jungle Birds at the bar, swings for seats, bare feet in the sand, stars overhead, Bob Marley thumping and a crowd of young, beautiful people?—Nicola was keeping untenable hours. And every week, a new and exciting opportunity seemed to appear.

She'd wanted to see Rosie. But it never felt like the right time to reach out. And after a while, Nicola knew it had been too long. Rosie had probably moved on. That was for the best. At least that's what Nicola kept telling herself.

She looked sideways, trying to read Rosie's expression. Rosie was quiet for a moment. "I was really surprised to hear that you'd granted the interview to my magazine. When you could have *Bon Appetit. The New York Times.* Any publication in the world, really. And, um, Oprah?"

Nicola had known this moment was coming. She'd

told herself it was about control. That was why she'd said yes to Rosie, not because she trusted her or missed her or felt guilty about the way things ended. Control was cleaner. Easier to manage.

Rosie was familiar enough to be safe, but distant enough to keep at arm's length. Maybe seeing Rosie would give her a chance to find out what had really happened between them. How real it was, when it all felt like a dream.

Nicola stopped just in front of the rose garden, where she'd have to part from Rosie for the kitchen. She turned to face her. "Better the devil you know than the devil you don't." The second the words left her mouth, she regretted them. Too harsh.

Rosie blinked, then laughed—a short, disbelieving sound. "Ouch!" she said. "Really? The *devil*?"

Nicola raised an eyebrow and tried for a smile. "I picked you because I like you. And because I don't like journalists these days."

"And why's that?"

"They care more about clicks than people. They forget there's a human sitting across from them." She did her best to keep her tone neutral.

Rosie arched a brow and tilted her head, unreadable. "And you think I'm going to go easy on you?"

"Let's save the questions for the interview," Nicola said, checking her watch. She hesitated, then added, more gently, "I'll see you at the demo?"

She noted a brief flash of disappointment in Rosie's eyes. And against her better judgment, Nicola felt the urge to walk it back. To offer something. Reassure her.

That was dangerous. Had she made a mistake inviting her? Would it have been easier, safer, to bring in some blowhard from Condé Nast who she had no problem keeping at arm's length?

The crayfish sides with the crab, she heard her grandmother's voice say. Her *halmoni* loved her proverbs as much as she did her afternoon soap operas and doled them out like a blackjack dealer. Rosie felt like more of a kindred spirit than any of those other journalists. Hopefully she'd side with Nicola. She just had to make sure Rosie's gorgeous eyes didn't slip past her defenses the way they were trying to now.

"See you then. And thanks for the coffee," Rosie said.

Nicola watched as Rosie walked back to her room, then turned down the path toward the kitchen. She tried to focus on the tasks ahead for the day.

But a familiar scene flashed in her mind. The reason she so strongly needed to protect herself—and Gabriel. The reason she'd had to get out of the public eye, until now.

It was a Thursday morning in mid-February, the worst time of year to live in Toronto, with the early creeping in of dark night skies, holiday lights long since packed away and the winter wind that cut like glass. Nicola had flown in that morning, hours after getting the call from Gabriel the night before. His voice had been shaky, stunned. His father—and Nicola's mentor, Alexi—was dead.

After arranging for a private jet to take her from Mallorca to Pearson Airport, she met Gabriel at Alexi's new restaurant, the one Alexi had opened only two weeks earlier. Nicola was invited to the soft opening but was too caught up in a week-long party celebrating the launch of her partnership with one of Spain's top Cava producers as well as her recent semifinalist nomination for her third James Beard award. She'd promised Alexi she would drop by the next time she was in town. But had no idea that by the time she arrived, Alexi would be gone.

Walking into the restaurant, she saw right away so many things that she would have told Alexi to change. The lighting. The orientation of the seating. The decor. A quick survey of the menu with its outdated dishes and overly ambitious fusion elements told Nicola it was wrong. All wrong.

Alexi had been a terrific French chef, but he had no business opening a fusion restaurant in a neighborhood that craved craft beer and uncomplicated, farm-to-table fare. The concept had been doomed from the start. Three brutal reviews from the city's top critics sealed its fate. His savings vanished almost overnight.

A lump formed in Nicola's throat as she recalled the moment she realized that her selfishness, the loss of her moral compass and her obsession with her celebrity lifestyle had cost, and was the reason, Alexi had died by a massive stress-induced heart attack. She could have helped her friend and former mentor. With some targeted changes prior to opening and one social media post recommending the restaurant to her million-plus followers, Gabriel's father would still be with them today.

Another one of Halmoni's favorite sayings rang in her mind: *The more the rice plant ripens, the more it bows its head.* In other words, the more accomplished you are, the humbler you should be. Clearly that had slipped right out of her head at that time in her life.

Nicola wiped the corners of her eyes and squared her shoulders. As much as the memories pained her, they were also her fuel. Today she would deliver in the kitchen. She'd show up, smile and give the demo attendees a day to remember. She would give Rosie something honest to work with. A glimpse of the woman behind the fame. The one who still loved food as much as she had the first day she put on a chef's coat.

The rest—her shame, her silence—was hers alone to carry. And she would carry it, no matter how heavy.

Chapter Five

"Right this way please, everyone, and just a reminder that this is a smartphone- and camera-free environment. In order to focus on the session and the incredible flavors Chef Kim has prepared for you today, we are adamant that everyone remain in the moment and be present in the here and now," Sebastien said as he led Rosie and a small group of guests into a private dining area adjacent to the main dining room of the Barn, which was set up with a number of workstations for the participants and a wide steel table at the front, where Rosie presumed Nicola would preside.

Rosie watched as a few disappointed guests slid their phones into their pockets, already prepared to snap some photos of Nicola for their Instagram or maybe a trophy of a selfie if they were to be so lucky.

There was some awkward mingling and polite small talk among the participants, whose eyes kept darting to the dining room entrance in anticipation of the chef they'd all come to learn from—but mostly gawk at.

At exactly two o'clock, Rosie watched as Nicola strode into the space in full chef's whites, carrying her knife bag and followed by two waiters holding trays of Champagne flutes. Nicola's gaze searched the room, pausing when her eyes met Rosie's. She offered a quick, dazzling smile that made Rosie catch her breath. Rosie returned it, warmth rising in her chest. The anticipation of spending the next hour in Nicola's orbit settled over her with a soft rush.

As Sebastien introduced Nicola to the group (as though they wouldn't know who she was), Nicola arranged her workstation deftly and methodically, her hands moving over her tools swiftly. Thoughts of those same hands handling her with the same purpose and precision filled Rosie with longing. How she was going to stay focused and professional during their time together was starting to feel beyond her.

A pin drop would have been audible in the room as Nicola began to introduce the demo to the group, who were either sipping on their Champagne or gaping at her, charmed by seeing one of their favorite stars in the flesh. Rosie noted that Nicola exuded a star quality. It was almost as though the room was glowing brighter with her in it, even though she seemed to take no pleasure in the attention.

Strange, Rosie thought. For someone who spent so many years seeking out the spotlight, now it seemed like it just made Nicola...*itch*.

"Thank you for joining me today, everyone. It's a real pleasure to be with you. For today's session, we're going to be starting with something that pairs perfectly with those glasses of Ruinart Blanc de Blancs you're holding. One of the planet's greenest sources of protein. And, I might add, something that has long been considered an aphrodisiac."

There was a titter of chuckling through the room, and Rosie couldn't help but smile when Nicola looked her way once again. She was exuding a self-assuredness that was undeniably sexy.

"Rumor has it that Cassanova threw back over fifty at breakfast," Nicola continued, a mischievous smile on her face. "Any guesses?"

"Tequila shots?" a man in the front row offered.

Nicola laughed. "Good for him if he were able to perform after that. No, our first tasting today hails from the coast of Prince Edward Island." She pulled a large tray from the cart behind her, covered with glittering shards of ice, topped with dozens of fresh oysters. "While it's convenient to order pre-shucked oysters, I've always maintained that there's a certain pleasure to shucking your own, right at the moment you're ready to consume them. Can't get any fresher than that."

Nicola spoke easily and with confidence. Her voice was smooth and sultry, and her hair was now loose from the bun she'd been wearing while cooking the night before and the hat she'd been hiding under that morning. It took everything in Rosie to tear her gaze away for even a moment. Nicola was even more beautiful, more magnetic than she remembered.

She shifted in her seat. What was the culinary equivalent of an *anti*-aphrodisiac? Gefilte fish? That was what Rosie needed.

Two waiters helped distribute oysters and shuckers

to each table, along with dishcloths and small bowls of mignonette, horseradish and a house-made hot sauce.

After Nicola's demo, she moved around the room, offering quiet pointers and generous praise. Rosie fiddled with her shucker, wrestling with a stubborn Malpeque, unable to find the "keyhole" Nicola had told them to look for.

"Relax your wrist a bit. Feel around with the tip of the shucker." Nicola's voice came from just behind her, low and calm. The small hairs on Rosie's neck stood up. "Here, do you want some help?"

"I can do it," Rosie said quickly, that familiar frustration creeping in, the sting of not getting something right on the first try. Nicola's nearness wasn't helping.

"You sure? I can—"

"I said I'm good." Rosie gave Nicola a tight smile. Those piercing eyes only unsettled her more. She felt both self-conscious and undeniably turned on, two sensations she knew didn't mix well with precision work.

After a beat, she sighed. "Okay, okay. What should I do?"

Nicola stepped closer. Her hand slid over Rosie's, gently adjusting the position of the oyster shell. With her other hand, she guided Rosie's grip on the shucking tool. The subtle pressure of Nicola's fingers sent a jolt up Rosie's arm. She nearly dropped everything.

Her heart was racing now, loud in her ears. Too loud.

"Here," Nicola said quietly, "take the dish towel. I don't want you hurting yourself." Rosie forgot about everyone else in the room as Nicola gently instructed her, her calm, steady voice guiding the movement of her hands until there was finally a small pop. Nicola's hand on hers, she turned the shucker until the membranes around the mollusk's side broke open. "Now take the blade of the knife and run it along the top," she said.

Rosie felt Nicola's eyes on her as she followed her instructions. "You're a good teacher," she said, holding up the finished product for Nicola's inspection.

"Nah," Nicola said. "I just have good students. Here." She took the small bowl of mignonette and spooned a small amount into the bowl of the oyster, then held it out to her. A current of electricity seemed to buzz between them. Could anyone around them sense it?

She took the oyster from Nicola's hand and tipped it back, the fresh briny flavor of the ocean filling her mouth, and she swallowed the small morsel. She opened her eyes and found Nicola looking at her with appreciation and desire in her eyes.

Casanova was onto something—that much was becoming clear.

"Thanks," she breathed. Had they been alone in the room, she would have had a hard time keeping her hands from finding their way back to hers. Letting Nicola guide her anywhere.

It wasn't until Nicola moved to the next table that Rosie relaxed her shoulders. She sat down on her stool for a moment, took a long draw of the Champagne, then pushed the half-empty flute to the other side of her workstation. A taste was nice, but she still had an interview to get through.

After an hour, they'd shucked oysters, prepared a velvety olive tapenade with rosemary-infused breadsticks and stuffed pillowy cremini mushrooms with a sausage, fennel and ricotta salata mixture. The guests were charmed, satisfied and all but eating right out of Nicola's hand.

Back at the front of the room, Nicola wiped her chef's blade with a dish towel, then placed it again so carefully back in her knife bag before addressing the group. "So that brings us to the end of the demo. I hope everyone feels like they have a few more recipes in their repertoire for the next time you're hosting happy hour. Just don't forget to invite me."

While it was a small group, the applause was loud, and it was clear that the guests would be leaving happy.

Sebastien stood up again in front of the group. "Before we wrap up, we have a few minutes for any questions anyone might have about today's recipes."

Rosie had a few questions—that was for sure. And none of them would be appropriate in front of a group.

She mentally kicked herself. Letting her mind go down that road was absolutely off-limits. She had a strict professional code to adhere to, and she wasn't about to throw the opportunity to get the biggest story of her career out the window all because it had been far too long since she'd felt that same electricity that she'd felt when Nicola took her hands in hers.

As always in a small-group setting, it took a few moments for a volunteer brave enough to ask her question.

"Thank you, Nicola! This has been a dream come true. My husband and I are here on our twenty-fifth wedding anniversary together." The crowd smattered applause, and Nicola smiled graciously at the couple.

"My question is," the woman continued, "where did you disappear to all those years? We missed seeing you on *At Home with Nicola*."

Nicola didn't flinch, but Rosie noted a hint of unease in her demeanor. "Any British television fans here? I've always been a fan of how they end shows before their shelf life expires."

There was a stillness in the air that clearly Nicola had hoped to be filled with laughter, but none came, and the entire audience was on the edge of their seats.

Nicola scratched her neck, and Rosie almost couldn't watch but, at the same time, felt herself internally goading her to answer and make her job easier during their meeting later.

"It was a busy few years," she continued, "and I needed some time to refill the well, so to speak, before coming here. Which has been a dream come true for me."

The woman sat back in her seat, clearly not fully satisfied but aware that's all she was getting from Nicola.

"All right, well, thank you all again so much for coming, and don't forget—it's worth the effort to serve some freshly grated horseradish with those oysters if you can find it. Hope to see you all again at dinner tonight. Take care." And with that, Nicola exited the room. Two of the restaurant staff started to organize her equipment, and the guests started to trickle out to the patio for happy hour drinks.

Rosie stayed behind as the room cleared, gazing out the window and trying to strategize how she could possibly get more out of Nicola than she currently seemed willing to give.

She thought back to one of her third-year courses at journalism school, an interviewing-skills seminar taught by a famous podcast host from NPR. "No one's ever finished talking when you think they are," he'd said. "Always leave some dead space at the end of someone's response. You'll be surprised by how often they'll have something to add."

Or how much more awkward that would make things.

Moments after the last guest had departed, Gabriel entered the room. He smiled as he approached Rosie. "How did you enjoy the cooking demo?" he asked.

"I found it really interesting," she said. She glanced over to where Nicola had disappeared into the kitchen with her staff.

"I have a few staff members to introduce you to, in case you have any questions for them about the experience working here. And then I'll escort you to see Chef Kim."

"Thank you," Rosie said, adjusting her grip on her notebook.

For the next twenty minutes, a cast of kitchen staff rotated through the room like an efficient, if slightly awkward, round of speed dating.

Leo and Karlos came together, clearly more comfortable with their knives than their PR duties. Leo was inked from wrist to where his rolled-up sleeves ended at his elbows, his arms crossed in easy confidence. Karlos was all charm, with bright emerald eyes that seemed to flirt even when he was just asking for a pen.

"Chef Kim's a beast," Leo said, with a tone that conveyed he was giving the highest praise. "In a good way. Like...she walks into the kitchen, and everyone tightens right up. Total legend."

"Untouchable," Karlos added. "I mean, no one would ever mess with her. Never. She might be petite, but she's *mighty.*" He grinned. "And her cooking? I don't even know how her brain works. It's like she lives in a matrix or something."

Rosie scribbled some notes. It wasn't much, but it was starting to paint a picture of life in Nicola's kitchen.

Next was Danielle, the sous chef. "I appreciate that Chef Kim doesn't breathe down our necks," she said. "She gives us lots of space." Rosie jotted that down in her notebook and wondered if it was freedom or distance.

Then there was the sommelier, Ynez, who didn't give her much, but Rosie politely jotted down the notes about how much of a connoisseur Nicola was, something that Ynez claimed made her life much easier.

Finally, Gabriel returned, his eyes bright with expectation. "I trust you got some useful information?" he asked. He looked so hopeful that Rosie didn't have it in her to tell him no.

"Great—thank you," she said. She was more interested in the next meeting anyway.

"Chef Kim is ready to meet you in the conference room, in the business center. I can show you the way," Gabriel said.

Rosie pulled her tote bag off the back of her chair and stood up. "I didn't know there was a business center on-site," she said. "Isn't this supposed to be an escape from that kind of thing?"

"I was hoping," Gabriel said. "But there's a real market for corporate wellness retreats these days. Meetings in the morning, yoga and spa in the afternoon. We don't really advertise it, but it's been a well-used space ever since we opened."

"Business and pleasure. Guess they do mix." *Or not*, Rosie thought. She would have to continue to remind herself of that.

Gabriel raised his eyebrows, then shook his head. "Not in my world! When I vacation it's phone off, laptop at home and only my mother knows my whereabouts, in case of emergency."

Rosie laughed. "Well, good for you. The rest of us should aspire to that."

Gabriel smiled. "Follow me."

They walked past the spa, past the building that housed Rosie's room and past the vegetable garden where apparently Nicola had been spying on her the day before.

Down a short stone path, a cottage-like structure appeared at the edge of a small river.

"This doesn't look like a business center," Rosie said. The building was right out of a *Town and Country* ad and looked like it belonged in a Dickensian village. It even had one of those small milk-delivery doors on the side of the building.

"It's the original house on the property. When I came to terms with the fact that people would be conducting business here, I thought at least it could be in as less of a sterile environment as possible. No fluorescent lights or bad carpeting."

Rosie stepped through the heavy oak door into a reception area that reminded her of a Thomas Kinkade painting. "I like your style," she said.

"Nicola will be waiting for you in the drawing room. Right this way."

Once again, her nerves started ratcheting up. She had to nail this interview. Get Nicola talking and offering more than the perfunctory pleasantries that she'd shared with the audience that afternoon.

An image flashed in her mind of her parents opening the newest edition of *Savorist* magazine, to see that their daughter had landed the biggest interview of the year. Maybe they'd share the news with their friends over brunch, a little bit of humble bragging about their daughter who, up to this point, had been regularly eclipsed by whatever her brother had been up to recently. She could feel accomplished. Important.

Suddenly, the nerves morphed and assembled sharply in the pit of her stomach, while a cold sweat prickled over her entire body. She willed away a deep desire to flee and did her best to pay attention to what Gabriel was saying. They entered the drawing room, where Nicola sat casually in a wingback chair by a fireplace. Seeing her, the intense pressure Rosie was feeling was slightly tempered by the warm yet guarded look in her eyes. Despite the invisible shield she wore, there was something about her that calmed her and made her feel at ease.

"I'll leave you to it, then," she heard Gabriel saying,

and felt herself nodding, and suddenly she was alone with Nicola in the stillness of the space.

Nicola looked at her expectantly, but there was still warmth in her eyes. *Snap out of it*, Rosie admonished herself.

"That was a lot of fun today," she said, scanning the room for the best place to sit. Close enough to gain some kind of trust, but not close enough to stoke the flame that had ignited the moment she ran into Nicola in the dining room.

"I'm glad you enjoyed it." Nicola was cool, collected and way more prepared for the interview than she was. Her gaze drifted over Rosie's figure, sparking sensation beneath her skin like the brush of a hand.

There was an identical chair to the left of Nicola's, but Rosie would have to crane her neck to talk with her. She settled on the couch opposite, with a small table beside. Between them, there was a coffee table, with a pitcher of ice water on top. Rosie had a fleeting thought that more ice might be needed to temper the slow heat building between them, a heat that flared the moment their eyes met.

Rosie rummaged around in her bag, then extracted her notepad, a pen and her recorder. "Are you okay with me recording?" she asked, preparing for the inevitable rebuke.

"Standard procedure, right?" Nicola asked. She was the picture of cool.

Rosie reset. Could it be that this wasn't going to be as challenging as she'd expected?

"Right." She set the device to record and sat back in

her chair, trying to project calm and confidence. Thank goodness she'd worn her black cardigan and not the peach one that was merciless in its revelation of sweat stains. "Okay."

She had her list of questions that she planned on asking, the list that she'd carefully curated with Jeremy's help. But that was before she'd been in Nicola's presence again. Before she'd felt the weight of her focused gaze, the way her full attention made Rosie shift in her seat and want to rise to meet it.

It was a rare and strange feeling, wanting to succeed and perform not because of some external pressure to live up to an impossible ideal but to succeed because she cared so much about someone's view of her. "This time three years ago, you told *The New York Times* that the most important thing about food was the story it told, about place and space and the culture in which it exists. Tell me about how, if at all, your view has changed and if your new situation has informed that view."

She looked up to see a huge, sexy grin on Nicola's face and felt the blood rushing to her cheeks in response. Was Nicola making fun of her?

Nicola cleared her throat and leaned forward. "I'm thinking a lot more about place these days. The environment and climate change will always, always factor into my choices. The good news is that those choices are also good news for the consumer. The closer to home your food is sourced, the better it will taste. And I always think that things taste better when they're good for the planet."

True. And hot. But it reeked with rehearsed, press

junket canned answer. It was time to set off down the road that she knew very well Nicola wasn't eager to accompany her on. "So that was three years ago. And here we are." She gulped and steadied herself. "There's a lot of interest in where you went the last few years."

"Don't I know it."

Rosie paused, waiting to see if she'd continue. But no luck.

"So what's your question?" Nicola said.

"My question is, where have you been?"

Nicola looked out the window, seeming to consider her answer. "I was staying with my sister and her two kids."

Okay, that was something. Rosie had read about Nicola's sister, a few years younger than her. She was a physiotherapist. A chiropractor? Somewhere on the east coast of Canada, was it? She waited again, but Nicola was clearly content with the response she'd given.

"Okay. And what did you get up to there?"

"The kids keep you busy. Soccer practice. Homework. Crazy eights and Go Fish. My sister works during the day, so I helped with school pickup and drop-off."

"And dinner duty, I'm sure? Lucky kids."

"They're chicken-nuggets-and-fries enthusiasts, I'm afraid."

Clearly Nicola was going to make her work for it. "I guess what I'm wondering is why. You went from all over the place, on every magazine, red carpet, commercial, billboard—an appearance at the royal wedding, even—and then you disappeared to small-town Nova Scotia to play cards?"

Nicola's face clouded over. "Not sure family time qualifies as a waste of time."

"That's not what I meant, I just—"

"You just what?"

"I don't recall you being this guarded," Rosie said.

Nicola's eyes narrowed. "I'm sorry?"

Rosie's heart pounded in her chest as she felt the interview starting to get away from her. She needed to retreat. "It sounds like you're really close with your sister. Can you tell me more about her?"

Nicola's expression softened. "The strongest woman I know. She's raised those two kids on her own, after her dirtbag ex-boyfriend left her for his brother's wife. Not only that, but she's built a successful massage therapy clinic and volunteers at the local retirement home."

It was sweet how much she clearly loved and admired her sister. But Rosie still wasn't convinced. Nicola had enough money to hire her a whole fleet of nannies, if that was what she needed. "So then how did you end up here? At Sugar Maple Farms? Can you tell me a bit about what went into that decision?"

"That was an easy one. Gabriel and I go way back. He's like a brother to me. And this place is really special."

"Tell me more about your history with Gabriel."

Nicola looked at her watch. Rosie had never seen someone more uncomfortable in an interview situation than Nicola. It was almost painful. How could this be the same woman who had been so easy to talk to and spend time with? A quick glance at her own watch told her that she had Nicola for another fifteen, maybe twenty minutes. And she had nothing so far.

Nicola took a deep breath. "All right. My parents always believed that young people should get a job as early as possible. I spent a lot of time babysitting and then shoveling neighbors' driveways in the winter. But I wanted something more regular, so when I saw an ad in the paper for a dishwashing job at Gabriel's father's restaurant, I showed up one day before opening with my resume, and after a ten-minute chat with the owner, Alexi, I was hired. And that's where I fell in love with the kitchen. I'd stay at the school after classes and quickly finish my homework in the library, then head to the restaurant and work from six until close."

She took a sip of her water before continuing. "My parents thought it was too much, but I kept my grades up, and I was saving enough money to make it worthwhile. Gabriel was always around, and we've been in touch ever since."

Okay, well that was something. At least she hadn't had to prod it out of her.

"And every night I got sent home with leftovers. My parents didn't love cooking—we went from having pizza or a basic stir-fry to cassoulet and boeuf bourguignon. They'd be up watching Letterman and Leno, and we'd all sit together and have a great French meal before bed." She smiled at the memory. "I think I put on five pounds in my first month. And was still the skinniest kid in my class."

"The wonder of butter," Rosie said.

"Exactly," Nicola said. "I used to pack a meal or two

for my neighbors as well. The husband lost his job, and they were going through a tough time financially. They were so grateful. No one appreciates food more than someone who's ever had to go without."

"Is that why you started your school-lunch charity?"

"Partly," she said. "And I can't stand hearing about the junk that kids can buy in their school cafeterias. It's criminal. If I ever have kids, that stuff will be banned in my house." She paused. "What about you? Do you want kids?"

"This interview is about you, not me," she said. And if Nicola didn't give her anything she could use soon, then she would be out of a job. And kids will be the least of her concerns.

"Okay, then."

"And maybe. Yes. One day. In the future."

Nicola cleared her throat. "Okay. Anything else?"

The way she was evading her questions and making Rosie feel less like a journalist and more like a professional interrogator. At this point, she wasn't sure who wanted out more. "How about the rest of your staff?"

"They're pros," Nicola said. "Highly competent. Most of them stay out of trouble, and those who don't do a good job about hiding it. They take direction and don't cut corners." She shrugged.

"I've always pictured a kitchen being like a family," said Rosie. "Like there must be a lot of fun stuff going on behind closed doors. I mean, to take the edge off the pressure."

Nicola was quiet for a moment. "We don't have a lot

of time for fun. A kitchen at this level is a really professional setting."

Something about the way she said it sounded... stunted? Rosie knew of other chefs—not as high-level as Nicola, to be fair—who had shared all kinds of stories about the pranks, hook-ups and late-night bonding sessions over drinks after the kitchen was shut down. Some of it was probably more suited to the younger staff members, but a lot of it sounded like a reward for hard work well done.

Rosie glanced at her watch. She had five minutes remaining. Time to wrap things up for today, and then she'd take stock and figure out where to take things during their next sit-down. "What does the future hold for you?"

Nicola paused, pensive. "I try not to think too far ahead. Making plans can make you miss the thing that's sitting right underneath your nose." She stood up and looked out the window. "Come here," she said without turning around.

Rosie stood up and joined Nicola at the window.

"Look," she said, pointing at a deer that was feeding on some tall grasses next to the entrance to the forest path. Another deer stepped out of the forest, joining its partner for a few bites, unaware that they were being watched.

"Wow," she breathed. The most wildlife she'd seen recently were the pigeons in Trinity Bellwoods Park. And even they seemed domesticated, eating leftovers from discarded Mandy's salad takeout containers and strutting along next to the city joggers and stroller-pushing parents.

"I'm pretty happy here, for now," Nicola said. "You can put that in your interview. Make sure people keep booking."

"I'm sure Gabriel will be happy to hear that too," Rosie said.

"Speaking of Gabriel." Nicola gestured toward the lane that led to the business center, and Rosie saw Gabriel approaching with his purposeful stride, no doubt coming to collect Nicola at precisely the agreed-upon time.

Rosie felt a sharp pang of regret, not only that her brief window of time to get something good out of Nicola had come to a close, but that their time together that day was ending as well. As infuriating as she was about the interview, being close to Nicola had ignited something in her.

She wanted to stay with her and ask her a million more questions. To hell with the interview. She was just interested in anything Nicola had to say, in that deep and vulnerable look in her eyes when she was speaking about her sister or her past, and in that mischievous expression that told Rosie she was fully aware that she was pushing her buttons.

"One last question, before you go," Rosie said, turning to look at her. "When's our next session?"

Nicola fixed her in her gaze, as though she was trying to figure her out. "I don't know. It's a pretty busy schedule." She checked her watch. "And I only have a couple of hours before I have to get back to the kitchen and check on prep for dinner service. I need a bit of downtime. So I hope you don't mind if I…" She motioned toward the exit.

She couldn't believe Nicola was going to get away with shaving time off one of their two measly sit-downs. So it was only a couple of minutes. It still felt like she was getting short-changed. "How about tomorrow?" she asked. "Same time?"

Gabriel poked his head into the room. Nicola stood up and extended her hand. "I'll have my people contact your people."

Rosie clenched her jaw in frustration but managed a smile as she accepted Nicola's handshake, her frustration immediately tempered by the feeling of Nicola's skin pressed against hers.

It lingered a beat too long for it to be purely professional.

Tomorrow at this time, Rosie thought. *Let it be a yes.*

Chapter Six

"So?" said Gabriel, after they'd walked in silence for two minutes down the gravel path toward the forest. "How'd it go?"

"Fine. Pretty standard," Nicola said, still feeling her nerves settle after the intensity of being alone with Rosie in the meeting room. A half hour in which she'd done everything in her power to maintain self-control. But it was damn near impossible with how incredibly beautiful she'd looked. And how was it possible that something as chaste as a handshake had made her more turned on than she could ever remember?

There was also the fact that she'd felt herself telling her more than she'd intended. The stuff about her childhood and their struggles with money? It wasn't something she'd planned on sharing or had ever really talked about in an interview. But there was something about Rosie that made Nicola desperately want to confide in her, the way she had the night they'd first met.

She remembered revealing her trepidation about the trip she was about to take and how she was leaving behind a great situation at Persimmon for the complete unknown. How she'd been lying awake at night, staring at the ceiling and imaging the many ways the trip was going to be a colossal error.

Rosie had been so easy to talk to, so nonjudgmental. Nicola wanted that again. She wanted to tell Rosie about the funk she was in. She wanted to tell her that she wasn't, in fact, totally okay with the division between her and her team but that after everything that had happened, she found it hard to trust new people. She wanted to tell her about Alexi and the guilt that weighed on her every day and now felt like a lousy source of inspiration for a job that required a true creative spark, something that came from a place of peace and confidence, not fear and regret. She wanted to really *talk* to her.

Maybe it wasn't just Rosie. Maybe the problem was her. This guardedness she wore like armor had once protected her. But now? It was just getting heavy.

But she's a journalist, she reminded herself. It was Rosie's job to get people to trust her. Rosie didn't really care about her. She just wanted the story.

And yet.

Nicola was completely torn between wanting to see her again and wanting to stay as far away from her as possible. What was she thinking, all but agreeing to sit through another half hour of probing her personal life?

"I'm glad to hear it," said Gabriel. "Because listen." Gabriel stopped. "I hate to put this pressure on you. But Calvin called this morning. The board met last night. And it sounds like the property evaluation didn't go in our favor."

"What does that mean?"

"It means our taxes are set to increase significantly

starting next year. We're going to have to raise resort prices as a result."

Nicola considered. The inn had steady bookings. Aside from Langdon Hall, the Restaurant at Pearl Morissette, the Elora Mill Inn and a little further afield, Manoir Hovey, it wasn't like there were that many places for people to travel close to Toronto for a truly upscale-dining experience in a beautiful natural setting. "People will pay. We've had no issues to date, have we?"

"Well no, but they're of the mind that there needs to be a renewed focus on the inn to make sure it stays in the public consciousness. Warrant the jump in price. You know just as well as I do that things can fizzle out pretty quickly."

Nicola considered. Constant reinvention, while maintaining the spirit of a place, was important. But surely her reputation was enough to sustain them, even through a slight price hike, was it not? And besides, didn't people with money equate price with desirability? The more it cost, the better it was perceived to be?

She took a deep breath in. Gabriel wasn't asking her for much. And besides, it was in her contract.

"How about this," Gabriel said. "Danielle can take the lunch service tomorrow. Take a few hours and take Rosie on a tour of Sunset County. Show her the sights."

Nicola paused. While she wasn't thrilled about the idea of missing a service on her scheduled day—Sundays and Mondays were her days off, and she didn't like to take extra time—her sous chef, Danielle, was the most talented that she'd ever worked with and would be ecstatic for the opportunity. Plus, there was the added benefit that a tour of the area would take the conversation in a very different direction than another one-on-one sit-down.

It wasn't perfect. But if she did it, she'd be doing it for Gabriel. For Alexi. For the chance that she might work her way out of this rut. "I'll think about it," she said. "What's the plan, aside from that?" Gabriel was sharp. Surely he wasn't banking on just one positive article.

He scratched his chin thoughtfully. "I've identified a couple of private equity firms that might be interested in investing. There are also some high-net-worth individuals in the area who might be willing to support a local business."

"Okay," said Nicola, furrowing her brow. "Sounds like there's a lot on the line." She studied his face—steady gaze, calm voice, no sign of stress. Gabriel always led like that. Just calm, easy. He set a good example for his team—that was for sure.

"It's not uncommon for a property like this to have a few bumps in our first year," Gabriel said. "The capital investment for this place was huge. We're still sorting out some inefficiencies, stabilizing operations. Attracting repeat guests, which—" he looked at her, smiling "—you've been a great partner in. The Barn is the jewel of the hotel."

Nicola swallowed. No pressure.

"Which is why I'm inviting some key potential investors to visit in a couple of weeks. We can meet beforehand to discuss the menu."

"Absolutely," Nicola said. For a dinner like that, it wasn't uncommon to do a bit of recon on the diners. Digging into diners' preferences, tailoring the menu—

that was way more in Nicola's wheelhouse than being grilled by journalists.

Nicola had always believed that her work spoke for itself. But now it seemed like the work wasn't enough. When had the rules changed? Or had she just been pretending they hadn't?

She glanced at her watch. Two precious hours before she had to be back in the kitchen. A bit of downtime, then a cool rinse in her outdoor shower.

"You just let me know what you need," she said as they reached the fork in the path. "See you later."

"See you later," Gabriel echoed before setting off in the other direction.

Nicola breathed deeply, walking toward her cottage, letting Gabriel's words settle. She'd faced tight financial situations before. In a high-end restaurant like the Barn at Sugar Maple Farms, where margins were razor thin and risks high, precariousness was expected. It was part of the game.

A shout across the field pulled her away from her thoughts, followed by cheers. Five of her kitchen staff were playing football. She watched for a few seconds, then smiled to herself, recalling the camaraderie she once shared with her team members in kitchens of her past. The head chefs who seemed were often at arm's length, who were enigmatic and sometimes even terrifying. The friendships—and sometimes more-than-friendships—that grew in kitchens weren't just about spending so much time together. They were survival tactics, a way to band together.

Today fun was clearly on the menu for this group.

"Chef!" Tim called out. "Go long!" He mimed throwing the ball her way, but she just smiled and waved him off. He turned back to the game.

Nicola thought about Rosie's statement. *I've always pictured a kitchen being like a family.* With Alexi, that had been the case, but she'd chalked that up to how well she gelled with him and Gabriel. At other kitchens, she'd made friends, lovers, partied, lived. But wasn't that just part of being young and inexperienced?

Was she too distant from her team? Too detached in the wrong ways? She knew they weren't afraid of her, in an unhealthy way at least. But was her disconnection part of what was holding her back?

Or was it prudent, keeping a safe distance? Her family, Gabriel—she trusted them implicitly.

Rosie's words rang again in her mind. *I don't recall you being this guarded.*

For the past few years, some distance felt like it kept things clean and simple. Now, watching her team laugh and play under the sun, carefree and enjoying one another's company, she wasn't so sure. Maybe Rosie was right.

Maybe the walls weren't protecting her anymore—just keeping her stuck.

Back at her cottage, Nicola grabbed a sparkling water from her fridge and a towel from the linen closet, then took her phone to her back patio and settled into the chair at the bistro table and opened the FaceTime app.

The pulsing chirp of the ringer sounded, and moments later, her grandmother's face appeared on the screen. Her eyes lit up behind her amber-rimmed glasses, her tightly curled perm likely just touched up at the salon. "*Aigoo*, finally!" she said. "You knew I'd be watching *B&B* right now, eh? You called at a good time. This *jalsaengin namja* is about to confess, and I don't trust him—*cheh!* He's too handsome to be sincere."

Nicola laughed. Her grandmother had been a devotee of *The Bold and the Beautiful* as long as she could remember. She and her sister had watched with her every afternoon for the long stretch of time her grandmother had taken care of them after school in their youth, likely way too young before it was appropriate. "Hi, Halmoni," she said. "I don't want to interrupt your show. I was just calling to say hi."

Her grandmother waved her away. "You can pause TV now, you know that?" There was a rustling in the background, and the only image on the screen was Halmoni's popcorn ceiling. Finally she reappeared again. "So how are you, *uri aegi*?"

Even hearing her grandmother's voice softened some of Nicola's anxiety. "I'm doing okay," she said. "You know, the usual. I want you to come and visit sometime soon."

"*Omo*, this old bag of bones is getting too old to travel," she said.

"Don't be crazy," Nicola said. "My parents said last time they went over they found you on a ladder outside washing the windows. Mine are looking a little dusty, to tell you the truth."

Halmoni hooted. "If I come to stay with you, I'll be in the president's suite!"

"No doubt." Nicola grinned. And it wouldn't even need to be Nicola who made it happen. Halmoni had a way of charming the pants off everyone she met.

One of the family's favorite stories came from the years Halmoni lived across the street from a used car lot. Instead of buying a car, she'd saunter over whenever she had errands, and the guy at the lot would hand over the keys to whichever vehicle she fancied. For nearly five years, she drove whatever caught her eye: first a blue Mustang convertible, and after that sold, a bubblegum-pink Cadillac.

If she hadn't given up driving decades ago, Nicola would've loved to buy her a car fit for the queen she was.

Mi-ja Kim was nothing if not Nicola's biggest cheerleader over the years. Her living room was a shrine to her granddaughter, with press clippings about Nicola's restaurants, photos of her with different celebrities and dignitaries, and in her kitchen, every single pot, pan or utensil was from the Nicola Kim product line, save for one item: her *ddukbaegi*.

That earthenware pot had pride of place on her stove, used for the dishes Nicola still associated with comfort and coming home: *kimchi jjigae*, *gyeran jjim*, *galbitang*, *bibimbap*—warm, bubbling meals she'd eagerly anticipated on every visit to Halmoni's home in Newmarket.

The irony was that the cooking gene seemed to have skipped a generation. Nicola's parents favored more North American tastes: frozen lasagnas, burgers, simple casseroles. Efficient, practical meals that kept the family fed while her parents focused on their careers.

So when their grandmother started taking care of her and her sister after school before their parents got home from work, Nicola remembered watching the clock tick toward the end of the school day in her classroom, practically salivating in anticipation before she could run through the school yard and through the neighborhood to Halmoni's house, where her grandmother would have a full meal waiting for her and her sister by the time they arrived.

What she wouldn't give right now to spend time with one of her most cherished family members.

"I'll talk to my parents and see when we can get you up here," she said.

"You're okay, though, *uri aegi*?" Halmoni asked.

"It's been hard," Nicola admitted. "But I'm doing okay."

Halmoni nodded. "Don't forget—after the rain, the ground hardens."

"Struggle makes you stronger," Nicola said. "I know. Love you, Halmoni. Talk soon."

She hung up and sighed. Her family was so far away. Was it time for her to branch out here, make one for herself?

As she set her phone down, she stared out at the sugar maples swaying gently beyond her patio.

Halmoni loved her proverbs, and she was usually right. After the rain, the ground did harden. But first she had to let it rain. Maybe it was time to stop holding back—from her team, from Rosie, from herself.

Chapter Seven

After changing out of her dress into a pair of jean shorts and a soft cotton tank top, Rosie grabbed her notebook and sat back on the plush couch in her room with a satisfied sigh, then flipped through the notes she'd taken.

There was some good stuff. And there was something about Nicola's responses that started to evolve over the course of the interview. She seemed to warm up. If only Rosie had more than thirty minutes.

She spent some time highlighting key points that might be usable. She wasn't sure what she'd expected from their first real conversation, but at least now she had a sense of what she was dealing with. There were at least a couple of inroads, a few threads to pursue that might result in something substantive.

With decent material and a full afternoon ahead, she figured she'd earned a small reward.

She remembered seeing the spa building on the way to the business center. Maybe there was a last-minute appointment available. A massage or a deluxe pedicure sounded perfect right about now.

The spa building was located at the edge of Lake

Shaughnessy. It was a cedar-shingled structure with sweeping views of the water, with seating areas and hammocks out front and various pools of different temperatures for a hot-and-cold-plunge circuit.

Rosie let herself in through the heavy wooden door and breathed in the welcoming scent of eucalyptus and lemon verbena. Soothing harp music played in the background as the front desk attendant greeted her with a warm smile. "Welcome," the woman said. She was dressed head to toe in white linen and had her blond hair pulled back in a sleek ponytail.

Rosie already felt more relaxed, and she hadn't even shelled out what she was sure was going to be an exorbitant amount for her treatment. But, she reminded herself, she'd finished her first interview with Nicola, and alone that was cause for celebration.

"Do you have an appointment today?" the attendant asked.

"I don't, actually," Rosie said. "Do you have any availability for a manicure?"

The attendant tapped on her keyboard and examined the screen. "Josie can take you in half an hour," she said. "In the meantime you're welcome to enjoy the amenities. There's a changeroom just down the hallway, with robes in the lockers." She passed Rosie a clipboard. "Please fill this out, and then you're all set. Josie will come and find you when it's your time."

Rosie felt as light as the terry cloth robe she'd just pulled over her shoulders as she exited the spa changeroom to the pool area, where she settled into a shaded lounger. She pulled a paperback from her bag and tried reading a few pages, but her mind kept drifting with different directions she could take the article. The stuff about Nicola's parents not enjoying cooking was fun and interesting. And the part about bringing food to her neighbor was humanizing. She'd put together a few paragraphs later that evening and send them to Jeremy for feedback.

She had a plan in place. Now it was time to take a break from her work and enjoy the blissful perfection of Sugar Maple Farms, which was even more idyllic than she could have ever imagined. Her only responsibilities for the next few hours were her spa appointment, maybe another walk around the property and then another dinner. She was there for work, sure, but when would she ever have the chance to enjoy a property like this again, all expenses paid?

Despite the serenity of the spa environment, she thought she knew the answer to that question, and it was keeping her from fully relaxing. If she could uncover something real, something about Nicola's disappearance, which increasingly felt like a story worth telling, one Nicola seemed to be guarding like a precious jewel, then maybe this wouldn't be a one-and-done opportunity for Rosie after all.

She pulled her straw hat over her face, closed her eyes and breathed in the warm air, listening to the far-off buzz of pleasure crafts buzzing on the lake and the call of a loon closer to shore, willing herself to relax.

At the sound of the door opening and the shuffling of flip-flops on the pool deck, Rosie opened her eyes slightly and watched through the basket weave of her hat as two robe-clad women claimed two other loungers under another umbrella, magazines and iced teas in hand. They looked to be about her age, two friends on vacation.

Gertie! Rosie sighed. If only her friend were here.

Maybe she could splurge sometime and come back. It would be a perfect girls' trip, and having an opportunity to see Nicola again felt promising. Something was clearly still simmering between them, and while Rosie knew it would never amount to anything, being in Nicola's presence was as addictive as the candied pecans in her room's minibar.

She felt herself drifting off again until the women's murmured conversation—something about lunch—piqued her interest.

"Yeah, but remember when we were at Cielo in Madrid?" said the one in the Chloé bucket hat. Rosie perked up a little. She recognized the voice from the cocktail reception. What was the woman's name? Kassie? Kylie? *Kerry.* Seemed like her friend had arrived for her one splurge night. Good to know Rosie wasn't the only one here on a budget. "You remember, right? And that woman came in and made a scene in the lobby?"

"It's a good thing their maître d' was basically a bouncer," her friend replied. "I heard Nicola was cheating on that woman with her sous chef."

"That's not what I heard," said Kerry. "I heard the woman was cheating on Nicola. Nicola dumped her, and she lost her mind."

"I mean… I get it," her friend said, fanning her face

with dramatic flair. "I've never been with a woman, but I definitely wouldn't say no to her."

"She's so hot," Kerry agreed. "And I guess she's not so messed up anymore if she's here. Although you can't take pictures in the restaurant or at the demo. Weak."

Rosie bristled. *Messed up?* Nicola wasn't messed up. She was private. So what if she didn't want her photos splashed all over the internet anymore?

"I read somewhere," Kerry continued, "that something weird happened with her and the dad of the guy who owns this place."

"What, like a relationship?"

"I have no idea. But the fact that she's here now? It all seems a little incestuous."

Rosie felt her pulse quicken. She almost spoke. Her instinct was to protect Nicola, but how would that work, if they ever found out Rosie was there to write an article about her?

She kept her hat over her face, listening intently, fighting the urge to tell them to shut up.

"Whatever. All I care about is that she keeps me well fed while we're here. The first night was forgettable. Last night was better. Hopefully tonight is the night. Otherwise I'm asking for a refund."

"Amen to that."

The conversation shifted to some other celebrity gossip from one of their magazines. Rosie tried to relax again, but a dull unease lingered. She was unsettled by how casually they dissected someone else's life.

But wasn't she just as bad? The whole reason she'd come was to get the scoop on the private details of

Nicola's life. A light sense of shame crept over her, followed by a feeling of confirmation that by delving into more stories like the ones Nicola had shared that afternoon, and allowing Nicola to direct the conversation, she'd be doing the right thing.

After her manicure—a light pink polish with a bit of a shimmer, and a paraffin treatment that left her skin feeling like spun silk—Rosie walked the paths of the property, eventually ending up at the games and equipment hut, where she decided to borrow a bike for a spin. A bit of exercise was in order before another indulgent meal that evening.

"Here's a map of the property," the chipper young attendant said, her tight curls as bouncy as her attitude. "It's a pretty simple loop, though. But there are a couple of turn-offs that look like you're going the right way but take you down another road."

Rosie examined the map. It looked simple enough. "I should be fine," she said. "Can I leave my tote bag here for a few minutes?"

"Of course!" said the girl. Moments later, after signing her life away on an insurance waiver, Rosie wheeled a red Dutch cruiser with a white leather seat away from the equipment hut. She admired her new nail polish as she tested the breaks, then set off on the trail, coasting down the path into the shaded woods and relishing the feeling of the warm summer breeze rippling through her loose hair.

The Inn at Sugar Maple Farms, Rosie decided, was truly heaven on earth.

As she coasted down the trail, she tried to remember the last time she'd ridden a bicycle. Probably not since her trip to Lyon, when her grandmother insisted they ride into town with big panniers strapped to the sides, ready to haul back all the treasures they found at the market.

Rosie smiled at the memory of the added challenge of the weight of the items, and how it required a new level of balance, especially on the days her grandmother wanted to re-stock her wine rack.

Between the dreamlike setting and her trip to memory lane, Rosie barely noticed how far she'd gone until the trail split into two nondescript paths just ahead. She slowed her bike to a stop, scanning her surroundings for the instructive markings that had populated the rest of the trail. Hadn't the girl basically implied only an idiot would get lost?

Rosie tried to recall the map she'd waved off, trying to mentally decipher where she was on the property, then thought about her phone, tucked into the zippered pocket of the purse she'd left at the activities hut. *Pick a path, any path*, she thought and pushed her bike forward again and started to pedal toward the path on the right.

She surveyed the forested area in front of her. Just beyond the thick swath of birch trees, she spotted a structure about a hundred meters away. Whoever lived there would likely be able to point her the correct way back.

She dismounted her bike, moving her foot to catch the ground, but her sandal caught in the foot strap. Her ankle twisted, shooting a sharp pain through her ankle. Rosie cried out in pain and tumbled to the gravel path, where she extended her leg and slowly tried wiggling her toes to make sure nothing was broken. “Damn it,” she gasped.

So much for her idyllic forest adventure.

Carefully testing out her ankle, which was painful but definitely not broken, Rosie got herself into a standing position. It hurt to walk on, but she picked up her bike and leaned it up against a thin birch just off the gravel path.

A narrower path led to the house. Rosie approached gingerly, not wanting to further damage her injured ankle by tripping on a rock or misstepping on an uneven section of the path. “Hello?” she called.

The house before her was small but cozy looking, almost fairy-tale like, but coupled with modern touches like large windows reflecting the forest, a solar-panel lined roof and a carefully manicured garden of snowball viburnums lining the exterior. Whoever lived there had a little slice of charming, modernist heaven.

She took a few more careful steps, trying to gauge if anyone was home. Whoever lived here also likely chose the remote location because they valued their privacy. Was a knock at the door going to be an unwelcome intrusion?

Rosie put a little more weight on her injured foot and gasped when a shot of pain stabbed. She looked down to see that it was already swelling.

Privacy be damned. Rosie needed ice.

She rapped on the door lightly and waited, then when there was no answer, she knocked again, this time with a little more force. Why had she left her phone behind?

Could she enter the little cottage, like Goldilocks, and just take what she needed?

A sound like spraying water was suddenly audible from the side of the building. Maybe the owner was doing some gardening.

Rosie hobbled a few steps down and moved gingerly along the gravel path to the side of the building, focusing on the path to make sure she didn't step on a rock or in a divot. Not only was her ankle twisted, but when she looked down at her elbow to see what was causing the burning sensation, she noticed she'd also scraped the skin there.

She rounded the corner, then yelped as she collided hard with a warm, towel-clad body and stumbled back. "Oh my goodness! I'm sorry—I just—" Rosie said, catching her balance. She glanced up.

Nicola.

She was clutching her towel to her chest, droplets of water still clinging to her shoulders and arms. Rosie glanced over her shoulder to find an outdoor shower connected to the side of the building, hidden only by a chest-high stone partition.

Surprise quickly gave way to recognition, and Nicola smiled. "Fancy running into you here," she said.

Rosie did her best not to let her gaze trail over Nicola's naked shoulders or the place where the towel hugged her breasts together. "Do you… I'm sorry—I just—" She paused, trying to compose herself. *Relax. It's nothing you haven't seen before.* Except it felt entirely different now.

"Isn't this a little beyond the journalist's code? Stalking your subject?" Nicola said, a mischievous glint in her eyes.

"I was out cycling and got turned around," Rosie said. "And I think I might have sprained my ankle."

Nicola's amused expression quickly turned to concern. She pulled on a gray T-shirt that was slung over the stone wall, then made her way over to where Rosie was standing, all of her weight on one foot. "Here," Nicola said, extending her hand. "Come in and sit. I'll get you some ice."

Rosie accepted Nicola's hand and allowed her to support her as she guided Rosie carefully toward the house. As they approached the steps, Nicola tucked her arm around Rosie's back right under her shoulder. The contact mixed with Nicola's care sent a rush of warmth through her. She breathed in the scent of her soap—something crisp and green—which rose up between them, momentarily distracting Rosie from the throb in her ankle.

"How did you hurt yourself?" Nicola asked as she assisted Rosie through the doorway.

Rosie scanned Nicola's living space. The inside of her cottage was as well-kept and pretty as the exterior. The most striking feature was the placement of the windows, which allowed the light in, filling the space with a warm glow and providing views of the surrounding forest.

"Apparently the old saying's a lie," Rosie said as Nicola helped her to the couch. "Turns out you *can* forget how to ride a bike."

"Here," Nicola said. She pulled over a camel leather

ottoman and shimmied it under Rosie's outstretched foot, allowing it to rest there. "I'll get you some ice. Do you want a drink? Something stiff to take the edge off?"

"No, no. I didn't mean to bother you. I'll just rest for a sec, then I'm sure I'll be fine to head back."

"You're not going anywhere with a sprained ankle. Just let me call Wes from the front desk to come and get you. The bike can go back later."

Nicola disappeared to the kitchen, leaving Rosie on the couch with her foot propped up. She listened as Nicola spoke with someone on the phone, trying to imagine her sitting alone in this room at night after the dinner service. Or not alone? The idea of Nicola being in the space with another woman sent an unreasonable current of jealousy rippling through Rosie's veins.

"See you soon," Nicola said, then reappeared in the entrance to the living room. "He's on his way."

Rosie looked around, taking in the peace of the surroundings. "So this is where you live? Not too shabby."

"Suits me fine. It's private." Nicola adjusted the sleeve of her T-shirt. "Usually."

Rosie felt her cheeks redden, even though Nicola's tone was playful. "I'm sorry. I really had no idea where I was."

Nicola perched on the edge of the couch. "I'll have to let Gabriel know that we'll need stricter guidelines for our journalists when they visit. Ankle tracking devices or something."

"How are we supposed to get our scoop without the freedom to do a little sleuthing?" Rosie said playfully.

"Ah, so that's what this is," Nicola said, her gaze

trailing down Rosie's bare leg to the ice pack on her ankle. "A clever ruse."

"My pride wishes I could say yes. But it's more like a bad sense of direction paired with lack of coordination."

Nicola grinned, then reached for the ice pack. She picked it up and inspected Rosie's ankle, gently touching the skin near the site of the injury, the heat from her fingertips warming her cold skin. "A bit swollen but nothing too bad," she said.

The softness in the way Nicola was tending to her was making her forget all about the light throbbing pain in her ankle. "Thanks for helping me out," she said.

"I'm not one to turn away a damsel in distress. Even if there's a slight chance she's here to spy on me."

Before Rosie could respond, the sound of Nicola's phone ringing sounded from the kitchen. "I'll be right back. Don't move," she said.

Rosie watched as Nicola left the room, then looked around at the living space, now able to take in the details without looking like she was spying.

There wasn't much of a personal nature, aside from whatever you could infer from a person from their choice in paint colors and couch fabric. Sleek, modern and clean, with warm colors, with everything arranged to face the fireplace as well as the view of the surrounding woods. The only photo was framed on the wall on the opposite side of the room, but it was too far away for Rosie to see.

The sound of Nicola's voice approached the room, and she continued her conversation as she stood in the doorway, leaning against the frame and looking at her.

Rosie shifted in her seat, suddenly self-conscious.

"Wait, Sunday?" she said to whoever she was talking to. Her expression changed as she continued to hold Rosie in her gaze. Was she thinking anything about her or just making sure she wasn't snooping? "All right, fine." She paused another moment. "Yep, ciao."

Nicola pocketed her phone. "Sorry about that. Just Gabriel."

"Calling to set up our next interview?" Rosie said.

Nicola raised an eyebrow. "No, actually. Just another event he's hoping I can show up to."

Rosie tried to mask her disappointment as well as her annoyance. "We can find another time, though, right?" she asked. She hadn't come all this way for a measly thirty minutes.

Or maybe it was better this way. Any more time with Nicola only felt like putting herself in temptation's path. Still, the idea that this could be the last minute she'd have alone with Nicola before she left Sugar Maple Farms was making a surprisingly large impact on her.

"I'll do my best. It's just a busy few days," Nicola said. "But how about Sunday evening?"

"I'm leaving Sunday morning. And you still owe me one more interview."

"Stay one more night. Gabriel will comp your room. I'd like you to come with me to a party Sunday. It's a local couple—you've probably heard of them. Will Hastings and Maya Monroe?"

"The film director?" Rosie asked, her mind racing. "And Maya's a writer, right?"

"Yes. They're both great. And I'd love for you to be

my date. I don't usually go to these things, but I can endure some small talk if you're with me."

"Why not just…not go?"

Nicola shrugged and looked out the window. "Gabriel just asked me to. The cocktails'll be decent." Something in the way she was brushing off the event but was still willing to attend didn't quite jive with the Nicola she knew. There had to be something important about this party. And the writer in her wanted to know what that was.

Nicola looked back at her expectantly, and Rosie hesitated. On one hand, going as Nicola's date would be amazing. She could picture herself on her arm and what she would look like dressed up. On the other hand, attending an event with her in public was exactly the opposite of maintaining professional boundaries. "I'd love to, but I can't." She saw what she thought was a flash of disappointment in Nicola's eyes. "I need to get back to the city. And I need our second interview before I leave."

"What's one more night?"

"I've got to get back to the office. And this place isn't exactly budget friendly for a publication like ours. It feels like you're stalling."

"Like I said, I'm sure we can comp a night."

"Then we have to publish that we were guests of the inn. Which immediately calls into question the objectivity of the article."

"So what you're saying is that it's a glowing review?" The twinkle in her eye told Rosie that she knew it couldn't be anything but.

"I still haven't finished the article. I don't really have a lot to go on, you know." She looked at Nicola pointedly.

Nicola was quiet for a moment. She shifted in her seat and looked out the window. "What you said about me earlier. About me being guarded?" There was something in the change of the tone of her voice that signaled something of importance was about to be revealed.

"Yes," Rosie said, hanging on her words. Was this it? Was she about to get what she came for?

Another beat of silence hung in the air. "I'm not guarded," she said finally. "I'm just not as interesting as people seem to believe." Then she grinned, seemingly loving her own joke.

For a moment, and even though she was irritated to be strung along like that, that very same mischievous smile transported Rosie back to Cantine, just before they'd left the restaurant to go back to Nicola's apartment. Nicola had grabbed her hand and pulled her down the restaurant's dark hallway and into the vintage photo booth where she'd pulled the green velvet curtain across, shutting out the outside world.

The combination of that same grin, the buzz of the cocktails they'd consumed and the promise of what was about to come next had woken up something daring in Rosie. She'd held on to her hand, pulled her closer and kissed her deeply as the camera popped and flashed four times before spitting out the photo strip that Rosie had hung onto all these years.

It was equal parts sensual and just-like-in-the-movies romantic, and after they'd grabbed their photos, they'd left the restaurant quickly, all but tripping down the street on their way to Nicola's apartment.

That smile. That face. Rosie could look at it all day and still feel like she was falling.

Nicola parted her lips to say something but was interrupted by the sound of the golf cart pulling up outside. She looked at Rosie, then paused. "Well, I'll look forward to reading it. I'm sure you'll put something great together."

Rosie searched for something to say, then offered a quick smile as Nicola moved to answer the door. She was half relieved at being let off the hook and half disappointed that she hadn't pressed further. And that now they'd be saying goodbye, and the only way she would be close to her would be trying to take the small threads she'd given her and weave them into a story.

Nicola returned to the couch and extended her arm. "Here, grab on."

Rosie took Nicola's arm, allowing her to help her to her feet. She tested her ankle, applying some light pressure. "It actually doesn't feel too bad," she said. "But I think I'll skip the heels for dinner," she added with a wry smile.

"I'll help you anyway," Nicola said, and Rosie was content to move outside with her arm over Nicola's shoulder, Nicola's arm wrapped around her waist.

"Hey, Wes," Nicola said. "Can you make sure this patient makes it back to her room okay? I'll bring the bike back on my way to the kitchen."

"No prob," the young man in a white golf shirt said,

flashing a bright smile. “And if you need more ice, you just let me know.”

“Thank you,” Rosie said gratefully. “I should be okay, though.”

“See you at dinner?” Nicola asked once Rosie was settled in the back of the golf cart.

“See you then,” Rosie said, trying not to smile too much.

Nicola leaned in a bit. “Tonight. After service. We’ll talk in the kitchen after cleanup.”

“Really? Perfect,” Rosie said, her spirits lifting. “See you tonight.”

Nicola took a few steps back and waved as Wes navigated away from Nicola’s place.

From the back of the golf cart, Rosie resisted the urge to turn around and look behind her. Instead, she cheered silently as they drove away.

She was getting her second sit-down. Tonight wasn’t just another interview. It was a chance—maybe the last—to finally understand Nicola’s story.

Chapter Eight

When Nicola returned to the kitchen, dinner prep was in motion. The familiar sounds and scents, so familiar and mundane, all working in tandem to create something extraordinary. Memorable. A dining experience that alone would warrant the drive to Sunset County.

"Chef," Karlos greeted her, looking up only briefly from the cabbage he was slicing into thin ribbons for a new dish they were trialing, a cabbage mille-feuille with brown butter and truffle. The ultrathin layers of napa cabbage would be stacked, compressed and baked until tender, then glazed with a brown butter reduction and finished with shaved black truffle and a spoon of celeriac purée.

"How's your hand?" Nicola asked.

"All good," said Karlos.

Nicola inspected his cutting board.

"That cabbage needs to be a layered, luxurious texture bomb," Nicola murmured, watching over his shoulder. "A little thinner, please." She did her best to keep her tone lighter than it had been last night.

"Yes, Chef," Karlos said, immediately adjusting the width of his slices.

She made her way over to the station where Tim was preparing the marinade for the miso-cured black cod. White miso, mirin, sake and sugar. "You're using the Iki na Onna sake, right?" Nicola asked. The floral, lightly savory choice was, in her opinion, a better option than the still refined and clean but less flavorful Dassai 39 they'd been using since they piloted the dish.

"Yes, Chef," said Tim. Nicola nodded, satisfied. Her own skills, techniques and inspiration might not have been at one hundred percent, but at least she felt like she could trust her team.

She continued through the kitchen, asking questions, giving notes and directions until she was satisfied.

Then she paused. Every interaction she'd ever had with her team members had been focused on the work. She cleared her throat and turned back to Tim. "Looks like you were good at more than Home Ec in high school," she said.

He looked up, confused for a moment, then his face broke out into a smile. "I played quarterback from the age of ten until I graduated," he said. He shook his head. "But really, these guys just made me look good."

"Whatever, Simpson," Karlos said, flicking a dish towel at his back. "You might have a good arm, but there's a reason my nickname's Larry Fitzgerald."

Laughter rippled through the kitchen as they turned back to their tasks. It was only a small thing, but Nicola felt the shift. A bit of levity in the room. In herself.

She left the kitchen and stood outside of Gabriel's office and rapped lightly on the door. She poked her head through to find Gabriel at his desk speaking with someone on the phone. He waved her in and motioned that he'd only be a minute, so she entered the office, sat down in the seat across from his desk and waited.

"I like the adjustments you made to tonight's menu," Gabriel said, right after hanging up the phone. "Although if you keep adding menu items that use that much top-shelf liqueur, I'll have to raise prices more than double digits."

Nicola smiled. "It'll be worth it. Trust me."

"I trust you implicitly."

"I just wanted to tell you," Nicola said, pulling her notebook from her tote and flipping to the page where she'd jotted down some notes before her shower and the surprise visit from Rosie. "I've already been thinking about that dinner. For the investors."

"Oh?" said Gabriel, his eyebrow rising only slightly.

She passed Gabriel the notebook, and he surveyed the page, nodding. "I like what I'm seeing here," he said. "Inventive. The smoked caviar with the oyster custard. Very nice."

"I've got more ideas. I just haven't worked them through yet," she said as Gabriel passed back the book. "You'll let me know when you've figured out who's coming?"

"I will," Gabriel said.

"All right," she said, standing up. "Showtime."

Walking back into the kitchen felt different. Rosie had done something to her—cast a spell, slipped some kind of a charm into the food, because Nicola was starting to shake off some of the fog she'd been living in.

Things in the kitchen felt…lighter. More fun.

Over the next two hours, every dish she sent out to the dining room was accompanied with a sense of anticipation. She watched Rosie's reactions to the plating and the flavors, and the few times they locked eyes between the kitchen and the dining room made Nicola feel buoyant, as if a spark had been reignited.

The mood in the kitchen was brighter too, even a little giddy. The music played louder, and Danielle cracked a smile when Nicola plated a scallop with a flourish.

After the last of the kitchen staff clocked out, Nicola found Rosie waiting patiently in the dining room with her notepad.

She wore another simple dress, pale blue with scalloped sleeves, but on her, it looked like a million bucks.

"I see you went with the flats," Nicola said, gesturing toward Rosie's brown leather sandals.

"Just a precaution. Luckily, I don't think I did too much damage." She grinned. "Another fabulous meal. Like how am I expected to go back to BLTs and Mr. Noodles after this?"

"I hope you didn't just say Mr. Noodles," Nicola said. The image of Rosie alone in her apartment, resorting to an easy dinner after work tugged at something in her.

"When I'm in a pinch, it does the trick," Rosie said, shrugging. She peered over Nicola's shoulder into the kitchen, which was now emptied out.

"Shall we?" Nicola said.

"Let's do it."

Welcoming Rosie into her kitchen felt oddly intimate. Stranger still, she felt more exposed than when Rosie had been inside her home. The kitchen was her sanctuary. Her domain. Now it felt like she'd invited Rosie inside to peel back her armor, without all the noise and action that typically filled the space as her shield.

Nicola watched as Rosie cast her gaze around the room. "Mind if I take a few photos?" she asked.

"Uh, sure," said Nicola. "Might be more interesting during the day, though."

"Is that an invitation to return?"

Nicola wanted to say yes. *Hell yes.* Having Rosie in her space was obviously doing something for her. But still, she felt a degree of protectiveness. The lines between them were already blurring, and Rosie hadn't even taken a note yet. The woman was here to push and prod her. She couldn't forget that. "You're funny," she said instead.

Nicola stepped back as Rosie took a few shots. "This is a really gorgeous kitchen," Rosie said. "Not a bad place to spend all your working hours."

Nicola nodded. "I got to be involved in the design," she said, trying to take in the space with new eyes and thinking about the decisions they'd made so that working in the kitchen would be as close to as enjoyable as eating the food that was prepared in it. "We put that marble prep counter near the north-facing window for cool, natural light." Then she pointed at the oven. "And that's a custom-built Athanor range. Timeless, cast iron and steel. You should get a shot of those bronze knobs. Beautifully aged, right?"

"How about the floor?" Rosie asked.

Nicola nodded. "Reclaimed wide-plank white oak with anti-slip treatment."

Rosie aimed her camera upward and snapped the hanging copper racks, where pans and dried herbs hung. "I love the exposed beams."

"Thanks," Nicola said, pride washing over her. "It's a great place to spend the day."

"And now the night," Rosie said, flipping open her notebook.

Nicola laughed, her pulse quickening. "The night, huh?" she said. "I promised you thirty minutes." But she wasn't sure if she was reminding Rosie or herself.

"Is it past your bedtime?" Rosie teased.

Nicola gave her a look, then pointed to a stool near a prep station. "Sit," she said. She was in control here. Rosie couldn't forget that.

"All right, all right." Rosie took a seat, then motioned to the one next to her. Instead, Nicola instinctively reached for a clean apron hanging from a hook on the wall and pulled it over her head.

She looked up at Rosie as she tied it behind her waist. "I can't be idle in here," she said. "Sorry."

She opened the pantry and took out the flour, sugar and cocoa and deposited them on the station, then set the temperature on the oven and continued to gather supplies. A mindless recipe was in order. A crack of an egg, a whisk in a bowl. The kind of focus that kept emotions at bay.

"Okay, then," Rosie said, flipping open her notepad.

"Wow, right to business," said Nicola.

"You're the one with a bedtime," Rosie said, light teasing in her voice.

"Fine, then," said Nicola, setting an aluminum bowl in front of her. "Fire."

Rosie cleared her throat. "Tell me more about your time in Spain," she said. "If I'm not incorrect, that feels like the time when everything was happening."

"That was…a time," Nicola agreed. Ahh. How much was she prepared to spill about *that* moment in time? And how much did she honestly remember? It had been such a whirlwind. "Let's just say I learned a lot. I was working twenty-hour days and existing on pure adrenaline."

"A lot of exciting stuff was happening."

"Probably too much, to be honest," Nicola said. "It was like everything I'd been chasing landed in my lap all at once. It was equal parts thrilling and terrifying. Some days I'd come off a sixteen-hour shift only to throw on something nice for a magazine gala or a product shoot. Sometimes I didn't even remember where I was waking up."

She leveled a cup of flour and turned it into the bowl and glanced up to see Rosie scribbling something down in her notebook. *Careful*, she thought. What she wanted, more than anything in that moment, was to just have an honest and unguarded conversation with Rosie. She sensed that Rosie would understand and be sympathetic. The legions of people who might read her article, however, would likely not. And would Nicola ever be able to say out loud the worst part of this story anyway, no matter how trustworthy the listener?

"I didn't know how to say no to anything," Nicola continued, measuring out some sugar. "It felt like these opportunities might stop presenting themselves, and I'd be stupid to turn them down. So I said yes to everything. Product endorsements. Guest speaking. Private events for royalty and celebrities. Dates with gorgeous women. Everything was a yes."

Nicola noticed Rosie's pen pause at that last time on her list.

"If you could go back, what would you have said no to?" Rosie asked.

Nicola considered. "Most of the endorsements. Every private event, except for the one in Marrakech. Cooking under the stars for a royal wedding, with string lights in the olive trees and truffles flown in from Piedmont? That was worth it." She laughed. "The crown prince was a huge Jordan fan. He gifted us all with custom silver Air Jordan Threes."

"Are you kidding? That's amazing. Love these details," Rosie said, still scribbling.

"Feel free to use them," Nicola said. She shook her head. "And definitely most of the dates. Most of those women were total users. They were always posting photos of us in their stories. When we went out to eat it was to be seen. There was always this expectation. A post, a call to someone in casting. It was exhausting. Beautiful to look at, but not so attractive to spend time with." She plucked a whisk from a nearby container and started to stir the batter. "So yeah. It's been a while since I've dated anyone."

Rosie let out a quick laugh. "You keep stirring like that, and I'm going to start feeling sorry for the batter."

Nicola grinned. "Every now and then, when I think about that time, I can't help but get a little worked up." She poured the batter into the waiting pastry mold, dabbed a clean towel to remove some of the drippings, then slid the tray into the waiting oven and clicked a timer for fifteen minutes.

Despite the quick trip down memory lane, Nicola felt calmer now, more relaxed with Rosie in her space. She pulled out the other stool and perched on it, awaiting her next question. *So far, so good*, she thought. Rosie seemed to like the sneaker story. Could she fend her off with some more anecdotes like that? She had enough of them to fill at least a few of those notepads.

"So was that what made you decide to disappear for a while?" Rosie asked, her voice softer, more understanding.

It was either genuine or Rosie was a skilled interviewer, because Nicola felt her voice catch at the back of her throat and tears threatening to form. She paused and looked away. "It was…a big part of the problem," she said. She cleared her throat. "But like I said. The chance to be with my sister and the kids, especially at their fun age? That was worth more than any high-paying corporate gig or custom shoe. So."

She did her best to shrug like it was no big deal, but something had shifted in the kitchen, and Nicola could tell Rosie noticed it.

She watched as Rosie flipped her notebook closed and put her pen down on the marble. A weight lifted off her shoulders. Were they done?

But Nicola couldn't ignore the sudden urge she felt to be honest. "I owe you an apology," she said.

Rosie blinked. "What do you mean?" She glanced at the oven. "You mean for the fact that whatever's in there already smells so delicious that despite how full I am already, I'm one hundred percent trying it?"

Nicola smiled. "No, not that," she said. "Can I speak…off the record for a second?"

"Sure," Rosie said softly. She deposited her pen on her notebook and pushed it away slightly, as if to affirm she had no intention of using whatever Nicola was about to tell her.

"I owe you an apology for never responding to your email. I did get it. And I have no excuse for not responding. No good one, at least."

Rosie nodded. "I figured you'd read it."

"It was just…" Nicola stopped and shook her head. "It was all too much. And bringing you into all of it—it just felt like it was going to go poorly, and it was going to tarnish that one perfect night we had together. I needed that memory to hold on to. You were…grounding for me."

"I wish you had just told me," Rosie said. "I felt like such an eye roll." A moment of silence passed. "Actually, forget it. That's not fair. You didn't owe me anything."

"I owed you the courtesy of a response," Nicola said. "So I'm sorry."

Rosie did her best to manage her reaction. The words that had just escaped Nicola's mouth felt like the most honest admission she'd made over the course of their two sessions—three actually, if the morning coffee walk was to be counted. Nothing about it could be used for her article, but the warmth in her chest was immediate, unexpected. A little dangerous. And yes, if she was honest, it turned her on.

Nicola had been thinking about her. Rosie hadn't been the only one dwelling on that night, on the perfection of their bodies tangled in the sheets, sure, but more importantly, that thick magnetism that felt like more than a physical connection. It was more.

The way Nicola was fiddling with her apron told Rosie it was up to her to keep this light and breezy. Clearly, Nicola had been through the ringer, although Rosie still suspected there was more to the story than she'd already let on.

"Don't feel too badly," Rosie said. "I ended up using the gift card anyway, after it was clear I wasn't going to be visiting you."

"Good," Nicola said. "I hope you went somewhere fabulous. Wait, let me guess."

Rosie laughed. "Wow. I kind of feel like these guesses are going to say a lot about what you think of me."

Nicola didn't break her gaze. "I think it's pretty clear that I think really highly of you."

Rosie held her breath, drinking in the compliment. "Thank you," she said softly. "Okay. Your best guess?"

"I can't say it now. Now that I know whatever I say is going to be overly dissected for meaning."

"Okay," Rosie said. "I ended up using it to go back to Lyon. I wanted to spend time with my grandmother there as an adult. She always came to see us, but I wanted to be back on her home turf. Relive my perfect trip." She studied Nicola's face for her reaction. There was a hint of surprise, maybe, tinged with respect.

"And how was it?"

Rosie remembered sitting in her economy seat on the plane. The voucher would have allowed to book business class, but somehow she had already felt like she was doing something wrong by using it for something other than its original intent, even though she was certain Nicola had forgotten all about her anyway.

She'd spent a good chunk of the flight staring out the window, imagining what it would have been like to have been flying out somewhere to meet Nicola, maybe a quiet village by the sea. Walking hand in hand through cobblestone streets, stopping to dine at some off-the-beaten-path restaurant frequented by locals, enjoying a great dinner and bottle of red wine and dessert—of course, dessert—before ambling back to a waterfront villa and making love with the sounds of the waves in the distance.

"I spent two weeks with my grandmother, which was unforgettable, in a very different way than a trip to see you might have been," Rosie said.

They were being honest at this point, it seemed. It felt good to say it out loud. "We visited the market together every day, just like we did when I was a teenager. We bought fresh ingredients, then cooked together. Never anything fancy, but the time chopping and sautéing was filled with my grandmother's stories about escaping her marriage and starting over in a foreign country, adapting to the culture and traditions and eventually feeling a part of something that had once been so foreign to her. I learned a lot about her. About life."

"That sounds incredible," Nicola said. "Grandmothers are so special."

Rosie nodded. "And each evening after she went to bed, I transcribed every last detail of my grandmother's stories in a leather-bound notebook as well as what we'd made together that day."

Nicola's gaze was fixed on her. Rosie felt interesting, worthy of listening to. It felt like an indulgence, speaking in detail rather than deflecting the attention back to the other person. A presumption that her own story meant nothing. "There was something so compelling about her life," she continued, an image of her grandmother so vivid in her brain. Blond hair, laced with gray, pulled back in a chic chignon. The flowing paisley dresses she wore every day and the large tortoiseshell sunglasses she wore, the kind that made people's heads turn and wonder if she was some kind of celebrity. "The resilience, the independence, the growth… that was so interesting." She paused for a moment, unsure of whether to reveal this last detail. "The kernel of an idea to write a novel inspired by her story was born on that trip. I've been thinking about it ever since."

Nicola's eyes sparked with curiosity. "You mentioned that before. And it sounds…amazing. Both the idea and the trip."

"It was kind of life-changing, actually," Rosie said. "My grandmother is an amazing woman."

"I'm glad you got to do something for you," Nicola

said. There were a few seconds of silence. "I wanted to reach out, more than once."

That idea that Nicola had thought of her made Rosie's heartbeat quicken, but it was tempered by the memory of how much the rejection had stung every time she'd thought of Nicola, when her phone had pinged with a text at an unusual time of day or when she'd combed through the junk section of her inbox *just in case* was still real. "I wish you had," she said, trying to keep her tone light.

But the fact of the matter was that it had hurt. As the would-be host, the provider of the means of travel, Nicola had the upper hand; it had been up to her to suggest a time and a place. To show any degree of interest in exploring what more could have come after that magical August night.

"Why didn't you?" Rosie said. The answer to this question was even more important to her than the ones she'd been sent here to ask.

Nicola sighed lightly. "Honestly, I was my own worst enemy at that time. Like I said before, sometimes I wonder if I had been ready to take on so much, so young. I was living in a whirlwind, and inviting you into the chaos felt...even more irresponsible than I was already being at the time. I just remember you being kind of, I don't know..." She paused, her eyes searching Rosie's. "Innocent?"

A light scoff escaped Rosie's mouth before she could stop it. "Wide-eyed, you mean? Inexperienced?" A pulse of indignation rushed through her. She shouldn't have asked.

"That's not what I meant," Nicola said. She reached over and took Rosie's hand in hers, the contact sending a light shiver dancing across Rosie's skin. Rosie drew back slightly. There was that old familiar feeling again. Ordinary. Middle-of-the-road. And just a little bit…boring.

"You meant something to me," Nicola continued. She was clearly trying to dig herself out of a hole, and Rosie just needed it to be over. "And somehow I knew I would screw it up, or you would come out and realize you didn't actually like me as much. There were a lot of people in my life at the time who made sure I couldn't trust easily."

Thick silence hung in her air again, and Rosie considered. Nicola had been burned, that much was clear. She softened. Maybe it wasn't all about her. "I guess being famous isn't everything it's chalked up to be."

Nicola nodded. "I was happy to be recognized for all the work I did. And it was fun and gratifying to build a brand. I liked a lot of it. But a lot of people like to try to come along for the ride, and their ambitions can be selfish. I had a couple of relationships that were pretty one-sided. And it was busy. It was so busy that I never had a minute to sit and take stock of what I'd done, and where we were going, and ultimately where I wanted to be." She scoffed and shook her head. "It's funny when I think about my actual job, and how so much of it depends on being incredibly thoughtful, diligent. Planning and executing. And how I just kind of got swept away. Being away from my family didn't help either."

Rosie considered. Hearing all of this, how lost Nicola

must have felt was soothing the sting from the slight that she'd carried for the last few years. She saw an opening, a crack—was it the crash after a whirlwind that had sent Nicola into hiding? Or was it something more?

She'd finally made it. And it was organic, not forced. She cleared her throat, ready to ask a probing question.

"But speaking of family," Nicola said, her expression brightening. "I want to know more details about your grandmother. And the trip you took."

Dammit, Rosie thought. Would it be too obvious if she deflected the question and tried to turn the subject back to Nicola? Yes, she decided. And it might go as far as to kill a nice moment. A *real* moment.

"They say olive oil is bottled-up sunshine, but it's not olive oil. It's Lyon," Rosie said, disappointment making way for nostalgia. "It's warm hay and geese honking and impossibly perfect loaf after loaf of fresh bread, fields of cornflower and buttercups and cold hunks of pâté. Bees and fistfuls of herbs and hens clucking. It's..." She opened her eyes and found Nicola looking at her intently. "It's heaven."

"Why didn't you stay?" Nicola asked. "It sounds like paradise."

"My grandmother loved having me around," Rosie said. "But she's an independent. She likes her alone time, and I'm pretty sure there was a certain 'gentleman caller' who was being kept at bay while I was visiting. It was time for her to get back into her...routine."

"Your grandmother sounds like a lot of fun," Nicola said. "You must take after her."

"Ha," Rosie said. "You just called me innocent, like, two minutes ago."

"I didn't mean it like that," Nicola said. "Trust me. I was there the night we..." A slow smile crept across her face. "I remember."

Once again, they were across the table from one another again at Cantine, candlelight warming Nicola's features as she asked Rosie if she wanted to come back to her place. Rosie took a sharp breath at the memory. All she wanted now was to ask Nicola to come back to her room. To disappear together into a sea of soft sheets.

But it wasn't just the fact that she was here as a journalist that held her back. There was still a division between them. Something unspoken, unresolved.

A timer dinged, and Nicola opened the oven. "Perfect," she murmured, sliding on a pair of mitts and extracting a tray she placed on the stove.

"That smells divine," Rosie said. "What is it?"

Nicola laid a placemat in front of her and, with the oven mitt still on, set down a small ramekin.

"Chocolate lava cakes," she said. "We'll have to let them cool. But part of the enjoyment is the wait." Her eyes sparkled with mischief.

Rosie's pulse quickened. Clearly, she wasn't the only one entertaining memories.

Nicola took the seat next to hers—not the one across, Rosie noted, where there was no danger of their legs brushing up against each other.

She passed them each a spoon, then used hers to break the surface of the dessert. She pulled it out, rich, gooey chocolate dripping from it. "Mmm," she said.

"Richard made that fabulous pêche Melba with spun sugar tonight. But there's something about the simplicity of a lava cake..." She blew lightly on the hot, runny chocolate and held it out for Rosie to taste.

Rosie allowed Nicola to tip the spoon into her mouth. Right away, the sweet chocolate melted across her tongue, making her moan slightly at the simple decadence.

She swallowed and opened her eyes. Nicola's delighted expression was now tinged with satisfaction. "I love how you look when you're enjoying food," she said. "I don't think I've ever seen anything more beautiful."

Rosie grinned. "I can't help it. You're too good." She broke into her own cake, spooned out a small amount and held it up for Nicola. "Here," she said. "Your turn."

Nicola paused a moment and then sampled from the spoon. She nodded and grinned. "Yep," she said. "Seven ingredients. Twenty minutes. Nothing fancy—"

"But damn, it's good," Rosie finished.

Nicola put her spoon down and turned to Rosie. "I really like having you here," she said softly. "I know you came with a job to do. But this is nice."

Rosie nodded, her heart swelling. It *was* nice. It was more than nice to have this alone time with Nicola, despite the nagging pressure of what she was there to do.

The warmth of the moment and the faint scent of cocoa lingering in the air made her job as a journalist feel like a distant memory. She allowed her mind to drift into a daydream as decadent as the dessert Nicola had just made for her.

In her imagination, Nicola leaned closer, her lips

brushing Rosie's softly, stealing her breath. She felt Nicola's hand at the base of her neck, fingertips grazing the fine hairs there. Her pulse quickened as the kiss deepened, hungry and intense. "Can I trust you?" Nicola whispered, her voice a low murmur against Rosie's lips. Rosie nodded, caught in the heat of the moment.

But a flicker of doubt pierced the fantasy. Nicola's question hung in the air, pulling Rosie back. She imagined herself hesitating, her breathing shallow, torn between desire and the uncertainty of what this kiss meant. In her mind, Nicola's gaze was wild, wanting, piercing through Rosie's remaining resolve and dissolving all doubt. Rosie closed her eyes again, sinking back into the dream, tasting Nicola's warm, soft lips, feeling the gentle probe of her tongue. A soft moan from Nicola sent a wave of heat through Rosie's core.

The daydream grew bolder. Nicola shifted, guiding Rosie back until she was perched on the counter, Nicola pressed between her legs. Their kiss deepened, urgent, as Nicola's hands slid slowly around Rosie's hips. The thought of someone walking into the restaurant, catching Rosie abandoning her journalistic integrity, flickered briefly, but in this fantasy, she didn't care. All that mattered was the heat, the hunger, her trembling need for Nicola.

The sound of a clinking spoon against a bowl made Rosie snap right back to reality. She felt her cheeks flush as she did her best to steady her breath. Nicola was still sitting beside her, spearing a piece of cake on her fork, seemingly oblivious to the vivid scene that had just played out in Rosie's mind.

Nicola glanced over, her eyebrow lifting slightly. “You okay?” she asked.

Rosie’s heart was racing as she nodded. “I’m…good,” she said, but that wasn’t entirely the truth. Every cell of her body buzzed with desire, and the weight of her real and highly inappropriate feelings, complicated by her job, by Nicola’s guarded nature, tugged at her again. There was only one place a daydream like that coming true could lead: the same fleeting perfection she’d experienced years ago, followed by seven years of longing for something that had never really been hers.

“I should go,” Rosie said, tentatively.

A flicker of disappointment crossed Nicola’s face. “Already?” she said, a light smile teasing on her face. “You haven’t finished your dessert.”

Rosie looked at her half-eaten plate. “It was delicious—thank you. Everything tonight was perfect.” And it was. As much as it killed her to walk away from Nicola, and the promise of even more pleasure, it was the right thing to do.

“Just give me a minute to clean up, and I’ll walk you back to your room,” Nicola said.

Rosie stood, breathing hard as Nicola set about moving the mixing bowl and their plates and forks into the sink, then draping her apron over a hook. “Come on,” she said. “It’s late.” She turned, and their eyes met for a long moment, a silent promise and a lingering regret hanging between them.

The night air was cool and calm, and stars twinkled in the inky sky overhead as they walked from the restaurant toward the main inn building. Rosie felt the weight of words unspoken pressing on her chest. She wanted to explain herself, her intentions, her feelings, but Nicola had said she understood. Maybe that had to be enough.

Still, Rosie couldn't shake the sense that she represented a threat. Not just to Nicola's privacy, but to her control, her carefully kept distance. And she still didn't fully understand why.

They reached the shadowed edge of the rose garden, just before the lights of the inn would cast them in full view. Nicola stopped.

"I'm going to say goodbye here," she said quietly. "But…tomorrow. It's your last day. Why don't you let me show you around the area? Some places that might be interesting to include in your article."

Who was this new Nicola?

Seeing her again, especially off the property, where they'd be away from curious eyes, felt…dangerous. But the prospect of new material had to win out. "I'd like that," she said. "Thank you again for everything," she said. "This place is…heaven on earth."

"You'll have to come back," Nicola replied. "For pleasure, not work next time."

"Not as the devil?" Rosie said with a soft smile.

Nicola's expression softened, her voice almost a whisper. "Exactly."

The way she said it sent a shiver through Rosie. It felt like a promise. One that had nothing to do with food or place. She could kiss Nicola, right here, right now, in the dim moonlight and bring her daydream to life.

But it also felt too familiar. Too much like that last

goodbye all those years ago. A glimmer of something real, fated to slip through her fingers.

Rosie hesitated. Then she stepped back.

"Good night, Nicola," she said, forcing a smile and stepping away toward the inn.

"I'll see you tomorrow. Nine o'clock, by Ayla's paddock. Stick with the flats."

"See you tomorrow," Rosie echoed.

An off-property excursion, just the two of them, with no danger of interruptions from staff or other guests. Could she manage that?

Rosie shook her head as she ascended the stairs to her room and let herself into the peaceful sanctuary and flicked on her lights.

And there it was. Her laptop, plugged in and fully charged.

Rosie let out a slow breath, her stomach knotting. She had no other choice, did she?

Chapter Nine

It was already warm and humid when Nicola approached the stables, coffees in hand, the morning sunshine streaming through the trees. She spotted Rosie right away, stroking Ayla's broad side through the fence, cooing at her and totally in her own world. Nicola stood for a moment watching the adoration with which she caressed the horse.

"She definitely trusts you," Nicola said, approaching the fence and taking in Rosie's fitted jean shorts and blue silky tank top. She noticed Rosie was also wearing a pair of docksiders, which she managed to make just as alluring as her high heels.

"At least someone around here does," Rosie said, turning around and fixing Nicola with a mildly accusatory but playful grin.

Good, Nicola thought. The way they'd left last night made her wonder if things were going to be at all awkward between them today. Rosie's light jab was a good indication that that moment in the kitchen, when it had seemed like things might be moving in a…not-so-professional place, had been a blip. Now they were back to friendly propriety.

Which was *not* the scenario Nicola had stayed up too late in bed imagining.

Nicola shoved that daydream aside and passed her the coffee. She'd poured a double shot of espresso in her own. "Hey, I'm missing lunch service for you. And you're about to be privy to some top-secret information." She joined Rosie in leaning over the fence and took a sip of the rocket fuel from her cup. "Do I need to make sure you're not bugged?"

"Ha," said Rosie. "I *am* here in the capacity of journalist today, right? If I'm recording anything, I don't need to hide it."

Nicola liked this version of Rosie. Years ago, when she was just starting out, she'd seemed like someone who'd be easy to rattle. Now, even without a byline in a top-tier publication, she carried herself with the ease of someone who knew what she was doing: steady, self-assured, with a quiet kind of confidence that wasn't there before.

"Thanks for the coffee," Rosie said. "So where are we going? I'm intrigued. Especially that there's a footwear requirement."

"You'll see. But here. Before we go. I brought these from the kitchen." She pulled three carrots and a Honeycrisp apple from her backpack and handed them to Rosie.

Rosie whistled to Ayla, who'd moved away from the fence, and immediately returned when she saw there were snacks available.

Nicola watched as Rosie cooed and fed the carrots to

Ayla one at a time. "There you go, sweetheart," Rosie murmured.

Nicola smiled. "Looks like she's adopted you."

Rosie laughed as Ayla took the apple right out of her outstretched palm. "Who doesn't like someone feeding them?" She glanced up at Nicola. "It's a very attractive quality in a person."

A flicker of heat caught Nicola off guard at Rosie's flirtation. But she reeled it back in quickly. *She's just looking for an in*, she reminded herself. "Come on," she said. "Let's go."

Nicola led Rosie to the employee parking lot, where her cobalt-gray Jeep Wrangler sat parked in the cool morning shade.

She'd driven some unbelievable cars over the past several years—a Maserati GranCabrio, a Porsche Boxster, a Mercedes-AMG—but the Jeep had always been a dream of hers in high school, and while it wasn't as fast or sleek or head-turning as her luxury sports cars, there was something about driving it that was just plain fun.

One of her first orders of business after arriving in Sunset County had been to visit a local second-hand dealer. She'd test driven the 2017 Wrangler, which had some light wear and tear, a few dents and a snag in the passenger-side seat fabric, but it only took a twenty-minute drive to sell her on it. She'd bought it in cash and had never loved driving a vehicle more.

Nicola took a moment to fold down the top, which was coated in early-morning dew. She wiped her hands on her jeans, then opened the door for Rosie.

The outing was business, but the air between them

carried a sweetness, something tender, like a first date. Rosie's gaze held a quiet softness, and Nicola wondered if her focus was truly on the article or on the moment they were sharing. Was it just her, or was this all feeling a little dangerously…nice?

Nicola slid behind the wheel and clicked her seatbelt in. "All set?" She stole a quick look at Rosie, who was fussing with her hair in her visor's mirror. "Don't bother with that," she said, a teasing smile tugging at her lips. "You'll have to settle for the windswept look today."

"I'm ready, as much as I can be given I have no idea where we're going. Where are you taking me?"

Rosie kept running her fingers through her dark waves, a playful glint in her eyes. Nicola caught the scent of floral shampoo and suddenly imagined kissing her right then. But it was only the beginning of their "date." "Aren't journalists supposed to be adventurous?" Nicola said.

Rosie narrowed her eyes slightly and smiled, revealing the tiny gap between her teeth. "We are adventurous. And inquisitive."

Could she kiss her? The faint memory of what they'd tiptoed into last night still lingered. Nicola could almost feel where it had been heading on her lips. "Don't remind me," Nicola murmured, her voice low and her eyes locked on Rosie's for a beat, until she revved the ignition and pulled out from the parking lot.

The drive to Bramblewood Farm was about ten minutes from the inn. Nicola appreciated that Rosie hadn't launched right into a series of questions. Or maybe it was the fact that the top was down and they'd have to yell to hear each other over the noise of the engine and the tires over gravel. Nicola looked sideways to see the wind whipping through Rosie's long dark waves and a contented smile on her face. She was enjoying herself. Nicola found herself feeling glad about that.

She pulled into the county lane that led to the farm and slowed the vehicle so Rosie could see the field in front of them. "What am I looking at?" she said, squinting her eyes out at the sandy brown expanse.

"Bramblewood Farm," Nicola said. "They grow soft wheat from imported seed from Burgundy." She'd stumbled across it one day at a local farmers' market, when she'd sampled a piece of baguette made by the farm. It was nutty, with a nice crisp crust and irregular crumb. She'd struck up a conversation with the man in the tent, and when she found out they were growing a heritage variety, she'd been intrigued. "You're looking at my secret stash."

"Of…"

"You know that bread that you liked from the first night's menu?"

"You mean *loved*? Would marry if I could marry bread?"

Nicola laughed. Rosie's zest for food was the best. "What you're looking at here is a crop of wheat from a very specific varietal from Burgundy. It's the secret ingredient in our bread. The wheat is grown here and milled by my friend Sam who owns the land. Just promise not to publish the location, or it'll get pillaged by weekend warrior foodies from the city."

When Rosie didn't say anything, Nicola looked over to see her gazing out at the fields, a happy but wistful look in her eyes. "Did you say Burgundy?"

"Avallon, to be exact. Why?"

"That first time I visited my grandmother, in Lyon—when I was a teenager? My parents were touring colleges with my brother—all the Ivys, of course—and needed to ship me away. I was so, so upset with them. But it ended up being a really incredible summer. We made day trips to Burgundy. My grandmother loved wine. It was the first time in a long time I'd been made to feel…special."

"Because of the wine?"

Rosie laughed. "I was allowed to have a glass with dinner. No. It was more that…" She paused, looking pensive. "It was the first time I could remember when I didn't live in my brother's shadow. He was an ocean away. And I guess it made me open up more, or something. Maybe it was just a grandmother thing. They're good at making kids feel in the limelight. Or maybe it was just the perfection of that area." She shook her head. "Heaven on earth."

"So you know how special it is."

"She gave me a decent introduction, I'd say."

Nicole smiled at the thought of a teenage Rosie swirling a full-bodied red in a wine glass. "So then you'll keep our flour supplier a secret?"

"Scout's honor," Rosie said, holding up her right hand.

Nicola grinned. So far, this little road trip was fun. She killed the Jeep's engine and pulled her backpack from the back seat. "Follow me."

She led Rosie into the field, which was organized in long rows, with tall, spindly swaths of wheat growing, all golden and a bit dry.

"I can see why now, about the shoes," Rosie said. The ground beneath them was dusty and dry.

Nicola nodded. "Here," she said, pulling some pieces from the stalk. "Smell this."

Rosie accepted the stalk, closed her eyes and breathed in. She cocked her head to the side. "It smells like… breakfast cereal."

Nicola smiled. "Yup," she said. She rubbed the husk in her hand until little grains fell into her palm, then held them up to her face and breathed in the grassy scent, like warm sun stepped in soil. "Once it's milled, it smells even better. Nutty, malty, sometimes kind of like vanilla."

"And then you bake it fresh every day?"

"Every day," Nicola said, shrugging one side of her backpack off her shoulder and unzipping it to remove a tea towel–wrapped loaf of bread, a small packet of butter and her Swiss army knife. "Well, to give credit where credit's due, our baker, Kaleigh, makes the bread. Here," she said, passing Rosie a lopped off piece. "Came out of the oven just a few hours ago. And the hand-churned butter's churned fresh too—they're our next stop."

"You're kidding me," Rosie said, looking at the morsel in her hand as though Nicola had just handed her a bar of gold. She allowed Nicola to sweep a small pat of butter across the surface before she held it up and took in a long draw of its scent. "Eating fresh bread in the field of wheat where it was grown? I could die and go to heaven." She took a small bite and sighed as she chewed and swallowed, then popped the rest of it in her mouth. "Mmm!" she murmured.

Nicola warmed with Rosie's enthusiasm. "So should the tour end now?"

Rosie chewed her bread thoughtfully as she gazed out onto the field around them. "Absolutely not," she said, reaching over and pulling another hunk off the loaf, then slathering it with butter. "I'm dying to see what else you have planned. Especially if it involves more of this."

As far as time spent with a journalist, Nicola had to admit this was not too bad. She silently patted herself on the back for how she was handling this, even if the day had been Gabriel's idea.

They sat in the field for a few minutes in the sun eating bread, while Nicola filled Rosie in on her own time spent in France and the influence it had on her cooking and the vintage cookbooks she'd started to collect on that trip. Rosie asked thoughtful questions about the flavors and techniques she'd learned during her stay, what her favorite regions of the country were, and if she'd picked up any French.

So far so good.

As long as Nicola could keep her entertained with stories and information about the food, Rosie might be content to leave the personal stuff alone.

"Ready for the next stop?" Nicola said.

"Is there a corresponding snack involved?" Rosie asked.

She grinned. "Of course."

* * *

They drove through the winding roads of Sunset County, and ten minutes later pulled into one of the few vacant spots on the Main Street, right outside of a pub called the Hidden Oar.

The downtown of Sunset Country was alive with a mixture of locals, who Nicola was more and more able to recognize the longer she lived in the area, and visitors to the local lakes.

Parents and children walked with coffee cups and dogs on leashes, couples lined up outside of Pete's Pies for a slice for an early lunch and a few of the local senior citizens sat out front of the Legion trading stories.

"Mmm," Rosie said, taking a long draw of breath in as she hopped out of the passenger seat. "If you hadn't fed me so well already and I wasn't saving room for dinner, I'd be following my nose to whatever that smell is."

Nicola fought the urge to grab Rosie by the waist and pull her in. Instead, she trailed her fingers along Rosie's wrist as she passed, just enough to stir something between them.

Rosie knew how to speak Nicola's language. Just the thought of seeing that blissed out expression on Rosie's face was almost enough for her to tell Rosie to change her reservation for the later serving that evening, but Rosie didn't know yet that Nicola had something a bit different in mind that night for her tasting experience.

"That's Flour Child Bakery," Nicola said. "Want to just have a peek inside?"

"Happy to feast with my eyes," Rosie said, grinning.

They entered the small bakeshop, the bell over the

door tinkling overhead. The owner, Maya Monroe, was behind the counter, which wasn't such a regular occurrence these days now that her writing career had taken off and she'd found a local to help her run the place. Lucas Foreman had started to work for Maya in his last year of high school and was managing the bakery while he took some night school courses at the local college in sports management.

Maya looked up when they entered and grinned. "Hey, Nicola," she said. "That tip on butter you gave me a couple of weeks ago—OMG! My croissants have never been crispier."

"Right?" Nicola said. While she liked to keep some of her providers close to the vest so they wouldn't sell out when she needed them, Copeland's Creamery had a larger operation going and was more than able to meet her needs as well as a smaller bakery like Maya's. "It's been a while. Are you guys in town for a bit?"

Maya nodded. "For a few weeks. I asked Will to make sure his shooting schedule didn't have us away for prime Sunset County time." She looked at Rosie. "Hi, I'm Maya Monroe. And you are?"

"Sorry," Nicola cut in. She struggled for a moment to find the words to introduce Rosie. Her crush? An old flame? A journalist who was trying to uncover all of her secrets? "This is Rosie Franklin-Smith," she said, simply. "An old friend of mine. She's visiting the inn to write an article."

"Welcome to Sunset County," Maya said. "It's not that we didn't have visitors to town before, but we local businesses are grateful to Nicola and the rest of the team at the inn for really putting us on the map. Lucas told me that last week he had customers who came through who were from Stockholm, San Francisco and Singapore. Sunset County's on a stop list in so many Canada tourist guides now."

"Well, lucky them that they ended up here," Nicola said, pointing to the case where Rosie seemed distracted by the offerings: macarons in all the colors of the rainbow, fudge brownies, Hello Dollies, macadamia-nut cookies and profiteroles.

"I'll second that," said Rosie, looking up. "It's so nice to meet you, Maya. I'm going to have to take something to put in my fridge back at the hotel. What do you recommend?"

"Sweet tooth or savory?"

"Both!" Rosie said, grinning.

Girl after my own heart, thought Nicola, doing her best to keep her own smile from spreading across her face.

She watched as Rosie and Maya chatted through some options, eventually landing on a cheddar-and-jalapeño scone in one bag and a brownie in the other. She really did have a way with people, and for a moment, Nicola could see her here in Sunset County. It was a foreign idea; Nicola liked her privacy and preferred space. But Rosie was fun to be around. Easy. And the way her shorts cut off at the perfect spot mid-thigh… well, she wasn't complaining about that either.

"Are we going to see you tomorrow night, Nicola?" Maya asked. She turned to Rosie. "Will and I are throwing a party tomorrow evening. Nothing too crazy—just a chance to see everyone we've been missing this summer. A couple of Will's associates are staying at the nearby lakes, so they'll come too," Maya said. "You both should join us."

Nicola noted the use of the term *associates*—she knew that was a veiled way of saying some kind of Hollywood bigwigs or actors in one of his upcoming films—but more than that she noted Maya's use of *you both*. Nicola experienced another flash of pleasure at the idea of her and Rosie being considered a duo.

"That sounds great, but tonight's my last night in town," Rosie said. "A big finale dinner tonight, I've been promised." She looked at Nicola and grinned that knee-weakening smile. "And then it's time for me to file an article."

"That's too bad, but I'll look forward to reading it."

"And I'll look forward to enjoying these later," Rosie said, holding up the paper bags with her pastries.

Maya turned to Nicola. "How about you, Nicola? Think you'll still be able to make an appearance?"

Nicola considered. It was Sunday evening, a night off for her from the kitchen. All she really wanted to do was grab a book and her bathing suit and spend a few hours switching between lying on one of the staff docks and swimming in the lake. But Gabriel had told her that a couple of the local investors he was targeting might be there, so she couldn't cancel. "Count me in," she said. She looked at Rosie. "And speaking of service, we've got more ground to cover before I need to get back to the kitchen."

"Nice to meet you," Rosie said. "I loved *Love on the Slopes*, by the way."

Back out on the street, Nicola motioned toward the other side of the street in the direction of the water. "I hope you don't mind if I get a quick caffeine hit before we hit the road again," she said.

"Of course," said Rosie. They strolled down the sidewalk, and Nicola felt the urge to reach out and grab Rosie's hand. But even in Sunset County, where people who recognized her generally left her alone, there was no telling who would snap a photo and make some kind of ridiculous fuss online about her being spotted with a gorgeous brunette. She shoved her hands into her pockets instead and fiddled with her keys and her phone.

Rise and Grind was busy as usual, given the time of day, before cottagers and visitors started to migrate to the pub and the restaurants with happy hour rather than looking for their next caffeine fixes.

Nicola held the door for Rosie. Rosie gave her a small grin as she passed through. "So chivalrous," she said quietly, her dark eyes sparkling. Nicola followed her in, treated by the sight of Rosie's bare shoulders, her skin smooth under the thin straps of her dress. Straps that she imagined herself moving to the side to get unencumbered access.

Cool it down, she told herself. But all she wanted was to indulge further in the daydream.

"I'll take a cortado, double shot," Nicola said to the barista, a young college kid with a faux hawk and bright eyes. "Would you like anything?"

“I’m good,” said Rosie. “If I drink coffee now I’ll never sleep.”

And that might be okay, Nicola thought as she considered the meal she had in store for Rosie tonight. If the woman happened to enjoy it the way Nicola was hoping, maybe she’d still be up when Nicola walked under her porch at the end of the night. Maybe she’d be interested in going for a walk around the property under the stars, while the other guests and staff were ready to call it a night. *Maybe...*

“Aw!” Rosie said, examining the cork board beside the cash register, where a few photos were pinned from the Sunset Country animal shelter. There was a tortoiseshell cat named Ella, who was looking for a new home, and a guinea pig named Motorhead.

Nicola almost opened her mouth to offer to take Rosie to see the shelter in the morning—she’d had been by a few times herself to see the animals, but with her hours had decided that the inn’s pets would be her own too.

But then she remembered. Rosie was checking out before noon. She would head back to the city, and to her life at *Savorist*.

Nicola felt a small pang of guilt that she hadn’t given Rosie what she knew she had come for. But at the same time, this day had been pretty perfect so far.

At least they had that.

Chapter Ten

Three hours later, Rosie was stuffed to the brim and had taken twelve pages of notes. After the wheat field, they'd visited Copeland's Creamery, where Nicola introduced her to Rayanne Copeland, who made the inn's butter as well as two of the inn's signature cheeses.

They did a tutored sampling of everything from creamy Bleubry to a smoky Fontina, then Rayanne took them to visit the sheep and goats happily in the pastures behind the barn.

After that, it was onto the shore of Robescarres Lake, where they'd sat on a dock overlooking the sparkling water and Nicola pointed out the best spots to fish for rainbow trout before getting back in the Jeep to visit a small boutique outside of downtown Sunset County to visit a chocolatier, who wouldn't take no for an answer when offering samples of all kinds of chocolates, including dark cocoa and fleur-de-sel, wildflower honey and lavender, and one filled with maple caramel.

"Enough!" Rosie had to say finally, laughing, as the kind woman with gray hair and a pink apron came around the counter with a second tray filled with the most gorgeous truffles Rosie had ever seen.

She waved off the woman, who disappeared behind the counter, then reappeared with a paper envelope of creamy, melt-in-your-mouth hazelnut truffles and two big dark-chocolate cookies. She nodded toward Rosie's purse, then extended the envelope toward her. "For later," she said.

"I may never eat again," Rosie whispered as they left the boutique to get back in the car. "Here, you take these." She passed the truffles and cookies to Nicola, who tucked them away in her bag.

"I don't know," said Nicola. "You might change your mind once you see what's on the menu tonight."

The idea of sitting down to dinner felt impossible. But Rosie knew that in a few hours, the heavenly aromas coming from Nicola's kitchen would beckon her in. "Hint?"

"You'll just have to show up and find out." Rosie felt Nicola place her hand gently on her back as they walked back together to the car. It was a simple touch—probably nothing, the way you touched someone when you were moving in the same direction. But it felt like more.

Everything about the day so far was giving serious date vibes. Jeremy wasn't paying her, or opening the coffers, for her to spend all day flirting with Nicola and stuffing herself full of Sunset County's best artisanal products.

It was time for her to make a move. Something small. Imperceptible. Get the ball rolling again, the way it had started in the kitchen last night.

But that chocolate... If Nicola's plan was to play defense by putting her into a food coma, it was working.

•

"How did you find all of these providers?" Rosie asked. "Had you spent time in the area before taking the job at the restaurant?" Innocent enough, but how Nicola had ended up here—in the middle of nowhere, really—was definitely a topic of great speculation. Of course, she knew Gabriel, but was that enough to get her to take a step away from what she was used to—working in the culinary epicenters of the world?

"Small towns are…small," Nicola said, navigating out of the parking area and back onto the county highway. Rosie took a moment to admire the way the wind whipped through Nicola's hair and the easy way she guided the vehicle, one hand on the steering wheel, the other arm draped over the open window. "The area isn't bursting with options, but luckily the ones we have are excellent. And when all else fails, you just ask around. People *love* to talk."

Just not you, Rosie thought.

"But if you're asking me how I ended up living and working in a place that most of the world has never heard of," Nicola said, glancing over and giving her a tight smile, "the answer is right in front of you."

Rosie's irritation flared again. She'd have to get better finding a way in, especially if Nicola was going to keep reading her like that. But the view made it hard to stay annoyed.

On one side, rolling hills of crops in tidy plots in different shades of green. On the other, a thick forested area with maples, evergreens and birch trees standing proudly, leaves fluttering softly in the breeze.

Sunset County might be known for its namesake sunsets, but Rosie was starting to wonder if the real magic happened before dusk. There was something special in the glow of the daytime sun here too, which made everything appear to drip with light.

Rosie glanced over. Nicola's arm still rested by the open window, and her fingers were tapping to the beat of the light music playing over the radio. She was carefree and seemingly unaware that she'd just blocked Rosie's line of questioning. That or she just didn't care.

Rosie shifted in her seat. She was regretting the last couple of hours of overindulgence. She needed to be sharper, and the thought that she was wasting her time made her take a sharp breath in.

"I think you'll like this next place," Nicola said. "I mean, they might be second to Ayla. But they're super cute."

Thankfully, the next stop didn't involve eating. From the road before they even turned in, Rosie could see the giraffe-like necks of a pack of—what were they, llamas?—bobbing through a fenced-in enclosure. They looked up with mild interest as Nicola navigated the Jeep into a small clearing beside a blue hut that had a sign reading *Alpaca Threads* above the doorway.

"This is where the wool for the inn's blankets is sourced," Nicola said. "There's a real commitment to sourcing as much as possible from local vendors. The Walker family requested that as a condition of the sale of their land. It's not something that's legally enforceable, but we're doing it anyway. It's a win-win for everyone."

"Based on what I've seen today, I have to agree,"

Rosie said, following Nicola into the small shop space, which had rows of sweaters hanging from racks, piles of folded blankets in different colors, and an assortment of winter accessories.

Rosie picked up a pair of mittens to tuck away for Gertie's Christmas gift while she calculated her next step. Something told her that this version of Nicola, seemingly carefree and chatty as ever, would shut down if Rosie made the wrong move.

After they cashed out, Rosie and Nicola stopped at the pen to look at the wooly creatures.

"Listen," Nicola said. "Close your eyes."

Rosie did as she was directed. "It's like it's humming," she said, and opened her eyes again to find Nicola nodding.

"Alpacas hum softly when they're curious, content or communicating with each other." Who was this Nicola? The cool-as-a-cucumber chef was now an animated nature guide?

This was a real turnaround, in both attitude and behavior, from their first interview. She seemed to actually want Rosie around, and there were a couple of occasions when Rosie found Nicola looking at her with a mixture of delight and curiosity, like she truly wanted to show Rosie a good time and was waiting at the edge of her seat to gauge Rosie's reactions to the places she was bringing her and people she introduced her to.

There was no need for Rosie to feign enjoyment. Everything had been amazing.

Sure, she still had no answers to the questions she was sent to ask, but Nicola was sharing some really good stuff about the local providers and the area in general. Maybe Jeremy would be okay with a new angle for the article. "The Supporting Cast of a Top Chef," or something like that.

"Up for one more stop?" Nicola asked. "Then I'll have to get back to the kitchen."

"If it doesn't involve eating, I'm game," Rosie said, hopping back into the Jeep and buckling her seat belt.

Minutes later, Nicola pulled the vehicle to a stop at yet another farm building, just as picturesque and quaint as the ones before. While Rosie was a city girl through and through, she was starting to see the appeal of the quieter, more natural setting of the countryside.

They walked beyond the farmhouse toward a sloping pasture lined with neat rows of grapevines. Fat clusters of green grapes hung heavy on the vines, their skins almost glowing in the late afternoon light.

"This is my kind of farm," Rosie said, shielding her eyes as she scanned the rows.

Nicola smiled. "This," she said, gesturing wide, "is my next project."

Her eyes sparkled with excitement as they swept the vineyard. Rosie imagined her looking the same way as she approached a new recipe. "And you're the first to know about it, aside from Gabriel, of course. You can include this in your article if you want."

It wasn't the kind of exclusive scoop she was looking for. But it was something. She followed Nicola away from the car toward the vines, the air sweet and sharp with the scent of sun-warmed fruit. Rosie ran a hand along a curling vine. "What kind of grapes are these?" she asked.

"Vidal. Nice thick skin, high acidity and can withstand the chill of the winters in these parts. Want to try our first harvest?"

"I'd love to." Rosie noted the excitement in Nicola's eyes. It was clear she was really proud of her work and was excited to share it with her. Top chef and budding vintner—another good angle for her article. She was starting to shed the weight of apprehension she'd been carrying since she'd arrived at Sugar Maple Farms.

In the barn, Nicola opened a small fridge and extracted a bottle, then grabbed two glasses from a cabinet.

Outside, they settled into two Muskoka chairs next to a firepit, and Nicola popped the cork on the labelless bottle.

"Does it have a name?" Rosie asked, accepting the glass of amber-hued liquid Nicola passed her.

"Martial Law," Nicola said. "Named after the Roman poet Martial." She held the glass up to the sun and squinted as she swished the liquid around. "Canadians love to think they invented ice wine, but he wrote about the importance of leaving the grapes on the vine until at least late November. Plus, he was a bit of a joker."

She reached into her bag and pulled out the paper bag with the chocolate cookies. "I like people who don't take themselves too seriously."

Rosie waved away the cookie but took another sip from her glass and sat back in her chair, sighing. "Never mind lunch—I'm going to be full for dinner," she said.

She took in the stunning vista in front of her. “I can see why you like it here,” she said.

“I love it. It’s pretty special,” Nicola said.

Once again, Rosie waited to see if Nicola would elaborate, give her something, *anything* of a personal nature, but she was quiet. “Thank you for showing me around. Ugh, okay, I’ll try one of those cookies.”

Nicola grinned and passed one to her, and Rosie took a small nibble. “Hope you got what you came for,” Nicola said. “What do you think of the wine?”

She took another long sip, savoring the ripe jammy fruit on her taste buds before swallowing. It was harmonious, satisfying, and just sweet enough that when she bit into the chocolate cookie again, everything came together in the perfect taste experience. “I think you have a winner here,” she said.

Nicola sat back in her seat, a satisfied expression on her face. “The real feat will be the cuvée,” she said, pointing through the open doors of the barn and gesturing toward a row of stainless steel. “They still need another few months.”

“And then you’ll need something to celebrate,” Rosie said.

Nicola smiled. “Exactly.”

The sun above was now slanted slightly westward in the sky. Their excursion had to be almost over—Nicola would be needed back in the kitchen soon.

Had this been a date, rather than a work outing, she wondered what might’ve happened next. Maybe they’d finish the bottle and walk through the privacy of the vineyards together. She imagined them in a wine-induced glow, her hands exploring Nicola's body, her lips on hers.

She looked over and saw Nicola smiling, then blushed, wondering if she'd read her mind. But this was no date. She was a journalist, and as a professional, even daydreaming about her subject seemed like a contravention of her code of ethics.

Nicola stood up and offered Rosie her hand. It might have been the wine or the stunning setting or just everything about Nicola herself, but she found herself powerless at her touch, and as she stood, she slid her hand so that it was interlocking Nicola's fingers. At the same time as she pulled herself toward her, she felt Nicola tugging at her, so that all she needed to do was to tip her head upward ever so slightly and Nicola's lips were on hers. Last night her imagined kiss had been soft, but this real one was hungrier. More immediate.

Rosie felt all her professional defenses coming down as Nicola kissed her ravenously, her hand grazing down the exposed skin at the base of her neck in a way that made her wish she wasn't wearing a shirt. She wanted Nicola to have access to every part of her body. To be hers again.

This wasn't just heat. This was history, and if Rosie wasn't careful, it might just be her undoing. "We shouldn't," Rosie whispered, pulling back and trying to control her breath, wanting to take the words back the moment they escaped her lips. The day had been so full of indulgence. One more wasn't a big deal, was it?

"Do you want me to stop?" Nicola said, her warm

breath in Rosie's ear making her shiver through her core.

Rosie breathed in the scent of Nicola's perfume or body lotion, whatever it was, as Nicola kissed her neck gently, making her moan quietly with pleasure.

"I don't want you to," Rosie said, doing her best to control her breathing. "But I just…"

The vineyard hummed around them, the bees buzzing out of sight, the sun lighting up Nicola's beautiful face until it was just her in front of Rosie, glowing.

"I know," Nicola said. "We should go." A soft breeze blew some strands of hair into Rosie's face. Nicola reached up and gently moved them away, then trailed her fingertips down Rosie's cheek. "Can I see you tonight?" she asked, her low and breathy voice making Rosie vibrate with desire. "After dinner?"

"Yes," Rosie said. "Yes."

They walked slowly back to the Jeep, the vineyard's warmth lingering on their skin. Once again, Nicola opened the passenger door for her, this time placing her hand on the small of Rosie's back as she stepped into the passenger side.

"I've had such a great day," Rosie said as they returned to the Jeep. "I can see the roots you're planting here."

"It's a special place. I'm glad you got to see it," Nicola said. "And I hope you enjoy this evening."

"I can't wait."

Nicola turned on the ignition.

"And Nicola," Rosie said as Nicola pulled out onto the street, her engine rumbling as she accelerated toward the highway. She knew she shouldn't say it, but she was going to say it anyway. "I hope you like what I've picked out to wear."

She felt Nicola press a little harder on the gas as she turned out of the vineyard onto the highway toward the inn. "You're making it hard to keep my eyes on the road," she said. The Jeep surged onto the country road, the wind whipping through the open windows, tangling their hair.

Rosie reached out, her fingers grazing Nicola's forearm, light but deliberate, feeling the muscle tense under her touch. "Good," Rosie murmured, her heart racing as Nicola's lips curved into a knowing smile.

The drive back to Sugar Maple Farms was a short one and a quiet one, but the electric heat between them didn't show any signs of dissipating.

"See you at dinner," Nicola said as she pulled the Jeep to a stop in front of her building. "Your last night here. I'll make sure it's a good one."

Whether she was talking about the dinner, or whatever was coming after the dinner, Rosie didn't know, but she was sure that either way, a very interesting night was ahead. She couldn't be certain, but was that a slight wistfulness in Nicola's expression, the same one she'd seen morning they'd said goodbye to one another at Nicola's Toronto condo?

Hard to say behind her dark sunglasses. And hadn't that last goodbye been misleading anyway? Did she want to go down that path again and be subject to that same feeling of left-behind dismissal?

This was a little vacation fling. Another highly inappropriate one at that. At least the first time around, she'd been the coat-check girl to Nicola's departed chef. She was pretty sure there were no HR issues there.

Up in the quiet of her room, she flopped onto her bed, trying to quiet the raging desire coursing through her. How had she possibly managed to let her defenses down so quickly?

Being alone with Nicola again was a terrible idea. A terrible, destructive, albeit positively magnetic idea. One that could take her from a journalist on the edge of everything she wanted to a hack with a reputation as a celebrity groupie.

She rolled over on the plush bedspread, which beckoned for an afternoon nap, and sighed, then sat up and pulled her notes from her bag. Raging teenage hormones aside, if she could get Jeremy some kind of draft before she left for dinner, just to get feedback on the overall direction, that would be ideal.

She was there to do a job, after all. Some writing would give her something to focus on.

Even if the subject herself was proving to be the biggest distraction of all.

Rosie flipped open her laptop, the same overwhelming sensation of staring into the void creeping over her. No matter how short or inane the article—a quick hit on the artisanal ice cream trend, a coast-to-coast roundup of the best shawarma, a throwback to menus of the eighties—the sight of a blank screen always felt like a mountain to climb.

Rosie leafed through her notes, summoning the flavors from her first dinner: The glow of the tree line at sunset, the respect and subtle awe with which Nicola's team spoke about her. The chatter of jaybirds, the stuck-in-a-better-time quaintness of Sunset County and the charm of its residents.

She closed her eyes, breathing deeply as she channeled the essence of the place. Of Nicola.

For the next two hours, she barely looked up as she filled three pages with her experiences and observations. It was like the article was writing itself, and for the first time since she'd accepted the assignment, she felt no fear, no pressure, no trepidation.

She felt pride.

Pride in the words on the page, which were landing with uncharacteristic umph. Pride in her ability to distill the perfection of the Inn at Sugar Maple Farms into something that someone hundreds of miles away would be able to conjure in their minds with all five senses. Pride in the woman who was so key in making it all happen.

And Rosie was doing it all without overstepping the concrete barrier that Nicola had erected around herself and her life. A barrier that Rosie was coming to realize was well within her right to have around a public greedy for details that didn't belong to them.

Her article felt fresh and dreamy. An escape.

Three hours and two thousand words later, Rosie sat at her laptop, smiling to herself as she completed a final proofread. She was excited to share her draft document with Jeremy, certain that he would be thrilled with the change in direction for the article. Not only had had she nailed her depiction of the ambience and rustic luxury of Sugar Maple Farms, but her time with Nicola, and the energy between them had allowed her to paint a vivid picture of her enthusiasm for her work, and the parts of the inn and the local community that contributed so much to her cuisine.

She read it over twice, tweaking words here and there, adding some extra sensory detail—not too much, just enough to be evocative, and then she sat, pondering a title.

Titles were hard. They had to draw a reader in, give enough information without sounding trite or trying too hard to be clever.

Rosie stood up and slid the door to her balcony open and stepped outside to the warm early evening air. It was almost time to get ready for dinner. Nicola would be in the kitchen, carefully creating the menu items for all the eager diners. And soon, Rosie would slip into the shimmery blue silk dress that she'd saved for her final evening and indulge in whatever flavor sensation Nicola was preparing.

She thought about Nicola, out in the garden, helping Shane pluck the smallest of flowers, the hundreds that would be painstakingly added to the dishes to add that extra level of elegance. The slightest wisp of extra flavor.

She went back inside and sat at her laptop and typed at the top center of the page, Sugar Maple Farms: Where Taste Takes Root.

One more read-through, and then Rosie attached a copy to Jeremy's email. Hope you like it! she wrote, confident that he would. How could he not? The article perfectly encapsulated the perfection of Sugar Maple Farms, its grounds, its people. Nicola.

Now, with her article all but filed, she was going to let herself free from the constraints of her work. It was time to celebrate.

Chapter Eleven

Nicola hummed to herself as she did a final walk-through of the dining space, examining the table settings and linens, straightening things here and there, just so. When she arrived at the table closest to the kitchen, the tree-side two-seater on a high top with a view of everything that was going on inside, she experienced a small thrill at the fact that Rosie would soon be perched there and Nicola would present her with the best meal of their life.

She was back. It was official. Her body practically thrummed with the idea of what she was about to execute with her team.

She'd woken up the night before and had spent an hour reimagining the menu for the evening. News of the changes had likely annoyed more than one person on her team, but she didn't care.

Because for the first time in as long as she could remember, ingredients and textures and flavors were fitting together in her mind like a Tetris board, and even the thought of the dishes in front of her was enough to make her heart beat faster as she lay in bed, staring up at the dark ceiling.

She was no longer at Sugar Maple Farms because she'd built a name for herself, and for the time being, that was enough to get people in and turn a blind eye to the fact that she was no longer great but really good.

Nicola could sense what was going to happen, and the electric excitement was palpable.

And then there was the kiss. Nicola couldn't help but emit a light groan at the memory of Rosie's lips, soft and sweet and probing with every ounce of intensity Nicola felt in that moment.

The electricity hadn't faded. If anything, Nicola felt an extra jolt in her step as she slipped into her station. And the moment her hands touched the first ingredients, it was confirmed. Rosie wasn't just a spark. She was an energy. An inspiration. A revelation.

The kitchen moved in rhythm with her heartbeat, sharp, fluid, alive. The perfect sear. The exact shade of caramelization. Every instinct landed with precision. It was as if her body already knew what to do, and her mind, for once, wasn't cluttered with doubt or distraction.

She'd never felt this tuned in before. And it was only first service.

Her staff must have felt it too. Everyone was sharp, dialed in. Tim was firing orders like a machine, and plates were hitting the pass with perfect timing. And when Sebastien came back into the kitchen, she heard him mutter something to Tim about a five-hundred-dollar tip given to him by a couple celebrating their anniversary, and Nicola knew that the energy wasn't just contained to the kitchen. It was out there in the dining room. The whole place was humming.

And soon, the woman who dialed her in would be there to witness firsthand what she was doing to Nicola.

Two hours later, Nicola looked up from her station just as Leo greeted Rosie at the entrance, and the air shifted.

Rosie's dark hair spilled over her shoulders in loose waves, her sun-kissed skin glowing against the soft shimmer of midnight-blue fabric. The dress. She hadn't been kidding about it.

Nicola swallowed hard, hand frozen mid-plating. Everything else in the kitchen blurred. Movement, noise, timing. For a second, all she could feel was heat.

She watched as Rosie followed Leo to her table, and indeed, Nicola very much liked not only the prospect of having Rosie at the tree-side table for the hour, sitting there with that dress that clung in all the right places, just low enough to hint at the curve of her cleavage.

Nicola's pulse ticked up. Rosie looked incredible. Poised, radiant, absolutely electric.

When she sat, her eyes found Nicola's. And in them, there was something more than heat. Something even more real than attraction.

Nicola put the plate she was holding down and turned her attention to the task at hand. Now it was *really* showtime.

Other diners had trickled in, but Nicola's attention was only on Rosie as she prepped the first dish she wanted brought out, a delicate foraged-mushroom tartlet with wild-leek aioli. She nodded to Seb, who came and swept up the plate, and a moment later it was being placed in front of Rosie, with a glass of lightly oaked Chardonnay delivered to the table by the bartender.

Rosie looked up at Nicola and grinned. They were off to the races.

Watching Rosie sample her food would never get old, and as the courses continued—lake-trout crudo with pickled wild blueberries, heirloom mushrooms with fresh burrata, lamb loin with saskatoon-berry jus, peach tart with basil ice cream, all with drink pairings, Rosie appeared to be wading deep into Nicola's seduction.

She put her spoon down on the table in front of her, then looked up at Nicola and shook her head slightly and smiled, approval mixed with a hint of incredulity in her eyes. When she picked up her spoon again and dipped it into the raspberry coulis, then tasted it, her eyes drifted closed for a moment.

Nicola felt it. It was time to visit Rosie's table.

She washed her hands at the sink, dried them with a clean dishtowel and paused by the mirror the servers used to check her appearance before leaving the brightly lit kitchen for the dim dining room.

Rosie looked up from her drink as Nicola approached, raising an eyebrow. She offered a quiet, playful round of applause. Nicola drank in the empty plates on Rosie's table and the dress, that, up close, more than delivered on its promise.

"Well, I might die of overindulgence," Rosie said as Nicola slid into the seat across from her. Nicola noticed the nearby diners pretending not to stare. She didn't care. "That was quite the parting gift."

"It's meant to tempt you to return," Nicola said.

Rosie shook her head slowly. "It was exquisite. Truly."

Nicola met her eyes. "It was for you."

Something in Rosie's expression shifted from complete satisfaction to something deeper. Wanting. Searching.

Nicola took a moment to break from Rosie's gaze to sweep her eyes across the dining room, and she was certain that it wasn't just Rosie who was swept up in the afterglow of a perfect meal. There was a contented buzz in the air, a subliminal satisfaction that pleasured Nicola right down to the core. She'd felt something approaching this before, but this? It was intoxicating.

Most of the guests had paid their checks and were taking the last sips of their drinks before retiring to their rooms. The dining room would soon be empty, but Nicola was desperate for Rosie to remember the invitation she'd agreed to earlier.

"Are you still up for hanging around for a bit?" Nicola said. "Why don't you get another drink, or a coffee or something. Wait for me to finish up. Cleanup's already well underway, so I just need to make my rounds."

"I can stick around for a few minutes," Rosie said. "I should probably get back soon to see if Jeremy sent any notes on the article, though. I filed it today. I know he's eager to get it in the next issue, so I might have some more work to do tonight."

Nicola raised an eyebrow as she stood up and pushed her chair back in. "Aha," she said. "Are you going to show it to me?" She tried not to sound too eager, but she was desperate to read Rosie's thoughts about the inn, the restaurant, about Sunset County as a whole.

"Not yet," Rosie said, dipping her chin just slightly and smiling. "I want to wait until it's perfect."

When Nicola disappeared back into the kitchen, Rosie leaned back in her chair, caught in a dreamscape.

Nicola had absolutely nailed that meal, and from the slight swagger in her step as she returned to the kitchen, she clearly knew it. Her quiet confidence, her satisfaction, the glow of someone fully in their element—it was an unbelievable turn-on.

That was the Nicola Kim meal she'd been expecting, and it was clear as day how Nicola had risen to the heights she had. The woman was an artist. An ingénue.

Rosie felt on the verge of sensory overload, caught between the perfection of the meal and the magnetic pull of Nicola herself. The promise of what the night might bring.

"May I join you for a moment?" a voice called from behind her. She turned to see Gabriel, still in his black suit but with the top button undone. His hair was just a little bit tousled; he had the mark of an elegant man who'd just worked a full and busy day.

"Please," Rosie said, nodding to the seat that Nicola had just vacated.

"How was your meal?" Gabriel said.

"Divine," said Rosie. "Honestly spectacular. Kudos to your team."

Gabriel visibly relaxed. "I've heard the same thing from a few other patrons tonight."

"No doubt," said Rosie. She felt another rush of pride for Nicola, then pushed it away. *She's not yours*, she reminded herself.

Despite the perfection of the day they'd had, that explosive kiss felt, impossibly, even more charged than their first kiss all those years ago, and the absolute theatre of what Nicola had just presented her, Rosie still had one foot planted firmly in reality. No amount of wine, butter or sugar could dissolve the truth.

After tomorrow, Nicola would once again be someone that she used to know. The thought sobered her, and for a moment, Rosie wondered if she should return to her room instead of waiting for Nicola to come out of the kitchen, like a fan waiting with an autograph book after a Broadway show.

"So your overall impressions?" Gabriel asked.

"It's..." Rosie searched for what to say to encapsulate her feelings about the inn. "The same phrase keeps coming to mind. It's heaven on earth. Truly."

Gabriel nodded, satisfied. "I know that we won't likely see your article until it's published," he said, his eyes searching hers. "And I can respect that, of course." He paused, and Rosie waited to see where this was going. Nowhere good, it seemed.

"It's just that...how do I say this?" He glanced at the kitchen, then folded his hands together on the table and leaned in. "There was a very poor review that came out earlier today," he said. "I'm worried it might make its way into Nicola's head. I was nervous about tonight's service—"

"Which you definitely didn't need to be, obviously," Rosie cut in. A bad review? How was that possible?

Gabriel cleared his throat. "I was just hoping, if at all possible, if there's going to be anything in your writing that's…unexpected, that you do me the courtesy of giving me a heads-up. So I can prepare Nicola." He glanced over his shoulder. "It's important that she's in a good space."

Rosie paused. Her article was more or less glowing. But she didn't want to make any promises until Jeremy had given it the stamp of approval. "I will give you a heads-up" was all she said.

Gabriel waited a beat and then gave a quick, satisfied shake of his head. "Okay, then. I hope you enjoy the rest of the evening. Be sure to look up when you're on your way back to your room." He stood up. "It's a full moon tonight."

A full moon. Strange things happened during full moons, didn't they?

He strode through the restaurant and out the door. Rosie could see through the kitchen that Nicola was talking to a couple of her staff, so she slid her phone from her purse and typed in Sugar Maple Farms + Nicola Kim. The first hit was from the *Toronto Tribune*'s Entertainment and Living section. Rosie clicked the link and was taken to a page with an article that had been posted that afternoon at three o'clock, right in the middle of their perfect day. She scanned the first couple of paragraphs. It all seemed positive. Was this the right article, or was Gabriel just incredibly…sensitive?

She knew Mark Marcellin. Had met him a few times,

actually, at various industry events. Her impression was that his head was on the larger side, but who was she to judge? He'd made it much farther in the industry than she had. Rosie, however, liked to believe that if she ever became a household name, her humility wouldn't evaporate overnight.

She continued to read about the property, the hotel grounds, the warm reception into the dining room that had been designed by an architecture firm who were responsible for a new symphony hall in Berlin, a flagship Cartier store in London and a boutique hotel in Napa.

There was a brief overview of the restaurant's ethos and a quote from Gabriel relating what they hoped to achieve with the space.

Rosie's stomach dropped when she got to the next part of the article: *While Chef Nicola Kim has been handed all the ingredients for an iconic dining experience, what's missing is the elusive spark, the secret sauce that once elevated her former ventures. The experience is like an overbaked soufflé—ambitious, promising, but ultimately deflated.*

Each sentence that followed was biting in tone and, truthfully, pretty unfair. Had the guy not eaten in the same restaurant as Rosie just had?

Had Nicola read the article? Rosie tried to imagine herself reading that kind of scathing critique of her own work. She definitely didn't have thick enough skin to endure that kind of public punishment. Maybe after so many years in the business, there was a chance it would roll right off Nicola's back.

She had a feeling that wasn't the case.

Rosie didn't know the details, but she got the sense that the inn was sitting on somewhat tenuous ground, that despite the pristine perfection of the inn, reviews like this one meant a great deal. The look in Gabriel's eyes—*please give me a heads-up*—confirmed it.

The article had nothing to do with Rosie, but it still felt like a gut punch. She scrolled back up, rereading a few sharp-edged sentences, each one ripping off the bandage all over again. She needed to be sure it was as brutal as she thought.

It was.

Mark Marcellin had it out for Nicola. There was no other explanation.

Just as she was about to bookmark the piece, a presence appeared over her shoulder.

"I knew you were stalking me."

Rosie flinched. She quickly turned her phone face down on the table, heart thumping in her chest.

Nicola stood behind her, hair loose and cheeks flushed, faint with perspiration from the kitchen. Her smile was light, teasing.

"What?" Nicola said, cocking her head. "I can't be a little cocky about finding a gorgeous woman checking me out online?"

That was when it hit Rosie.

Nicola hadn't read the review.

"Hey!" Rosie managed, way too enthusiastic. "The dinner tonight was…wow. A feat." She meant it, but Nicola's narrowing eyes said she wasn't buying the deflection.

"Thanks," Nicola said, looking back at Rosie's phone.

She turned it over quickly on the table. “Wait, what were you just looking at?”

Rosie covered it with her hand. “Nothing important.” She tried to be playful, but Nicola wasn’t fooled.

“It’s the review, isn’t it?”

Rosie hesitated. Then nodded.

Nicola held out her hand. “Let me see it.”

“I…” Rosie’s stomach twisted. “It’s pretty unfair, honestly.”

Nicola said nothing. Just waited.

Reluctantly, Rosie turned over her phone and tapped in her passcode, then passed the device to Nicola.

She couldn’t watch as Nicola scrolled, her face still, unreadable, until her shoulders tensed and she handed it back.

“Honestly, it’s not that bad,” Rosie said quickly. “And anyone who knows anything will see right through it. Plus—”

“It’s a terrible review, Rosie,” Nicola said flatly. “And maybe I deserve it.”

She looked back at the kitchen, then at Rosie. Her voice softened. “I’ve gotta go. Sorry about tonight. I hope you sleep well. It’s been nice to see you.”

With that, she turned and left Rosie sitting at her table. “Wait!” Rosie called, but Nicola disappeared behind the kitchen door.

Should she go after her?

Rosie felt sick with complicity. Look what that journalist had done to Nicola, seemingly with no care about her as a human being. No wonder Nicola was keeping her at arm's length. Of course in this moment Rosie would be the last person she'd want to associate with.

Rosie stayed where she was, the silence of the dark dining room stretching out around her like a punishment.

She hadn't written the review, but she might as well have.

With a hollow ache settling in her chest, Rosie turned off her phone, slid it into her pocket and left the restaurant alone.

Nicola fought the lump in her throat as she stepped back into the kitchen, which was spotless and quiet. She leaned against the counter and tried to steady her breathing, unable to believe how fast one of the best nights she'd had in ages had unraveled.

Get it together, she told herself, exhaling shakily. Rosie had stuck around for her. She hadn't done anything wrong. *Go back out there*, she thought.

It was one review. One person's take. The review said it was flat, but she'd just watched as an entire dining room fell in love with her food. That was the real her. But now, with the weight of the knowledge that the inn was on shaky ground, she needed people to know that what had happened in the restaurant tonight was the real deal.

You're good, she told herself. *You're more than good. You're great.*

Tears pooled in her eyes, but she blinked them back quickly, reaching deep inside to do her best to dust off the hurt, straighten her shoulders and get back out to the dining room to join Rosie. She took a deep breath and reached for composure like a clean dishtowel.

She rounded the corner toward the staff washroom and nearly collided with Danielle, who was on her way out.

"Whoops, sorry!" Danielle said in the dim light of the hallway, her cheeks still flushed from the frenetic service. "That was some night!" she said, grinning.

"Uh, yeah," Nicola said. She knew she should say more, compliment Danielle. The woman had executed her role seamlessly all night. Clearly she hadn't read the review.

Not that anyone would blame Danielle for the disastrous write-up anyway. That was the beauty of being in a supporting role. You didn't get all the glory when things were good, but it was easier to sidestep the bad.

"Some of us are going to do a night swim to celebrate," Danielle said tentatively. "Would you…want to join us?"

Nicola wished she could absorb Danielle's joy, but all she felt was the sting of those printed words. The only thing she wanted was to pull her duvet over her head, close her eyes and escape into a dream world where Mark Marcellin didn't exist. Where she could indulge in the memory of what she'd felt earlier that night. Where she still had the whole night ahead of her with Rosie and all the promise that held.

"Yeah, maybe I'll meet you at the lake," she said. The noncommittal tone oozed out before she could correct it. Danielle's lips dipped slightly and the light in her eyes flickered. Nicola didn't need to say it. They both knew she wasn't coming.

"All right, well, hope to see you there," Danielle said with a tight smile and a quick wave before disappearing toward the back entrance.

Nicola glanced out toward the dining room. Empty. Rosie was gone.

Now she felt not only like a failure but also like a total jerk.

They'd finally started to click as a team. Nicola had pulled off a fabulous meal. And the woman who'd sparked it all had been sitting right outside, waiting for her.

It should have been a night to celebrate. A return to form. But all Nicola could feel was that she was a ghost of herself in her own kitchen.

Chapter Twelve

Rosie woke early and reached for her phone on the side table. Her inbox was empty save for her phone bill and a promotional email from Jenny Bird advertising a twenty-five-percent-off sale. Nothing from Nicola.

She let out a sigh and flopped onto her back, staring at the ceiling. What now?

What Rosie wanted to do was get dressed, pick up two coffees from the lobby and walk over to Nicola's cottage and knock on the door like it was nothing. Like they still had that ease between them.

Maybe Nicola had slept on it and had a chance to digest the review. Maybe she'd be ready to talk.

But showing up uninvited felt presumptuous. Intrusive.

Still, leaving things hanging like this felt worse.

She tapped her phone screen to open a new email and typed, I think you're incredible. And not just your cooking. Thank you for everything. She stared at it for a long minute, her thumb hovering, then hit Send without even adding a subject line.

She might never hear back from Nicola, but she wanted her to know how she felt and at the very least feel some semblance of reassurance that Rosie's article wasn't going to follow in Mark Marcellin's footsteps.

Regardless, the dull ache of disappointment, the one she'd told herself repeatedly that she was setting herself up for, settled in. Of course it hadn't panned out. What was she expecting?

She navigated back to her inbox. Jeremy hadn't responded yet. Maybe she should just go back to bed. She could leave town, although she didn't want to depart Sunset County until she got the thumbs-up from Jeremy that her work was done.

Another cloudless sky greeted Rosie when she pulled back the blinds, the early sunshine lighting up the mist from the sprinklers over the vegetable garden and the morning glories winding along her balcony railing trumpeting a rich purple *good morning.*

She could order room service for breakfast. But that bakery they'd visited, Flour Child, and another cup of coffee from Rise and Grind called to her. She'd take a car into town, spend the morning poking around the adorable-looking shops, and by the time she returned, Jeremy would no doubt have left her some light revision notes in her email inbox, but until then, a trip to the Sunset County main strip felt like a perfect way to pass the time.

And maybe, just maybe, Nicola would write back too.

Rosie pulled on a white sleeveless jersey dress with camel leather slip-on sandals, then packed a paperback and a water bottle in her bag and descended to the deserted lobby. The other guests, clearly, were still enjoying their Cadillac mattresses.

The concierge looked up from his computer and smiled. "Good morning," he said. "Can I help you with anything?"

"I remember something about a car service?" Rosie asked. Part of her felt badly for asking, like she'd be putting someone out by asking them to do a job they were paid to do. But the way the man reacted, like they would actually be thrilled to take her into town, put her at ease. "I'm hoping to go into town for an hour or so."

"Of course," he said, reaching for the phone. "Let me call Anderson. He'll meet you out front."

Rosie stood in the early morning sun, listening to the sparrows and the faint murmur of gardeners tending the hydrangeas along the main building.

Her eyes drifted toward the trails she knew Nicola walked each morning. They were empty. Rosie half expected to see her there, head down, hands in her pockets, enjoying the grounds but keeping a low profile. She wanted to wave. To catch her eye. To have the chance to say *I'm still here*.

An ache of loss pulsed as she remembered their walks. Their easy banter and the quiet pride in Nicola's voice as she showed Rosie around her new home.

Now it all felt like a dream.

A white SUV rounded the corner and pulled to a stop in front of Rosie. The driver rolled down the window. "Ms. Franklin-Smith?" he asked.

"That's me," said Rosie, and before she could even make a move to open the back door, Anderson had exited the vehicle and was holding the door open for her.

The small details made all the difference, and Rosie

wanted to make sure they shone through in her review. She'd have to go back in and mention this too. Doing right by Nicola mattered. Maybe their time together hadn't turned out the way Rosie had hoped, but at least she could feel good about that. She was determined to enjoy her last morning in Sunset County.

Anderson dropped Rosie off in front of Rise and Grind, where she lined up among the other townspeople and cottagers, all looking relaxed and sun kissed, the golden glow of those who either lived in or were lucky enough to spend time in this idyllic summer paradise.

She bought a latte, then walked down the street to peruse the display at Flour Child. A young man stood behind the counter wearing a nametag that said *Lucas*.

"Hey," he said as the bells above the door chimed. "How's your morning going?"

It was the mumble of a teen mixed with the moving-toward-maturity of a young man who was learning the customer service ropes. "I'm good—thanks," Rosie said, surveying the day's offerings.

There were gingham-tea-towel-lined wicker baskets of fresh-baked sourdough and rye loaves, piles of cheddar-and-jalapeño and white-chocolate-and-raspberry scones, golden-crusted croissants and pain au chocolat, three key lime pies, carrot-cake cupcakes drizzled with cream-cheese frosting and coconut macaroons with dark-chocolate bottoms. "I'll take one of those," Rosie said, pointing to the macaroons.

"Those are fire," Lucas said, sliding one into a paper bag and passing it across the counter. "Enjoy."

"Can I ask you a question?" Rosie said. She felt a little bit strange doing it, especially with this young kid, but curiosity got the better of her. "What do people in town think about the Inn at Sugar Maple Farms?"

Lucas raised an eyebrow. "In what sense?"

"I don't know," Rosie said. And she didn't really know why she was asking. Part of her wanted to know that she was leaving Nicola in a good place. After what she'd seen last night, the sense of protection that had started to grow the day she'd overheard the woman talking about Nicola in the spa had only grown. That sense of loneliness that Nicola had spoken of, from the time before she'd disappeared from the public eye—was that what Rosie was going to leave her to exist in? "I guess I'm just curious about all the attention. Especially with the restaurant and everything."

Lucas's expression brightened. "I've watched every episode of *At Home with Nicola*," he said. "If you'd have known me a couple years ago you'd never have believed it. But then I got into all this—" he gestured toward the bakery display case "—and I've kind of gotten obsessed with it. Cooking and baking and stuff. I think people around here think it's pretty legit. And she's come in here a few times. She's chill."

Rosie nodded, doing her best not to smile at the thought of this teen boy, who looked like he was going to grow into quite the heartbreaker with his sculpted cheekbones and Jordan Catalano–esque swooped hair, being a superfan of Nicola's.

Sunset County, it seemed, might just take good care of her.

For the next hour, Rosie wandered through a women's clothing boutique called Wish, flipping through racks of airy linen and soft knits. She tried on a dress that was a bit dressier and more revealing than she typically wore. Maybe it was the tan she'd developed after spending the last few days in the sunshine, or maybe it was the lighting in the dressing room, but the dress fit her perfectly.

"That dress was made for you," the shopkeeper gushed, as Rosie examined herself from different angles in the dressing room mirror. "Oh, and all sale items are fifty percent off this weekend."

Rosie flipped the tag. The once expensive item had already been steeply marked down, and with the additional discount, they were practically giving it away.

"I'll take it," she said after she changed back into her clothes and passed it to the shopkeeper, who smiled and wrapped it in tissue paper.

Rosie called the number the inn had given her to call when she was ready to be collected. "Anderson will be there in fifteen, Ms. Franklin-Smith," the front desk attendant said.

Could Rosie ever travel like a regular person again? It wouldn't be easy.

She had fifteen minutes to kill, so she ducked into the local bookstore, where the children's section was tucked inside an old bank vault and the cookbook aisle was so thoughtfully curated she could have spent the entire afternoon there.

Sunset County was just as charming as the inn was elegant, and if Rosie could have designed her perfect day, this might have been it. *If Nicola were here too,* she thought, the sharp pain of her absence still not dulling.

Rosie brought an easy weeknight Mediterranean cookbook she'd heard good things about to the till—no more Mr. Noodles for her, she was resolved, not after this trip—and was about to check out when she noticed a stack of newspapers by the cash register. Curious, she unfolded the Entertainment and Living section of the *Toronto Tribune*, and there it was in print. Right smack dab on the front page of the section. The review.

"Not a great look for the inn," the store employee said, shaking his head. "I haven't eaten there myself, but I doubt it's as bad as that guy's making it out to be."

"It's not," Rosie said, too quickly. "It's actually… nothing like that."

Without thinking, she scooped up the only other three copies of the paper and added them to her book pile. Back in her room, she'd shove them into the recycling bin. Out of sight. Three fewer people to read that reviewer's nonsense account of his visit.

This wasn't healthy, she reminded herself. She was still meant to be presenting a fair, objective profile of Nicola Kim, and nothing about her behavior right now suggested a professional distance.

But still. She was only human. And she knew now that Nicola Kim was much more vulnerable than first met the eye.

Buying them felt like a small act of defiance, as if she could keep those words from spreading any further. It was the very least she could do.

* * *

The moment she'd returned to her hotel room, Rosie opened her email and clicked on Jeremy's reply to her article draft. Where there would usually be a paragraph or so summary of his overall thoughts about the strengths and areas for improvement were only two words: Call me.

Her stomach lurched. Jeremy was not happy with the new direction, and a phone call confirmed it.

"It's just not what we sent you there for," he said. "The writing works. But it reads like a love letter to Sunset County. And Nicola's just a background figure. A host, a tour guide."

Rosie steadied herself. "This is Nicola's life now. I think readers will want to know about how drastically her life has changed. She went from jet-setting around the world to living on a quaint farm in rural Ontario. All these places, the people that make up the fabric of her life." She could picture the less-than-impressed expression on Jeremy's face. No matter how much she believed what she was saying, Jeremy wasn't going to buy it.

"You know as well as I do that the real story is what happened before she got there."

"We're a food publication, not a tabloid, Jeremy," she said, her boldness surprising her. She knew he was right. But suddenly, she felt protective of Nicola and her privacy. So what if she didn't want the intimate details of her life broadcast to the entire world?

Rosie closed her eyes. Or maybe she was just making excuses for her own inability to execute.

"You're right—we're a food publication. A food publication on the brink of shutting down unless we can get some web traffic to satisfy our advertisers. Are you sure you can't get anything else out of her?"

Rosie sat on the sofa beside her half-packed suitcase, one foot resting on the coffee table, staring out at the gardens. The black-eyed Susans shifted in the breeze, and sunlight danced through the tree canopy overhead—this little slice of paradise she was about to lose. The thought of leaving it all behind, empty-handed, made her chest tighten.

The other end of the line was quiet, and the all-too-familiar feeling of mediocrity washed over her. If she had any iota of talent as an interviewer, she would have been able to get Nicola talking. Now she felt foolish, wrapped in a buttery-soft terry-cloth robe that should have been draped over the shoulders of a real journalist.

Then, she remembered the promise she made to herself on the drive from Toronto. She was going to make this happen. Come hell or high water.

"One more night," she heard herself saying.

"We've already spent—"

"I'm paying for it out of pocket. There's a party tonight. Nicola invited me." Her mind raced. Could she actually show up at that party? And would Nicola even go? If she was still as deep in her blue spell as Rosie guessed she was, there was a more than significant chance she would blow off the event.

Jeremy was quiet on the other end.

"I'll get the story." The assuredness with which she said it surprised her. Hopefully that confidence would carry forward into her next moments with Nicola.

"Add the one night to our bill," Jeremy said finally. "I was on the fence about telling you this. I don't want to add more pressure than I know you're already feeling." Rosie's stomach sank as she fought an irresistible urge to tap the screen to hang up. This didn't sound good. "I guess your presence at the inn has been noted by more than one high-profile organization. I've had calls from both *Hello!* and *Entertainment Weekly*, both promising enhanced distribution. Digital, print, video segments." He hesitated. "This was already big for us. Now?"

Rosie lay back in the bed, mind spinning. "Massive."

"Massive," Jeremy echoed.

No pressure. Suddenly her head throbbed, but it was more than a headache. Was it possible for a brain to hurt?

"Just do your best. I know you will. Good luck, Rosie."

"Good night, Jeremy," Rosie said.

Her mind raced. *Massive* didn't feel superlative enough. It felt like a molehill. The publications Jeremy had just mentioned would be Rosie's ticket to a new echelon of journalism. She would be *known*.

And there was a less than zero percent chance that they were going to syndicate Rosie's "love letter" to Sunset County. At this point, it felt like a grade-five book report, not a serious contender for the scoop of the year that everyone was expecting.

What had she been thinking, getting sucked back into the spell of Nicola Kim? It was like she'd forgotten her whole reason for coming to Sugar Maple Farms.

Was she that average? That *weak*? No. She was stronger than that. This was her chance to be great. To taste one iota of the success that Nicola had found. The idea was even more intoxicating than any of the wine she'd tasted over the past few days, wine, she knew now, that had likely been presented to her to dull her senses. Lull her into complacency. Keep her from accomplishing her mission.

Maybe her approach had been wrong this whole time. Talking to Nicola on her turf. In her kitchen. At the places where she sourced all her ingredients. She'd been on grounds where Nicola felt comfortable, confident. She had the upper hand.

A party off property might be the place to get Nicola talking. A cocktail or two. Dim lights and music, a stolen moment by the water under the moonlight.

Rosie shook her head. Was she actually thinking of seducing Nicola for the story? Given what she'd seen of Nicola over the last few days: her vulnerability, the high esteem in which her staff held her. The way the bad review seemed to have chipped away at something deep inside. The hushed gossip of the women at the spa. Was leaving her alone the way to go?

Her phone buzzed again beside her. Did Jeremy just have another quick read-through and was calling to recognize her brilliance and say he was firing it off to all the major pubs and encourage her to attend the party to celebrate, just for fun?

Doubtful.

She flipped it over to find an incoming call from her mother on the call display. Rosie stared at her phone. She hovered her thumb over the screen, ready to send the call to voicemail—she had to get ready for the party and get her head in the game with this new information—

but she reconsidered and hit Accept. It would be nice to hear her mother's voice and get the scoop on the inane neighborhood gossip. Who was getting new interlocking in their driveway. How many people showed up at the town meeting to express concerns about the condos being planned just outside of their subdivision which would no doubt increase local traffic. Which author the book club was reading next.

"Hey, Mom," Rosie said, flopping down onto the bed and tapping the screen again to activate speakerphone. She lay back on the heavenly pillow and closed her eyes. Would the housekeeper notice if the room was one pillow short after her checkout?

"Hi, sweetheart!" her mother's voice called, filling the room with her eternal optimism and energy. "Your dad and I are both here. And Ashton too, and Liana!"

Rosie pictured them all in her parents' sitting room, with the view of their rose garden. There would be iced tea and biscotti on the table, the cribbage board and a deck of cards ready for Ashton and her dad, and Michael Bublé playing over the sound system. Everyone would look dressed for a yacht party.

"Oh wow. Hi, everyone," Rosie said. It was a bit odd, them all calling on speakerphone.

"We thought we'd call you so you could celebrate some big news that your brother just shared with us!" her mother said.

Rosie winced. She could just picture Ashton, lips pursed, fully embarrassed and aware that whatever this news was about to be shared not just to Rosie but to the many group chats his mother was a part of. Her sisters and sisters-in-law. Besties from the fitness club that she belonged to. Her hairdresser, probably even her gynecologist. Because when Patricia Franklin had news to share, *everyone* was privy.

"Wow," she repeated. "So what is it?"

"Tell her, honey," Patricia said, and Rosie could feel her mother grinning at Ashton.

"Hey, sis," Ashton said. "Guess what? I got the Wordle in two today."

"Oh stop it!" Patricia called. "Okay, fine, I'll spill. Ashton has been promoted to partner. The youngest in his company's history!"

"Oh wow!" Rosie said. She needed to find another exclamatory word.

"And not only that," Patricia said, her pride oozing through the phone. "But Ashton and Liana are *engaged*!"

Rosie closed her eyes as her mother rattled off the details of the promotion. Company car, shares in the firm, two weeks a year at the villa in Turks. And then the engagement, which had happened in a hot air balloon over Cappadocia.

"I'm thrilled for you, bro," Rosie said. "And Liana. Wow. I'm finally going to have a sister." There was laughter on the other end, maybe tinged with relief. And Rosie's words were genuine. She was happy for her brother. He was legitimately amazing and deserved the corner office and brainy and beautiful wife.

She forced out "amazing" and "so, so great" like a pro, even managed to keep her tone bright. A tiny part of her was proud of the performance.

“Looking forward to seeing you guys,” Rosie said. For half a second she thought about telling them where she was and the assignment she’d been sent on. But doing so would invite questions and follow-up, and when it settled that there was a not-so-insignificant chance that Rosie was going to be going home empty-handed and she’d soon be explaining to her family that she was looking for a job, she clamped her mouth shut until it was time to say goodbye.

There had to be a way to turn this around. To write something bold enough, brilliant enough that Jeremy couldn’t deny it, and force the big media conglomerates into a bidding war. She stood and walked to the window, scanning the grounds of Sugar Maple Farms like a battlefield. Was the story truly dead? Or had she stopped chasing it the moment she stepped into Nicola Kim’s orbit again, gravitating toward a pull she hadn’t fully escaped the first time?

Rosie stood in the shower, letting the warm stream from the rain spout trickle through her hair and down her body. She could do this. She *had* to do this.

She pictured her article, amassing views by the hundreds of thousands. Millions? Reposted by the who’s who in the journalism and culinary worlds.

The look on Jeremy’s face when she strolled into the office and hearing that his phone was ringing off the hook with advertisers.

Rosie’s inbox, flooded with requests for guest speaking, media appearances and offers for representation.

Her novel, finding a home.

Maybe there was a way.

Her gaze landed on the dress she'd just bought in town, the soft gold threads catching the light even from across the room. She almost hadn't bought it. Too dressy, too revealing, maybe too much for a casual lakefront party. But tonight it felt like armor. Strategic? Maybe. Manipulative? She wasn't sure. But when it came to Nicola…her heart was already bending the rules.

She wasn't here to seduce a quote out of someone, but she couldn't ignore the tug in her chest every time Nicola looked at her like she was something more than a passing curiosity. It had started out as a story. It was still a story. But somewhere along the line, Nicola had stopped feeling like just a source.

In service of the story, she thought, doing her best to reconcile this cognitive dissonance. Nicola might've been guarded, but she *had* invited Rosie to the party. A time when she was off the clock. She was aware and obviously okay with Rosie seeing her outside of her professional space. And that had to count for something.

Chapter Thirteen

Nicola kept her head down as she entered the kitchen, where the staff were busy with pre-service prep, taking directions from Danielle. She wasn't scheduled to work, but old habits died hard.

They were busy, but it only took a few seconds to notice that the air had shifted since last night. No one was trading barbs, and none of the younger prep chefs were blaring music the way they tended to during these times when the dining room was empty.

They, too, must have seen the review.

"Hey, Chef," Karlos said, flashing Nicola a quick smile then turning right back to the turnips he was slicing into delicate rounds on the chopping board in front of him.

"Hey," she said. "Any allergies, VIPs tonight?" Even though she wasn't on the roster, she was curious, especially after last night.

He glanced up from his station. "Just your friend from that magazine," he said.

Her stomach clenched at the mention of Rosie. A twist of shame and something else she wasn't ready to name. "She's checking out this morning," Nicola said.

"I don't know," said Karlos. "It's on the rundown for the day. First seating."

A mistake. But she wasn't going to correct it. Better they stayed sharp, even if she wasn't on the line tonight.

But the fact that there would be no one else of note was surprising. There were usually at least three or four other guests they needed to be in the know about—repeat customers, either of the inn or of Gabriel's father's restaurant. Some influencer or another. A notable chef from a restaurant in the city.

"Are we already bleeding customers or something?" Nicola said, mostly to herself, but at her words, she sensed the energy in the room shift, and more than one staff member glanced up slightly.

Her presence wasn't helping. She had to leave.

She slipped into Gabriel's empty office, closed the door behind her and flopped onto the couch.

The article was already open on her phone. She didn't need to read it again. She knew every line by heart. Still, she couldn't help herself. She typed in her passcode, and there it was, staring at her.

Blood pounded through her veins. She was ready to whip the phone right through the floor-to-ceiling window when Gabriel appeared in the doorway, a look of alarm on his face.

"Nicola," he said, his voice tentative. "It's not as bad as you—"

"It's worse," Nicola cut in. "That piece of shit trampled on this place. It's completely uncalled for and unfair."

Gabriel poured her a glass of water and brought it to where she was sitting. "It's one review, Nicola."

She felt a lump in her throat, which she tried to wash down with some water. She knew how much damage a bad review could do.

Gabriel sighed, then scratched his head. "We'll just have to make sure another article gets published with a different viewpoint," Gabriel said pointedly, a light grin on his face. "It's clear she likes you. Will you see her today?"

She wanted to. Desperately. But shame clung to her, over how she'd acted last night and over the article itself, which had cut her down in ways she wasn't ready to admit. The idea of facing Rosie now felt impossible.

"Maybe," she said, noncommittally. "She's probably already checked out."

"She…didn't tell you she's staying another night?"

Nicola met his gaze, suddenly alert. "What?" she said. "What do you mean?"

"She called down to the front desk this morning and asked if her room was available for another night." She felt Gabriel's eyes searching her. Did he have an inkling of what had developed between them and what might have occurred had Nicola not read the review the night before?

Nicola set the water glass down, her fingers tightening around her phone.

"Okay," Nicola said. Her mind was racing. Should she text Rosie? Should she already have texted her? Why was she staying?

She didn't know.

But Rosie had made a decision this morning.

And now Nicola would have to make hers.

"If you're going to bring Halmoni, let me know," Nicola said, standing in front of her closet and absent-mindedly flicking through the hangers. "I'll make sure you get an accessible room."

"Are you sure you want us to bring your grandmother?" Nicola's father, Jason, said. "You know she'll spend her time working the dining room and soliciting praise for her role in raising such an amazing granddaughter."

Nicola laughed. He wasn't wrong.

"I can't wait to see you guys," she said. "The last time you were here was the soft launch. You'll be amazed by how things have come along."

"And how are *you*, honey?" her mom's voice called through the speaker.

Nicola winced. There was a one hundred percent chance her sister had hung up after their late-night call last night and called their parents immediately to ring the alarm bell, even though she'd asked her not to. She could be mad, but really, she knew she was lucky to have a network of people looking out for her, even though she was fine.

Was she fine?

"I'm great, Mom," Nicola said. Her parents, her mom especially, required a lot of reassurance these days that their daughter wasn't about to go off the deep end again. It had been them who had suggested she stay with her sister on the East Coast, despite how much they would have liked to have hosted their eldest daughter. But they lived downtown Toronto, and staying in their house in Toronto's Annex neighborhood would mean she'd be trapped at home if she wanted to avoid running into someone she knew. So the friendly streets of the small-town Nova Scotia, with the proximity to hiking trails and ocean front felt like a better move.

"We saw that ridiculous *Toronto Tribune* article," her dad started, tentatively. "I hope you dusted that one off your shoulder. That loser doesn't know what he's talking about."

"Part of the business, Dad. You know that," Nicola said through gritted teeth. She didn't want her parents to worry about her. "And I've already forgotten about it. Thanks for bringing it up."

"I'm sorry. I—"

"I'm teasing. Relax," Nicola said. For a moment she considered telling them where she was going that night. Not the party itself, although she knew her father loved Will Hastings's movies.

She felt a small tug to tell them she was going to a party where someone might be in attendance, someone who, amazingly, had come back into her life after so many years, and unexpectedly, it felt like there was still something there. What it meant given how far they lived from one another was something to consider. But right now, she was just looking forward to seeing Rosie and knew that if her parents met her, they would love her. *Don't get ahead of yourself,* she thought.

"Listen, I'd better go. Text me when you talk to Halmoni, and let me know the dates. Can't wait to see you guys."

She dropped her phone onto her bedside table and pulled a black tank and her favorite jeans out of the closet. Another thing she loved about living in Sunset County: No pressure to dress up. But she did want to look good for Rosie.

After getting changed, she made her way over to the kitchen to make sure she wasn't needed for anything and to check in on how Danielle was managing.

"Hi, Chef," Danielle said, flashing her a big smile. "This is supposed to be your night off."

"Just thought I'd say hi," she said. "I hope you don't think I'm breathing over your shoulder."

"Never," said Danielle. "That's not your nature. I told the journalist that. You trust your team."

It had taken everything in her not to ask Rosie for a preview of the article. That fact that it was written and filed was a big part of why she was looking forward to this evening, without hesitation.

"That was some dinner last night," Danielle said, looking up sideways as she chopped an onion. "Everyone's still talking about it."

"Great team effort," Nicola said. She didn't need to add that the whole experience had been ruined by that cretin Mark Marcellin.

Not just the meal, but what might have been an incredible night with Rosie.

Nicola winced, thinking of how she'd just left her there at the table, alone. But she couldn't let Rosie see her cry, which was exactly what she'd done as soon as she'd reached the safety of the kitchen. Crouched down, back to the door, weeping.

It felt dramatic now. But in the moment, it was a release.

And now, Nicola thought, pulling her phone from her pocket, it felt like a promise.

She opened her email app, to where Rosie's message sat, still unanswered.

You stayed, she wrote. I hope to see you tonight.

She hit Send, then without thinking, replied again with the address for the party. There was a chance Rosie wouldn't come. Nicola didn't want to ask, didn't want to force a yes or no. If Rosie wanted to be there, she would be.

Chapter Fourteen

As soon as the sun started to dip toward the tree line, Rosie asked the front desk to call her a taxi. She stood waiting in the front foyer as Gabriel entered from outside, this evening in a dove-gray linen suit with a light blue button-up. He smiled. “Good evening, Rosie. We’re so glad you’ve decided to extend your stay.”

“You’ve made it hard to leave,” she said. “It really is a special place.”

Gabriel nodded. “I’m happy to hear that. You’ll have to return again when you’re not working.”

That would all depend on what happened over the next few hours, Rosie knew. Could she show her face again after a spectacular flub of a chance to make her mark as a serious writer? Or would she be welcomed back with open arms, delivering an article that would make both *Savorist* and Sugar Maple Farms proud? A light current of nerves traveled through her core. “I hope so,” she said. She looked over Gabriel’s shoulder to see a car pulling up. “That’s my ride,” she said.

Gabriel moved to the exit and swung open the door for her. “If I might say, Rosie, you look lovely this evening.”

Rosie drank in the compliment. Something about Gabriel's polished appearance, his Parisien air and the cut of his perfect suit—the compliment meant something. "Thank you," she said as he took another step ahead and opened the car door for her. "Have a good night," Rosie called through the open window.

"Enjoy the party," he said, waving as the car pulled away.

The car took her through the winding country roads, passing a lake with a number of turn-offs. Through the breaks in the trees, she caught a glimpse of all of the different cottages: some smaller and timeworn, likely passed down through generations, old canoes tied to docks sagging in the water, and others, show-stoppers that had been built in the past decade, with glass walls and boathouses three times the size of Rosie's apartment in the city.

Sunset County seemed to be a place where tradition and ambition coexisted, where family legacies floated next to weekend escapes in polished mahogany speedboats.

As for the party she was attending? Something told her that Will Hastings's lakefront home, which he shared with his wife Maya, a romance novelist, would be the latter.

"Here we are," the driver said. Rosie looked out the window as the driver navigated down a pebbled lane toward what she supposed was technically called a "cottage," given where it was, but looked more like a lakefront estate.

Overlooking the shore of Lake Shaughnessy, the cottage—estate—home, whatever it was, seemed to glow in the setting sun.

The path that led to the entrance was lined with thick bushes of tiger lilies, lavender and echinacea. There was a wide flagstone porch with deep rattan sitting chairs and wooden paddle fans overhead where Rosie could imagine curling up for a lazy afternoon of reading.

Through the windows, she could see the silhouetted figures of several party guests. “Thank you,” Rosie said to the driver as she exited the car, to where faint music and laughter sounded in the air. The party seemed to be well underway. Was Nicola already there?

The door swung open just as Rosie was ready to knock, and Maya appeared, wearing a bright blue slip dress, her red hair piled in a bun on top of her head. “Oh!” she said. “Hi! Sorry to startle you. I was just coming out to light the tiki torches!” she said, nodding to the speared torches at the edge of the driveway. “Glad you could make it. Rosie, right?”

“Yes,” she said. “Thank you for having me.”

“The writer,” said Maya. “My kindred spirit.” She winked before padding barefoot down the path with her barbecue lighter, and Rosie relaxed a little. Maya was beautiful and successful, but her warmth and the fact that she wasn’t wearing shoes made Rosie feel comfortable.

She watched as Maya lit the torches, which on some properties might’ve looked a little kitschy but here they added another layer of elegance to the show. She smiled at Rosie. “Will doesn’t love the idea of flames burning on both sides of the property. The only pyro he’s into is on film sets. But they look nice, right? Come on in.”

“They look great,” said Rosie, smoothing her dress

and adding another quick swipe of lipstick from her purse as she followed Maya into her home.

The inside was just as refined as the exterior, and whatever was coming from the kitchen—something barbecued or smoked—made Rosie's stomach growl in response.

She hadn't eaten since her late breakfast, which she'd squeezed in after talking to Jeremy and the snap decision she'd made to stay another night. There had barely been a twenty-minute window to grab food, and lunch had come and gone.

Rosie spotted a tray of deviled eggs, some flaky puff pastries filled with something cheesy and a heaping platter of pink shrimp beside a bowl of cocktail sauce. Mr. Noodles was truly a thing of her past.

"Help yourself to anything to eat," Maya said. "Bar's outside. If you need anything, just let me know."

"Thanks," said Rosie, peering through the windows to the wide deck overlooking the water, where most of the partygoers were assembled.

Rosie scanned the crowd. Will Hastings might've been a celebrity—she'd seen most of his films—but judging by the easy vibe and Maya's warm welcome, this wasn't a red-carpet crowd.

She stepped through the doors onto the porch overlooking the lake and accepted a flute of Champagne that a young server in jeans and a black button-up passed her. The rest of the crowd was a real mixture of people. Some appeared to have arrived dockside, with Sperry Top-Siders and T-shirts with craft brewery or local sailing club logos. Others, she noted with relief, had also dressed up for the occasion. She was glad not to stick out like a sore thumb, especially since Nicola was nowhere to be seen.

Had she already left? Or had she blown off the party completely?

Rosie wouldn't be surprised. In fact, the only thing that surprised her was that Nicola had plans to come to the party in the first place, given her apparent new aversion to social settings.

But when she rounded the corner to a quieter section of the wraparound porch and found Nicola speaking with a man in horn-rimmed glasses and a trucker hat, the real surprise wasn't that Nicola was there, it was the expression on her face when she saw Rosie.

Rosie gave her a light smile and wave and watched as Nicola seemed to do her best to focus on ending her conversation. Seconds later, she crossed the porch to where Rosie stood, drink in hand and heart in her throat.

Nicola wore a sleeveless black silk shirt and jeans and had small diamond studs twinkling through her hair that fell loose around her face. Rosie had never seen her look so beautiful, not even in the professionally styled ads she remembered coming across so frequently only a few years earlier. "I heard you were staying another night," Nicola said, her dark eyes sparkling. "Part of me wondered if you'd actually come."

"You guys don't make it easy to leave," Rosie said. It wasn't the full truth, but it wasn't a lie. Telling Nicola that Jeremy had rejected the article wouldn't just make her shut down again, it would put those emotional walls right back up, just when they'd finally started to lower.

Admitting failure to someone like Nicola—so confident, so accomplished—felt unbearable.

She wanted Nicola to want her. Not pity her. Not see the cracks.

And if the slow sweep of Nicola's gaze, the way it trailed over the fabric of her dress, in all the places it clung just so, Rosie was getting just what she'd hoped for.

"I didn't mean to interrupt your conversation," Rosie said.

"That was Mark Wilson," Nicola said. "I knew him from way back in the early days of my show. He was one of the producers. He moved into film after that. He's on some project with Will now," she said, nodding toward where Will Hastings stood with a small group, telling a story. Maya had joined his side and was looking at him with pure adoration.

Rosie was dying to ask about the show. It felt like a natural in. But she didn't want to arouse any suspicion that part of the reason she was there was to unearth some more details.

And the other reason…was thrumming through her core. A magnetic attraction.

If Rosie didn't already know how compatible she and Nicola were on a physical level, it might have been easier to step away.

Just then, a server came by and offered Nicola a drink. She glanced at Rosie. "Not sure I should have another," she said.

"Why's that?" Rosie said.

Nicola paused, and the air between them hummed with magnetic tension.

"Or maybe I will," she said. She plucked a glass from the tray without breaking her gaze from Rosie's. She held her drink up for a moment after the waiter disappeared. "I don't have to keep my guard up around you anymore."

"You were before?" Rosie asked, feigning innocence.

She leaned in, and Rosie caught the soft, clean scent of her shampoo. It made her body quake in the subtlest, most traitorous way. "Maybe."

What surprised her more was how comfortable Nicola seemed, this close, this cozy, in such a public space, especially for someone so fiercely private. But no one was watching.

They might as well have been alone on the deck, until a man and woman holding hands approached. "Hey, Knox," Nicola said. "Andie." She turned to Rosie. "This is Knox Walker. His family owns Sugar Maple Farms, the farm right next to the inn. Andie's his fiancée."

"You're Ayla's owners, right?" said Rosie. "Nice to meet you. What a beautiful horse."

"We adore her," Knox said, grinning. Knox was handsome, with a strong build and a kind smile. Andie, with her dark hair, cutoff jean shorts and white tank top looked like she'd walked right out of a J.Crew ad. They were an attractive couple.

"Why don't you bring the boys around next week?" Nicola said to Knox and Andie. "The inn's bringing in a falconer on Wednesday morning for a demo. If you think they'd like it."

"Really?" Andie said. "I know you guys don't usually have kids around."

Nicola waved her away. “You guys are neighbors. Practically family. No one will mind.”

“Awesome,” said Knox. “Nice to meet you, Rosie. Enjoy the party.” He tipped his glass, and the couple moved to say hi to another group.

“That’s Georgia O’Neill,” Nicola said, pointing to a blonde woman in a white eyelet dress, holding the hand of a dark-haired woman in khaki pants and a gray T-shirt. “And her wife, Mel Carter. Mel is the town vet. Andie’s sister.”

“I can see the resemblance,” Rosie said.

Rosie liked this side of Nicola. Clearly she’d integrated well into her new community. Content. Connected. At ease. “They seem great,” she said.

“Salt-of-the-earth people around here for the most part,” Nicola said. “It’s a nice change.”

Again, Rosie felt the urge to press, to ask about Nicola’s time abroad, the TV show, the product line that bore her name. The people she’d met that made her see this as a nice change. Everything that had made her famous. But she stopped herself.

It wasn’t the time. And in this moment, she felt like she was seeing the real Nicola. No chef’s whites, no cameras, no fans clamoring for photos. Just Nicola. She pushed the pressure of the article back into the deep recesses of her mind.

“I have to apologize,” Nicola said. “For last night. I’m sorry I left the way I did. But I really enjoyed cooking for you before that. I felt—” She stopped, her eyes searching Rosie’s. “I felt more like myself than I have in a really long time.”

She paused, and Rosie hung on every word. The flood of sensation from the evening before returned, each flavor, each glance. The way Nicola had watched her, eyes intent, like Rosie was a private performance and she was savoring every second.

"And it's been a while since I've cooked like that," Nicola said.

"What do you mean?" Rosie asked. "Your cooking is unbelievable. I hope you're not taking that idiot's article too much to heart."

Nicola shook her head gently. "The thing is, he picked up on something. I've been off. It's been a long time since I've felt…" She turned toward the lake for a moment, then back at Rosie, her gaze sharp and shining. "Since I've felt truly excellent. I know that sounds…silly. But I've been chasing that feeling for a while. And over the last two nights, I think I finally caught it. Because of you."

Rosie watched as Nicola reached out and grazed her fingertips across the sensitive skin of Rosie's wrist. The slight brush sent a rush of electricity up her arm.

If they'd been alone, there was nothing in the world that could have stopped Rosie from leaning in and closing the space between them. She knew already that Nicola's lips were sweeter than any dessert could ever be.

Instead, she just breathed in the moment. The touch.

She searched for the words. She wanted to tell Nicola she'd felt it too. Not just the perfection of her cooking, but the connection, the way Nicola made her feel vividly, undeniably alive.

But before she could speak, a crackling sound cut

through the air. They both turned as a burst of color exploded over the lake.

"A little early for fireworks," Nicola said.

The sky was still tinged with light, but somehow the fireworks held their own, brilliant streaks against the soft blue, their echoes rippling across the water. The faint smell of sulfur drifted in the breeze as more bursts followed, one after another.

Without a word, Rosie slipped her hand into Nicola's. Together they moved to the edge of the balcony, joining the rest of the party to watch the show across the lake.

"They beat us to it!" Maya said as the last firework faded. "We'll just call that the warm-up act."

Nicola turned to Rosie. "Is that something you want to stick around for?" she said, her voice quieter now.

Rosie held her gaze, then gave a small shake of her head. "No," she said softly, Nicola's earlier words still echoing in her ears like a promise. "I'd love to see those cookbooks you were telling me about." She needed to be alone with Nicola, back in the secluded privacy of her cottage.

The way Nicola's eyes flashed told Rosie that she knew very well this wasn't about the cookbooks. Nicola glanced over at the rest of the partygoers. The deck had filled in, and there were several people migrating down toward the water, where a series of Muskoka chairs were set in semicircles, some around a fire pit where flames danced invitingly. It was a perfect spot for a party. And when Nicola's grip tightened lightly around her hand, Rosie couldn't wait to leave.

"I'm parked out back," Nicola said, low and intent.

Chapter Fifteen

Rosie followed Nicola wordlessly through the party and out the back door, where the tiki torches lit their way along a gravel path. The sounds of the gathering faded as they moved into the forest, shadows thickening around them.

They reached a small clearing where several cars were parked. Rosie spotted Nicola's Jeep. The top was down, moonlight catching on the windshield.

Her pulse quickened as she climbed into the passenger seat. They drove in silence, the night wind whipping through her hair as Nicola navigated the winding country roads.

As they pulled into the inn's grounds, Rosie tensed for a moment. Was Nicola going to stop in front of her building?

But the Jeep rolled past. Rosie exhaled, a quiet rush of relief in her chest, as they continued into the woods, toward Nicola's hidden home behind the trees.

Nicola pulled up beside her house, a soft light glowing in the window. She cut the engine, and for a moment the only sound was the steady chorus of crickets.

"Do you ever get scared out here at night? By yourself?" Rosie asked.

Nicola let out a quiet laugh. "Yes," she said. "Not so much anymore. But those first few weeks? I barely slept. I kept a baseball bat by the bed. Totally ridiculous." She smiled. "Now I sometimes forget to lock the door at night."

Rosie looked up at the sky as they walked to the door. "Look at the sky," she breathed. A spread of stars sparkled above, the moon a crisp crescent.

"I don't know if I'll ever be able to leave," Nicola said quietly. She pushed open the door and stepped aside. "Come on in."

The inside of Nicola's cottage was cozy, lit up with soft, dim lighting, far more romantic than when Rosie had stumbled across it in the daytime. In this little corner of the woods, the rest of the world felt miles away.

Rosie removed her sandals.

"Can I get you something to drink?" Nicola asked.

"Water, please," said Rosie. She'd only had one glass of Champagne but felt a bit buzzed. Or maybe it wasn't the drink at all. Maybe it was the thrill of being alone with Nicola.

Nicola disappeared into the kitchen, leaving Rosie standing alone in the living room, unsure what to do with herself. She approached one of the bookshelves and let out a small laugh when she spotted two whole rows of CDs.

"What?" said Nicola, entering the room. "It's a solid collection."

"I just love that you still have CDs." Rosie skimmed

the collection, grinning. "Adele is well represented. Lana Del Ray. John Mayer. Backstreet Boys. I'm sensing a theme."

Nicola joined her at the shelf and passed her the glass of water. "What? Good taste in music?"

Rosie looked back at the shelf. "Elton John. Norah Jones. *Celine Dion?* I didn't peg you as…sappy."

Nicola narrowed her brow, but it was clear she was fighting back a smile. "Whatever. This is a thoughtfully curated collection. Laugh all you want."

"I'm not laughing," Rosie said. "I like it. Play me some music."

Nicola cocked her head slightly. "I still think you're making fun of me," she said. "But fine. Sit."

Rosie took a seat on the couch and watched as Nicola thumbed through the CDs, pulling one out every now and then and returning it to the pile. She was choosing this thoughtfully.

Rosie waited with anticipation as Nicola pulled out a case and brought it to the audio console underneath the television. "How long have you had that thing?" she asked.

Nicola popped in the disc and pressed the button for the tray to close. "Since I was ten," she said. "So, twenty-six years."

"That thing must have seen some solid mix CDs."

"You know it," Nicola said as a familiar opening sounded through the speaker.

A familiar melody drifted into the room.

"Wait. Is this—"

Nicola grinned. "Only the most iconic make-out music of all time."

Rosie blinked, then laughed. "Oh, so that's what this is? A make-out trap? And here I thought you might be about to make another dessert."

Nicola just smiled, slow and unreadable. "I can whip up a pie," she said. "Blueberry? Peach?" The pretense that they hadn't come back here with an agenda was almost laughable.

Rosie raised her eyebrows. "Now I can't tell if you're taunting me or just trying to make me nervous."

Nicola's eyes danced with delight. "You don't have to be nervous around me." She cleared her throat, and her expression shifted slightly. "I don't..." she started. "I haven't brought anyone back here before."

Was that a hint of regret in her voice? Or was Nicola concerned about her colleagues knowing that Rosie was there? "We could go to my room, if you'd prefer," Rosie said.

"Definitely not," said Nicola. "I just wanted you to know that."

Rosie understood. It was important for Nicola to know that even though she could land anyone she wanted, that she probably had women throwing themselves at her on a regular basis, that this invitation mattered more than a fun night together. She reached over and took Nicola's hand in hers. "Thanks for having me over," she said.

Nervous was the last thing Rosie felt. She was turned on and completely in the moment. She wanted this night to stretch out forever. So while she could have stepped right through the door Nicola had just opened—melted right into the promise of a kiss, maybe more—she chose, uncharacteristically, to delay gratification. "I thought you wanted to show me some cookbooks."

Nicola stood and opened the cabinet at the bottom of the bookshelf. She slid out five of the six books stacked inside and laid them carefully on the coffee table in front of Rosie.

"Feast your eyes on these," she said.

She sat down beside Rosie again, closer this time. Rosie picked up the top book, keenly aware of Nicola's warmth beside her. The air between them seemed to shift.

Rosie did her best to focus on the words on the page. She traced her fingers over the table of contents, which listed recipes such as *panelle*, *fregola* with clams, *braciole* and *polpette al sugo*. Now all she could think about was she and Nicola on some kind of sailboat, coasting through turquoise waters past jagged limestone cliffs, docking in Capri with whitewashed villas shimmering in the distance.

It reminded her of the same daydream she'd had so many times before, years ago, when she thought she might really travel to see Nicola, join her great adventure, be part of something bigger.

But it had never happened.

The memory pulled her back. This magical evening, this moment with Nicola. It felt like the same flicker of hope, the same flash of magic. Was she about to walk down that road again?

"Where did you go?" Nicola asked, breaking the silence.

Rosie looked up and caught the soft glow of Nicola's skin, the way her hair brushed the line of her jaw, her perfect pink lips slowly curving into a smile.

"I'm here," Rosie said lightly, returning the smile while her stomach suddenly twisted in a knot. She put the book down and removed the next one from the pile. "*Chez Panisse Menu Cookbook*," she read aloud, tracing her fingertips over the beige cover with the stenciled typography and linocut-style depiction of a restaurant.

"I got that for my nineteenth birthday," Nicola said. "Alice Waters is one of my heroes. Open it up to that bookmarked page."

Rosie flipped it open and scanned the page. "*Crostata di Perrella*," she said. "Yum."

"Seriously yum," Nicola said. "It's like a calzone. And the crust is so golden. I almost forgot—" She stopped and shifted in her seat so she was facing Rosie. "Now, there's a restaurant I would love to take you to. You would die and go to heaven."

A restaurant I'd love to take you to. Nicola's words melted over Rosie like a delicious promise. She let herself imagine it. Traveling the world with Nicola, dining at beautiful restaurants, places where Nicola worked or knew other chefs, where they'd get a front seat to the action, extra plates brought to their table. Visit farmers' markets and pick up fresh bread and cheeses and sit in the sun with a good bottle of wine and a view.

But that fantasy was like the Meyer-lemon éclairs Nicola had flipped to next: too sweet, too beautiful and never meant to last. Rosie turned her attention back to the conversation.

"I'm glad we pulled this out," Nicola murmured, tracing her fingers over the page and seeming to disappear into another universe. "I've been trying to figure out the third course for this dinner I'm prepping for next week, and I…" She trailed off and then after a moment looked up and grinned. "What?"

Rosie smiled. "Nothing," she said. "I just like seeing genius at work."

"Ha," Nicola said. "Hardly. But the wheels are turning again, and I just…" She shook her head and placed the book on the coffee table in front of her and then shifted slightly, her knee brushing the bare skin beneath Rosie's dress. She reached out, fingers grazing the sensitive skin at the crook of Rosie's elbow, her eyes locked on hers.

Rosie's breath caught, the air between them warm and electric. Without breaking eye contact, she breathed in deeply as Nicola trailed her fingers along Rosie's arm. "You've done something to me," Nicola breathed, her voice now a little huskier. "You know that?"

You've done something to me too, Rosie wanted to say, but something in Nicola's expression told her that the conversation was over.

Nicola's chin dipped as she moved to close the space between them. Rosie closed her eyes and let out a soft sigh as their lips met. When they'd first tumbled into Nicola's bed together, so many years ago, it had been under the haze of several cocktails and a few glasses of wine. She'd wondered for years if that night had carried so much meaning for her alone.

Now, clear-headed, Rosie luxuriated in the soft intent of Nicola's kiss, the firm grip on her arm, the faint moan that slipped from her lips. This wasn't just a lusty hookup. Nicola wanted her—that was clear. But it meant more.

It might be just a night, but she would sort out any feelings later. Now she wanted Nicola.

Her heart thrummed in her chest. Heat bloomed low in her core as Nicola's lips traced a path across her cheek, landing on the sensitive skin of her neck. "You're beautiful," Nicola said softly as Rosie's hands found the small of Nicola's back, pulling her in closer as Nicola kissed her again.

Rosie moved her tongue gently against Nicola's, and when Nicola pressed lightly on her chest, she silently acquiesced and lay back on the sofa, Nicola following her down, not breaking the kiss.

Only hours earlier, she was ready to pack her things and leave Sunset County empty handed, the lingering desire for Nicola Kim still burning. Now she found herself tugging at the hem of Nicola's top, testing to see if she was okay with Rosie pulling it over her head. She was.

The other thing that she hadn't been able to enjoy their first night together was the pleasure of seeing Nicola's naked body as they fell into the sheets at her apartment. It had been late at night, and when they'd arrived, the intensity of their desire had prevented them from doing anything as time-consuming as flicking on a light.

So when Nicola allowed Rosie to reach behind her back and unclasp her bra, letting it slide from her chest onto the floor, Rosie took a moment to indulge in the sight of Nicola's breasts, soft and flushed in the dim light, rising and falling with her shallow breaths.

She lifted her head slightly off the pillow, enough to take one of Nicola's perfect nipples into her mouth.

Nicola sighed with pleasure as Rosie slowly explored her, raising her hips to meet the place where she was certain Nicola was burning, just like she was.

"I want you," Nicola breathed, and every cell of Rosie's body reverberated with pleasure.

Rosie kissed Nicola's lips again as she felt for Nicola's belt. Nicola pushed her hand to the side gently, and for a moment Rosie wondered if she'd gone too far, but Nicola wasn't patient enough for Rosie to be fiddling around. She pulled Rosie off the couch, into her bedroom and onto the bed, and within seconds, she'd unhooked her belt, unbuttoned her jeans and was guiding Rosie's hand past the waistband of her silky underwear, where Rosie found Nicola fully ready for her fingers to enter her.

Rosie caressed Nicola with her fingertips, stroking her gently and eliciting a gentle moan. "Yes," Nicola said, grasping on to Rosie's forearm as she lay beside her on the bed.

"Take your jeans off," Rosie whispered, not stopping her work as Nicola slowly shed her jeans and her underwear, now completely naked next to her, eyes closed, luxuriating in Rosie's touch.

Nicola was coasting on a breathless wave of bliss and was willing herself to make this perfect feeling last. Rosie knew just how to touch her: gentle enough, but with enough building pressure to cause her breath to catch in her throat as she focused only on the perfect sensation. "Is that good?" Rosie whispered.

Nicola allowed her eyes to flutter open momentarily to see Rosie, next to her, wearing the only thing in the world that might come somewhere close to the perfection she knew it covered. The second she'd seen Rosie walk into the party with that dynamite dress, it was game over for her, a miracle that she'd made it this far in the night without trying to get where she was now. "So good," she panted, and before she could pull Rosie's hand back, just slightly enough to hold on, to ride this pleasure until the wave crashed, Rosie circled her finger just so, and Nicola bucked forward slightly, gasping as she quaked in Rosie's hand.

"Mmm," Rosie hummed, sliding two fingers deep inside her, in and out as Nicola rode the aftershocks of her orgasm.

"That was…" Nicola said, breathing deeply and opening her eyes to find Rosie gazing at her with adoration mixed with desire, "fast." She let out a light laugh. Had she ever finished that quickly? "I'm like a teenager or something."

Rosie grinned. "I liked that. A lot." The smile faded as Nicola moved from her position lying down. She slowly straddled Rosie, intent on savoring every last bit of her. And now her own hunger was satiated, she planned to do so slowly. Methodically.

"Turn over," Nicola ordered quietly. Rosie didn't ask any questions, she simply turned onto her stomach, her dark waves cascading across her back. Nicola put her hands on Rosie's shoulders, sliding her fingers along them gently to her elbows, then her hands, pulling them up toward her face and extended across the pillow over her head. With her fingertips, she raked Rosie's dark hair aside, the silky strands moving through her fingertips. She kissed the base of Rosie's neck, then slowly, slowly, one inch at a time, pulled the zipper of her dress down, all the way to her hips. Rosie squirmed under her, a silent plea to hurry up, but Nicola wasn't deterred. She'd finished too quickly, and she was determined to take her time with Rosie. They had all night.

Nicola parted the fabric of the unzipped dress, then dipped down and trailed her tongue lightly along the exposed skin on Rosie's back. She drew in a deep breath of Rosie's sweet scent as she savored Rosie's soft skin, then pulled the fabric back further, allowing her to kiss the base of Rosie's back.

At the same time, she trailed her fingertips softly along Rosie's inner thighs, which were parted just enough to allow Nicola to touch her all the way up, where she reached the lacy fabric between her legs.

"Please," Rosie whispered, wriggling again and opening her legs a touch wider.

Nicola smiled, breathing in Rosie's intoxicating desire. She didn't think she would like anything more than cooking for the woman, but this was dangerously addictive.

She moved down the bed slightly, then used her tongue to trace the places where her fingers had been moments ago. Nicola glanced up to find Rosie was breathing heavily and gripping the pillowcase in her hands.

Finally, she pulled Rosie's dress up her torso, still in no rush, and over her head. She unhooked her bra and nudged her lightly to turn over, then rose onto her knees to take in the perfection of Rosie's body before she gave the woman what she was practically whimpering for at this point. Rosie moved one hand to touch herself, but Nicola pushed it away. "Okay, gorgeous," Nicola said, drinking in the flush of Rosie's cheeks. "You've been patient."

Rosie moaned as Nicola found the place she knew was aching for her the most and moved her tongue lightly but intently as she held Rosie's shifting hips in her hands. Rosie's breath quickened and became shallower.

When Nicola sensed that Rosie was on the brink, she flicked her tongue just the slightest bit more quickly, and within seconds, Rosie was sitting up, her back arched, gasping and shuddering lightly before she lay back on the pillow, taking deep breaths.

Nicola took a moment to watch as Rosie caught her breath and lay back on the pillow with her eyes closed before moving up to join Rosie, moving some strands of hair from her face that were caught in her light perspiration.

Satisfying people on a sensory level was something she did every day. And she'd slept with her fair share of women. But this was different. It was vulnerable and laced with emotion, and suddenly Nicola was overcome. When was the last time she'd trusted another person like this? Trusted *herself*?

She turned to the side and found the smooth skin of Rosie's neck and kissed it gently, then raked her fingertips lightly along Rosie's side, from her ribcage down to her hip. Rosie sighed contentedly. "I told myself I wasn't going to do this," she murmured, her lips turning up in a light smile.

"Do you regret it?" Nicola asked. She prayed the answer was no.

Rosie laughed lightly. "Regret? No. No, no, no."

"And wait—you've been thinking about this?"

Rosie propped herself up on her elbow and gazed down at Nicola. "I've been thinking about this since the moment I walked out of your apartment," she said quietly, reaching out and brushing a light touch on Nicola's cheek. "I know you forgot about me, but there's no use denying that I thought about you my fair share." She paused. "I mean, it didn't help that your face was plastered on billboards and on the front of cookbooks at my local bookstore."

Nicola narrowed her eyes slightly. "Why are you so sure I didn't think about you?"

Rosie gave her a look. "Come on. Think about what your life was like. It's no wonder you forgot about me. I mean, I can't blame you."

Something shifted inside Nicola. She could laugh

it off, roll her eyes and pretend that yes, she'd been so consumed with her exciting life and all the interesting people and women. But Rosie deserved the truth.

"I did think about you," she said softly and paused. Rosie said nothing, and for a moment Nicola wondered if her words had gotten lost in the gentle whirring of the overhead fan.

"When?" Rosie asked.

Nicola paused. How much was she willing to share? She'd spend the last few days asking herself that question, but she was done with it now. "I vividly remember thinking about you when I saw a beautiful woman on the steps of the Trevi Fountain. She had hair like yours—long, wavy and a little bit wild. She looked so perfectly at home in the setting, like she was there to be photographed by all the tourists. I remember thinking she was beautiful. But that you were even more so."

Rosie opened her mouth to speak, but Nicola wasn't done.

"And I remember one night, after a big restaurant buyout by some member of the royal family of Singapore. It was a big splash: caviar, white truffles, king crab, salt-marsh lamb and cocktails with gold flecks. A little over the top actually. I remember looking out at the dining room, and the guests were either angling their cameras to take a photo or were so caught up in who was sitting at the next table that no one seemed to even notice what they were spearing on their forks. I thought about what it would have been like to have you there. You would have been in the moment and tasted everything."

The floodgates had opened, but something about it felt so right. Lying there under the gaze of Rosie's deep brown eyes…she didn't want to stop.

"And one last time," Nicola continued, "although there are more, but I don't want you to think I'm psycho."

Rosie laughed as she nestled further into the crook of Nicola's arm. "I could listen to this all night."

Nicola luxuriated in the feeling of Rosie's closeness, her attentiveness. She kissed her lightly on the head. "I remember one night, at home after the ICAP Awards. I'd won the Trailblazer Award. I was alone. I put the trophy on the desk of my hotel room and stared at it from my bed. I hadn't seen my parents or my sister in over a year. My phone was buzzing with people wondering why I'd left the afterparty, and I realized that none of them really cared about if I was okay, they just wanted to be seen with me, grab a late-night story for their Instagram."

She felt Rosie nod lightly. Could she tell her this next part of the story? Nicola swallowed. "Alexi had invited me to his restaurant's soft opening, and I'd missed it and was feeling guilty for not being there for him." She felt her voice catch. That was as far as she could go. But the next part she wanted Rosie to know. "And I remember thinking about you. And what you were doing. Just thinking about you made me feel…calm."

And saying it out loud made her feel even more so. How had she let herself tumble so far down the fame tunnel, wasting so many of her precious days with people who thought they knew her but were really only enamored with the idea of her?

She gazed at Rosie. It wasn't like they'd known one another forever, but Rosie was so authentically herself that it didn't matter. To know a woman like Rosie for five minutes was to know her an entire lifetime.

"I like that," Rosie said, looking up, eyes filled with emotion. "Thank you for telling me."

In that moment there was a lot more than Nicola wanted to tell Rosie. Now that the article was complete. Now that it was just the two of them, in the privacy of her space, in this small town that felt like being wrapped in a warm blanket.

But Rosie yawned, and Nicola felt a wave of contented fatigue wash over her at the same time.

"Do you want me to go?" Rosie said, sitting up slightly. "I totally understand. I can—"

"You're staying right here," Nicola said, moving her arm over Rosie's naked body and pulling her in close. She kissed her head again and breathed in the floral scent of Rosie's hair. She didn't want her to leave—not tonight, not ever.

In the morning she would float the idea of Rosie coming back to visit sometime soon or Nicola coming to the city. They could visit some of Nicola's favorite old haunts, and with Rosie by her side, she wouldn't worry about running into anyone she knew.

Maybe they could just…see.

For now, she was ready to give in again as Rosie kissed her, bathed in the moonlight streaming through the shutters.

Chapter Sixteen

Rosie lay awake in Nicola's bed, her breath steady as Nicola slept beside her, mouth slightly open, an arm draped across Rosie's waist.

She'd been so tired she'd expected to drift off into a dreamless slumber after Nicola had invited her to sleep there, but Rosie hadn't slept for even one minute, which was unusual for her. She was generally lights-out as soon as her head hit the pillow.

But now events of the evening continued to replay in her mind. She didn't mind that—that was for sure—but being a zombie in the morning didn't hold much appeal.

At home, on the rare occasion when sleep evaded her, she'd pull a book from the eternal revolving stack on her bedside table and read until her eyes gave in.

There was no such stack here. Nicola's room held only their clothes, scattered on the floor, and two neat, sparsely decorated nightstands.

Rosie's mind flicked to the Lyon cookbook, buried somewhere in Nicola's vintage collection. They'd barely made it past *Chez Panisse*. Hadn't there also been *Flavors of India*?

A few minutes of quiet page-turning might shift

her from this place of restless awareness to something steadier—calm, tranquil and content. Sleep would come. And she needed sleep.

Because tomorrow, over breakfast, was her last chance. Her final pitch. She had to believe that after the night they'd shared, Nicola would trust her to tell the story with care.

There had been a moment, just before they drifted off, when Rosie thought Nicola might say more—something deeper—but she hadn't. Rosie hadn't pushed. If Nicola chose to tell her story, Rosie wanted it to be entirely on her terms. A hot flash of guilt washed over her when she remembered getting ready in her hotel room after the conversation with her parents and brother. Was she that desperate for external validation? The idea now felt so petty.

As quietly as possible, Rosie extracted herself from the sheets and willed the floorboards not to creak under her as she stood up, then felt around at the foot of the bed for the cashmere blanket she remembered seeing there. It wasn't cold in the cottage, but it was too dark to find her clothes, which were scattered on the floor somewhere.

Switching on a light would for sure wake Nicola, so instead, Rosie found her phone on the side table and used the faint brightness of the screen to navigate out of the room. When she got to the couch, she turned on the flashlight and picked up one of the cookbooks from the coffee table.

For the next twenty minutes, Rosie flipped through the pages of the cookbooks, starting with the one featuring Lyonnais cuisine. She drank in all the familiar sights, instantly transporting back to the cozy *bouchone* where she and her grandmother had enjoyed *cervelle de canut* before walking the cobbled streets to take in the Renaissance architecture of Vieux Lyon. After this quiet trip down memory lane, she set the Lyon cookbook aside and picked up the Indian-cuisine cookbook, still using her phone to illuminate the vibrant images of the coconut palms and lush spice gardens of Kerala, the misty tea plantations in the Nilgiri hills and the majestic palaces and desert vistas of Jodhpur.

Rosie closed the book and placed it gently on the table. This had probably been a bad idea. Her senses were going nuts. Did Nicola have a phone book she could read? She felt as wired as a freshman gearing up for club night on his third Red Bull.

Then she remembered the other book tucked away in the cupboard, the one that had been at the bottom of the pile.

Curious, she grabbed her flashlight, aimed it at the shelf and slid out a canvas-bound album. She carried it over to the couch and sank down with it.

She opened it to find a printed menu from Persimmon. She examined it closely. It must have been from the time Nicola was head chef there. The place they'd first met, when Rosie was working the coat check at Nicola's going-away party. The first and only night they'd spent together, until now.

She flipped to the next page. Another menu, this one from a restaurant called Corail & Ciel in the Seychelles.

Rosie was desperate to know the stories behind all

these menus. Who had she cooked for? Cooked with? What did she do after service? What was her life like in all these places?

Now her curiosity wasn't journalistic. She wanted to know everything about the gorgeous woman sleeping in the other room, because she'd fallen for her all over again.

Suddenly, she knew she was invading Nicola's privacy. There was a reason Nicola had left the book in the cupboard when she'd taken out the others to look at.

Rosie closed the book quietly then stood up to return it to the shelf, but as she did, something floated from the book's pages to the ground.

She picked it up and aimed her flashlight at the piece of paper in her hand.

The handwriting was that of an older person, she could tell. They didn't teach cursive like this anymore.

The ink had faded, but the message was now clear.

Dear Nicola, it read. *How I've been overjoyed to witness your success from afar. Your presence in the culinary world is something so many aspire toward, but so few have the discipline, diligence and admirable creativity to be able to reach the heights you've scaled. It would be my honor if you were able to visit my new restaurant, Foundry, in advance of our opening next month. Recognizing you are a busy woman, but your boldness has been an inspiration to me and having you here to share this moment would mean a great deal.*

Alexi

Rosie blinked. Foundry. She recognized the name. She looked at the date on the letter. It was four years ago. Right around the time Nicola had disappeared. Hadn't Nicola said she'd missed the opening?

Had Nicola mentioned the name of the restaurant? Rosie tried to think of if she'd done a round-up of Parkdale restaurants for *Savorist* or something similar.

Then she remembered. She hadn't written it, but *Savorist* had published a profile of three Toronto restaurants that had opened and closed the fastest in the city's fine-dining history. Foundry had been one of them. And it had belonged to Alexi, Nicola's mentor?

It seemed strange to her. Nicola always spoke about Alexi's cooking in such glowing terms. Classic. Refined. Timeless.

Then she remembered that look in Nicola's eyes when she'd spoken briefly of Alexi. *Died of a heart attack.* Wass that why the restaurant had met such an early demise? Was Alexi, like so many chefs, living the unhealthy lifestyle of so many in the business? Little sleep, high stress, drinking, maybe drugs?

A rustling across the room made her jump, and she dropped her phone onto the floor.

Before she could retrieve it, a light flicked on. Rosie looked up to find Nicola standing in the doorway, wearing a short cotton robe and an expression of sleepy confusion.

"What are you..." Her eyes flitted across the table, then settled on the letter sitting atop the open book.

"I was just—" Rosie stopped, her heart pounding. It dawned on her how bad this looked. "I couldn't sleep, and I—"

I wanted to know you better. I wanted to know what you were hiding.

"You wanted to go through my stuff," Nicola said, her voice dripping with contempt. "Was that your plan? Come here, wait until I was asleep, then rifle through my belongings? Find material for your *stupid article*?"

Rosie's pulse raced. "That's not at all what I was—"

Nicola crossed the room and snatched the note off the table, then slammed the book shut. She glared at Rosie, those same eyes that only hours ago had been heavy with adoration.

"I think it's time for you to leave now."

Rosie's eyes filled with tears. "I came out to look at the books again. That's all. I promise. I know how this looks, but I—"

"And then you just happened to photograph a personal item? Forget it, Rosie. I said leave."

Nicola disappeared into her room, then returned with Rosie's bag and clothes. Rosie watched, her heart in her throat, as she dumped them onto the coffee table. "I trusted you," Nicola said, her voice cracking, just for a second, before the walls went back up. "I let you in." She picked up the book and the letter, returned to her room and slammed the door shut.

Rosie shuddered. She should have known better. Nicola had left that book in the cupboard for a reason. Her burning curiosity, her intense desire to know was no different from anyone else's. She could pretend it was innocent, but was it? Or was she just like every other celebrity gawker, poking around where she didn't belong? Worse yet, was she someone who would deceive another person just to get ahead?

She stood for a moment, unmoving, staring at Nicola's door and willing it to open again. A hot tear fell down her cheek as she reached for her clothes.

Rosie held back a sob as she quickly dressed and stepped into the cool night air, pulling the door of Nicola's cottage closed behind her. It was going to be a long walk in heels, but all she felt as she made her way down the path back to the inn was shame.

Chapter Seventeen

Two weeks later

"Karlos, can you try this?" Nicola asked.

"Yes, Chef," Karlos said, looking up from his cutting board of shallots before dropping his paring knife and approaching Nicola's station. The air in the kitchen was thick with the scent of roasting bones, tomato paste and something not quite right.

She passed him a spoonful of the *sauce espagnole* and watched as he took a thoughtful sip, then narrowed his brow just slightly, enough to know that it was a fail, but like everyone else in her kitchen over the past ten days, he struggled to figure out how honest was too honest. Her collar behind her neck was damp with sweat as she waited for his assessment.

It was her second attempt of the day, after the first batch had a slightly cloudy nature to it and wasn't coating the back of her spoon like velvet the way she liked it.

Cue the eggshell walking.

"A touch more port?" Karlos suggested, but the tone of his voice told Nicola she needed to start over again. She glanced at her watch. Two hours until the investors were set to arrive. The private dining room was set for a group of eight, and it was time for Nicola to shine. The menu was audacious—a seven-course meal with the aged duck breast that was meant to be swimming in the demi-glace she was trying to make happen. The meal *hinged* on it.

Nicola yearned for the days this kind of pressure ignited her. It was like every instinct, all her years of experience had evaporated. Not only that, but over the past few days her mind had been swimming with tweaks to the menu. Not the same inspired onslaught of ideas from when Rosie was here, but ideas fueled by second guesses and uncertainties. She hadn't slept more than a couple of hours each night.

And in the moments before the swirling ideas was the softness of Rosie's voice. The click of her pen. Her inhale before a question. The curiosity of her gaze across the table in that meeting room, watching Nicola squirm under the surface and pretend she was fine.

It wasn't happening. In fact, it was so not happening that every time Nicola closed her eyes and recalled all of the lessons she'd learned at culinary school, then from every renowned chef she'd been privileged to work with over the years, the only image she could conjure in her mind was of Rosie Franklin-Smith, taking a spoon and bringing it to her mouth. But in this daydream, instead of that perfect sublime expression of enjoyment, Rosie spat the food out, the only expression on her face one of abject disgust.

Before Rosie's arrival, she'd been tentative. Now she was a total mess. And in two hours, she was meant to deliver the meal that could make or break Gabriel and Sugar Maple Farms's fortunes.

Frustration boiled up in her as she ripped off her apron and tossed it on the counter. "Have a stab at it, will you?" she muttered. "I'll be out back."

She left the kitchen where her team was busy preparing the other menu items, grateful that they didn't seem to be experiencing the same block as she was.

Nicola exited the side door to the sitting area outside, where restaurant staff often took their breaks. No one was there. Good. She wouldn't be forced to make small talk.

She slumped in the chair by the firepit and closed her eyes. There was a cool breeze in the air, which she breathed in deeply as the sun warmed her skin.

This meal was important. One of the most important of her career. Gabriel had been more than antsy over the past few days, quietly seeking reassurance that the visit would go well, the investors would be charmed and Sugar Maple Farms would get the cash injection it needed to continue to build up its reputation without having to raise prices too much in the process and risk alienating potential guests.

Sugar Maple Farms wasn't just a beautiful country escape, a place for visitors to unwind and relax and soak in the natural beauty of the landscape and hopefully enjoy a few amazing meals.

It was Gabriel's everything, and in that, it was Alexi's legacy.

And for Nicola, it was home.

A place she'd never imagine she needed.

Nicola continued to breathe deeply, in her nose, out

through her mouth, trying to channel any last ounce of confidence.

That fleeting feeling that she'd experienced the moment Rosie had stepped on the grounds of the inn. That feeling had been washed away the moment she'd seen Rosie with her phone pointed over her letter from Alexi, that tangible reminder of how she'd let him down. She'd let not only his restaurant die but Alexi too.

And now she was about to let Gabriel down.

Tears sprung in her eyes. Rosie had felt for a moment like a promise. She'd brought life not only to Nicola's craft but to everything.

And then, it was clear that Nicola had made a terrible mistake by letting her in. Being so vulnerable, turning herself over, body and mind to a person she'd thought she could trust but, like so many before her, was just using her.

Just as she sat up and started to wipe the tears from the corner of her eyes, the door to the patio swung open and Gabriel appeared in the entrance. He was about to say something, but his expression shifted when he realized she was crying.

"Nicola," he said. He furrowed his brow and stepped out of the kitchen. "I just wanted to check on you. Karlos said he didn't know where you'd gone. Are you—"

"I'm fine," Nicola said, standing up and forcing a grin, but the unchanging expression of concern on his face told her she wasn't fooling him.

"Mr. Levain and Ms. Otis have both arrived on property with their colleagues," Gabriel said. "Could we get the team together to go over the last details?"

"Of course," said Nicola.

She tried to pass by him through the entrance and return to the kitchen, but Gabriel reached out and gently grabbed her arm. "Nicola, I—" He paused, his eyes searching hers. "Are you sure everything's okay?"

"More than okay, boss," she said.

She'd cooked through harder things. An extreme heat wave in the South of France with no air-conditioning, when the staff had taken their turns hosing each other down with the dishwashing hose turned to cold so they wouldn't completely overheat during service.

A Japanese-inspired meal for a private party when they'd discovered only an hour before service that the entire rice supply they'd shipped out to the estate two hours from any grocery store was coated in a thick mold.

The time a plane of dignitaries had been unexpectedly grounded at Kelowna International Airport, and the prime minister himself had called Nicola, humbly asking if she could feed them.

All one hundred forty of them.

They'd made a quick deal with the elementary school across the street, who allowed them to set up folding tables in the gym. Her sous chef decorated each table with wildflowers that the hostess and bartender picked from the field out front, and at the end of the meal, each guest departed for the roadside hotel where they were put up for the night with a brown paper bag filled with a fresh-baked muffin and fruit compote they could eat in the morning.

Nicola had done hard things.

Tonight was nothing.

Impressing a group of investors? In her own kitchen, with her team at full force and perfect conditions and supplies?

This was child's play.

But as much as she tried to psych herself up, she couldn't manage to temper the panic.

Twice Nicola mistimed the duck, and as a result, service was backed up and they'd received more than one complaint from the dining room about the timing of the service. They were prioritizing the private room, of course, but from her station in the kitchen, Nicola not once but twice observed two of the investors casually engaging in conversation with some of the other diners, no doubt doing some reconnaissance about the other patrons' experiences.

Nicola flinched at the thought of it. Had her restaurant turned into Cirque? Had she committed the cardinal sin of treating her VIPs so markedly better than her everyday clients?

She couldn't be that chef.

"Champ every table," she barked when Adam passed by with a tray of empty glasses. He looked at her, confused.

"Are you sure?" he asked. "Most tables are ready for last course. Many already have the wine pairings. It might be—"

"Do it," ordered Nicola. "Everyone loves Champagne."

"Okay," he said uncertainly. She watched as he returned to the bar to let the bartender know the plan. Nicola could feel his eye roll from across the room.

It was misplaced. It was desperate. It was, she knew,

an unmitigated disaster. One of the biggest nights of her career, and she had failed.

The rest of the dinner service felt like survival mode. They fired one dish after the other—edible, yes, but as Nicola watched them being marched out by the servers, she imagined them missing the soul, the energy, the panache that had lit up the dining room only days ago.

After the last diner left the space, Nicola looked up from the station she'd just finished clearing to see Gabriel shaking the hands at the investors' table. He walked them to the door, and once they'd all disappeared, he retreated to his office with an unreadable expression on his face.

A knot tightened in her stomach. She slammed her hand down on the counter and squeezed her eyes shut. Had she let him down?

Nicola ripped off her apron, ignoring the looks of concern from her team as she passed through the kitchen and knocked on Gabriel's door.

"Come in," his voice sounded.

She entered the office to find him on his laptop. His eyes were weary, and he'd shed his blazer, which was uncharacteristically flung on the sofa beside his desk rather than neatly on a hanger.

Gabriel looked just as undone as she felt.

"Can I talk to you for a second?" Nicola asked.

Gabriel nodded. The moment she stepped in and the office door clicked shut behind her, Nicola let out a shoulder-shaking sob. "I'm sorry," she said, burying her face in her hands. "I'm letting you down. I'm letting your father down."

"Nicola, I—"

With her eyes squeezed shut she could hear Gabriel's shoes crossing the floor quickly. Within seconds he was hugging her, allowing her tears to fall on the shoulder of his expensive dress shirt. "You don't need to apologize," he said. "I'm worried about you, Nicola. What's going on?"

"I'm failing you. I know I am," Nicola said through tears. "Just like I failed your father all those years ago."

She watched Gabriel's expression shift from concern to confusion. "What do you mean?" he asked, brows furrowed.

Was she really going to have this conversation now? Clearly Gabriel was licking his own wounds and didn't need her to hash up painful memories and float the idea that she could have saved his father from his early fate. But before she could stop herself, then words started to flow out of her mouth.

She said it all out loud. And Gabriel listened quietly without reaction, passing her tissues and turning away two staff members who knocked at the door looking for Nicola with questions.

"I know you probably hate me now. I would," Nicola said. She blew her nose, then looked out the window at the now dark grounds of the inn, her eyes stinging from tears.

"Nicola," Gabriel said softly. "My father loved you like a daughter. He would have been thrilled to have you there, but he never expected it. He knew that you were busy chasing after your own dreams, and he couldn't have been prouder. He had a photo of the two of you together taped above his stove."

He placed his hand on her shoulder. "My father was also a stubborn man, as I'm sure you remember. Others tried to help him with the vision of the restaurant. And goodness knows enough people tried to help him change his diet and his exercise. But…the man died doing what he loved. He probably wouldn't have listened to you anyway." Gabriel chuckled quietly, then shook his head. "You don't need to feel any guilt. You were a joy in his life."

Nicola sniffed. "I just wish I'd been there for him. Even just to see him again before…"

Gabriel nodded. "I know. But make no mistake—he knew you cared. Remember that time you mentioned his restaurant, when you were on *Jimmy Fallon*?"

Nicola nodded.

"The phone rang off the hook for weeks. He had to hire extra staff to keep up with the reservations. And do you know that crate of Amalfi lemons you sent him for his birthday a few years ago?"

Nicola remembered. They'd cost more in shipping than an economy plane ticket, and she'd half wondered if she could pay a flight attendant to strap the little wooden box in for the flight from Naples International to Pearson. But she'd known that the just the scent of the lemons' perfect citrus perfume once he unwrapped them from their delicate tissue paper, printed with bright Mediterranean colors, would light Alexi up more than any expensive wine she would order to be delivered to his place, so she'd forked over her credit card and scrawled a handwritten note that she tucked in the crate.

"What you probably don't know is that he sat with that box beside him on the table beside his recliner for a whole week, picking up the lemons and just smelling them," Gabriel said, laughing, and Rosie couldn't help but smile at the idea. "I finally had to force him to make something with them before they rotted."

"And what did he make?" she asked.

"I remember vividly, because it was so ridiculous, and he told me all about it during our weekly phone call. He made a lemon beurre blanc for the scallop appetizer," Gabriel said. "It lasted all week. He wanted to share it with others."

"That's so him," Nicola said. Stubborn as burnt cheese on a nonstick pan, but also inventive and always generous to a fault.

"So what I'm telling you," Gabriel said, "is that you need to let go of this guilt you're carrying."

Nicola shook her head. "But I don't want to let you down either."

Gabriel scoffed incredulously. "Nicola. I've said this before, and I'll say it again. Having you here…is an honor. I wish you could accept that."

"But the review—"

"Is yesterday's news," he said firmly.

"But then, with Rosie and *Savorist*, I had the chance to share my story, and I totally screwed it up. It would have not only given the inn so much more attention and all the bookings we need to stay afloat, it—" She stopped and, through her tears, recognized the weight that had been lifted from her shoulders.

"Nicola, the investors had a great time tonight. There might have been a few mistakes here and there—a few more than usual. But honestly? Those guys were more concerned with whatever business talk they were engaged in. They're not true connoisseurs like you and I are. I promise you it's all good. And as for Rosie?" Gabriel hesitated, searching her expression. "I can't help but wonder if there's still time."

Maybe there was still time, at least when it came to the article. She could call *Savorist*, maybe speak to Rosie's boss—Jeremy, that was his name—and lay out everything, do whatever it took to settle her debt to Gabriel.

But when it came to Rosie?

No. That door had already closed.

The way Nicola had acted, not even pausing to understand, unlike Gabriel, who was offering Rosie space and grace now—that had sealed their fate. That was the final blow, and Nicola knew it.

"Listen," said Gabriel. "The past week has been stressful. I know that."

Nicola nodded. Maybe the most stressful in her career.

"I think I know what we need to do."

"What's that?" Nicola said, pulling another tissue to wipe her nose. "What are we doing?"

"Get changed and meet me outside," Gabriel said. "We're doing something we should have done a long time ago."

* * *

Music, laughter and the clink of glasses drifted through the trees as Gabriel and Nicola approached the lakeside cabins, tucked around the point and well out of view and earshot of the inn's guests and neighbors.

Not all staff lived on-site. Those with families usually rented nearby, but the younger crew, new to long hours and eager to save money, stayed in the cabins. And as Nicola knew from kitchen chatter, they threw some legendary parties. It was a smart move on the property planner's part to tuck them away where their attempts at blowing off steam wouldn't be a nuisance to anyone.

Tonight, it seemed, there was much steam to blow off.

"Are you sure they want us here?" Nicola asked. She knew that her heightened vigilance in the kitchen that night was likely a contributor to her staff's need to let loose a little.

"Trust me," Gabriel said. "If we don't make a habit of it, a guest appearance here and there will actually mean a lot to them."

Nicola considered that. The magic of Alexi's kitchen had everything to do with his skill, but more than that, wasn't it how he treated his team? How seen and valued he made her feel?

"Okay," she said, still uncertain but willing to play along.

As they neared the bonfire, Leo and Sebastien looked up from their chairs. Sebastien blinked as though he thought he was hallucinating, then after a second let out a whoop. "Look who it is!" he called through the night. Soon the rest of the staff joined in with cheers as they registered who had just arrived. Nicola blinked, startled by the warmth of their welcome.

Gabriel had been right. They were wanted here.

Minutes later, Nicola had a cold can of Moosehead in hand and was amused to see Gabriel drink straight from his too. He'd unbuttoned his collar, hair slightly mussed, a bit of sweat shining on his brow. He fit in seamlessly. Gabriel was deep in animated French with Richard, the pastry chef. Nicola didn't catch a word, but whatever it was, it had them both in stitches.

"Nicola, do you play poker?" Richard turned to her and asked.

Nicola chuckled. It was clear Richard had already had a couple of drinks during the couple of games they'd played between lunch and dinner service. "You think I'm fresh meat or something? You're going down, *mon ami*," Nicola said. She followed Richard inside where a game was being set up.

An hour later, Nicola threw down a full house and grinned, pulling a big pile of chips toward her. "Sorry folks, but I play to win."

Richard cursed, something in French, and the rest of the group groaned.

"You brought this upon yourself, *mon ami*," Nicola said, laughing. From across the table, Gabriel was grinning at her.

Thank you, she mouthed across the table.

By the time tequila shots were being poured, well past one in the morning, Nicola knew it was her cue to leave.

After she and Gabriel finally said their good-nights, they stepped out to the group chanting "Legends! Legends!," laughter ringing through the cabin as they shook their heads and exited into the cool night air.

"That was something," Nicola said.

"It was fun," Gabriel agreed. "Hopefully they'll shut it down soon."

"I'm expecting more than one bleary face tomorrow," Nicola said with a shake of her head. "Though at that age, I could pull an all-nighter and still make it through a shift. Barely. Just barely."

Gabriel chuckled. "Not me. Always been a lightweight. Come on. I'll walk you home."

They strolled down the forest path in silence. Nicola had a buzz in her chest but a lighter heart than she'd ended her shift with. "Thanks again for taking me there," she said. "I think I needed that." She paused. "Maybe we all did."

Gabriel nodded. "Some of my best times in this job have been with the people. Remember the time on that slow service day, when my dad was out at that wedding—"

"And we blew up the caramel?" Nicola said, laughing at the memory of the dessert gone wrong. "You held up that baking sheet like a riot shield!"

"And good thing," Gabriel said. "I almost lost an eye!"

"We stayed hours after closing, remember?" Nicola said. She smiled at the memory of the two of them, cleaning rags in hand, scouring the walls of the kitchen and then, after borrowing a ladder from the convenience store across the street, the ceiling, which was speckled with candy. "Do you think your dad ever found out?"

"No, definitely not," Gabriel said. "I would have heard about it for sure."

"'*Mais enfin!*'" Nicola said, miming the old expression Alexi used to use when chastising his son or a member of his kitchen staff if they said something ridiculous or made a stupid mistake.

They both laughed as they reached the path from the road to Nicola's house.

Gabriel turned to face her. "You're a good person, Nicola. And a great chef. I'm starting to understand the pressure you've been putting on yourself. I want you to do your best to let it go. It's not serving you or our restaurant."

"What are you, my boss or something?" Nicola said, smiling lightly.

Gabriel grinned. "Happy to pull rank in this instance."

Nicola's instinct was to wave him away. But the couple of beers had made her feel light. Honest. Airy. "You're right," she said. "I've been starting to wonder if I'm past my peak. But maybe I've been my own worst enemy."

They were quiet for a moment, the only sound the light breeze through the tree canopy above, and the faint whir of June beetles.

"Get some sleep," Gabriel said. "We'll talk again tomorrow."

"'Kay." Nicola opened her arms and hugged Gabriel tightly. "I just want to do right by you. And your father. I want to be great again. I'm sorry if I've been anything but."

Gabriel pulled back and shook his head as he held

her shoulders. "Even at your worst, you're still the best," he said. "Good night, Nicola."

"Good night, Gabriel," she said.

He started walking away, and just as Nicola was about to close her door, his voice sounded again from down the path.

"Oh, and Nicola. Call Rosie," he called. "She's good for you."

Nicola took a sharp breath in at the mention of Rosie. "*Mais enfin!*" she shouted, doing her best to add a note of humor. Gabriel's laughter echoed down the lane. She pushed open her door and entered her dark and quiet cottage.

She stood in the dark hallway, remembering what it had felt like to have Rosie in her space. She'd always thought of the cottage as a retreat, her one piece of the world. Private, sacred. Letting someone in had seemed like a risk. A loss of control. But Rosie had surprised her. Even after just that one night, the cottage felt quieter now. Emptier. As if something essential had gone missing.

Had she overreacted? In some way, she felt like yes. But still. It felt like a betrayal, and she wasn't sure she could move on.

Should she take Gabiel's advice and call Rosie? What would she say? Did Nicola owe her a chance to explain?

If she was honest, what she wanted to say was that losing Rosie—again—felt like more than just regret.

It felt like grief.

Chapter Eighteen

Rosie stared at the blank screen in front of her, trying to conjure up some excitement about the street festival happening in Cabbagetown next weekend, a series of food trucks and tents operated by some great local shops and restaurants. She had a quote from the owner of St. Jamestown Steak and Chops, and she'd just gotten off the phone with one of the organizers to fill in some details about the event.

She closed her laptop and surveyed her office, which was a complete mess. Maybe some mindless organization would help clear her head, and she could take another stab at the article once she'd cleaned up some more.

She started with a file folder full of odds and ends that was sitting on top of a pile of books from her undergrad, style guides that were out of date and old journalism textbooks.

Why she'd kept any of this junk, Rosie didn't know. But somehow, tossing the old notebooks filled with notes she'd taken on location when out doing research felt wrong, as if somehow she'd need them one day.

So one by one, she stuffed them into an old banker's

box in the small office at *Savorist*, which in two weeks' time would host a not-for-profit dedicated to protecting the marshlands of the Greenbelt.

In the adjacent office, Rosie could tell from the drawers opening and closing and the sounds of stacks of paper being deposited into a recycling bin that Jeremy was doing the same thing. The sounds of Crosby, Stills, Nash and Young wafted over from his office. Rosie would miss the music. Jeremy always played music, and it was comforting to Rosie.

He'd done his best to assure Rosie that moving their operation online had been in the plans for a while, but Rosie wasn't fooled. Jeremy was old school. He loved coming into the office, spending the first part of the day chatting, spitballing ideas for features in an ad hoc, organic manner rather than on a planned Zoom meeting.

Rosie's article had even done reasonably well. It hadn't broken the internet in the way they'd initially hoped when the marketing department at Sugar Maple Farms had reached out. But their analytics showed twice as many page visits as usual, and several higher-profile publications had re-shared the link on social media.

But that was a week ago, and now it was back to business as usual, and Rosie would be writing her next piece about the upcoming gourmet-food-and-wine trade show from her home office or the coffee shop around the corner instead of *Savorist*'s office in Cabbagetown.

"I'm going over to the LCBO to get a few more boxes. Need any?" Jeremy called from the other room.

"I think I'm all set," said Rosie. "I'll be back tomorrow with my parents' car to pick up my stuff."

Jeremy appeared in the doorway. "Lunch after that?" he asked. "I heard the new pho place on Carleton is next level."

"Sounds great," Rosie said. She felt the urge to apologize to Jeremy again for the third time, but she knew she'd had enough, and she'd just start to cry anyway and they'd both just feel awkward about it all over again. "See you tomorrow," she said instead.

Jeremy's footsteps sounded down the stairs and moments later, the door closed. Rosie stood standing in her empty office. She shuffled through the last pile of papers on her desk, and the strip of photos of her and Nicola fell onto the table.

She picked it up again, and her heart bottomed out at the sight of their happy faces. That had been seven years ago, but she'd seen that look in Nicola's eyes again the night they spent together at Sugar Maple Farms, before Rosie had completely blown it.

If Nicola hadn't woken up, would Rosie have used what she'd seen to try to get more information from Nicola? Innocently, over breakfast?

She wasn't sure. So part of her felt like Nicola's outburst was warranted. Still, she hadn't even given Rosie a chance to explain.

The door creaked open again downstairs. Jeremy must have forgotten his phone or wallet.

Footsteps sounded again up the stairs as Rosie tucked the photograph into a file folder, placed it on top of a box. "I'll walk out with you," she called to Jeremy. She grabbed her purse from the hook on the back of the door.

She swung it open and came face-to-face with Nicola, holding a bouquet of lavender, cosmos and nigella.

Rosie blinked. Inhaled sharply. "I—you're—" Her heart thudded again the same way it had the first time she'd been alone with Nicola. She hadn't expected this. Not now.

She wore olive-green cargos, a white T-shirt and a very different expression from the last time Rosie had seen her.

She took in the hopeful look in Nicola's eyes, the perfection of her face, her soft, glowing skin.

Nicola extended the bouquet slightly. "I brought you these," she said. "From the farm."

Rosie accepted the bouquet and looked quizzically at Nicola. "Thank you," she said. "What are you doing here?"

She fished some papers out of her back pocket and unfolded them. Rosie's article. She'd read it.

"This was really good," she said, hesitantly. "And I behaved really badly."

Something caught in Rosie's throat. But Nicola wasn't done speaking.

"You did a beautiful job capturing the essence of the inn and of Sunset County. I've read it like ten times now, and honestly, if I ever have to leave the area, I'll bring this with me. So I can feel right back in the place again."

The words soaked in slowly, warm and unexpected. To hear Nicola speak so effusively about her work felt good. More than good. It was vindicating.

"But I know that wasn't supposed to be the point of

the article," Nicola continued. "It was meant to be about me. And I gave you nothing."

"That's not true," Rosie said softly. "That place is a part of you now. You gave me that."

Nicola shook her head. "I should have told you everything. I just..." Her voice faltered. She reached for Rosie's hand.

The warmth of Nicola's skin and the firm clasp of her hand assured Rosie this moment was real and not a figment of her imagination.

"I still haven't forgiven myself for a lot of things," Nicola continued, her eyes shining with sincerity. "And I wasn't ready to say them out loud. I'm really sorry you didn't get what you needed from me. And I'm sorry for how I behaved. I didn't even give you a chance to explain."

Rosie shook her head. It was everything she'd been waiting to hear, but now that Nicola was saying it, Rosie felt for her. The pain in her voice was clear, and all her armor was now fully shed. "I'm the one who should apologize. You're under no obligation to tell me anything. You deserve your privacy."

"Well, I want to tell you now," Nicola said, releasing Rosie's hand. "Will you have dinner with me? I want to tell you everything, no matter what you do with it after. I just want to share it with you, because you matter to me."

Rosie's grip tightened slightly over the bouquet. She hadn't expected any of this. The flowers, the apology, the softness in Nicola's voice. She didn't think she'd ever see Nicola again. And now Nicola was inviting Rosie to sit with her and hear her story.

"Okay," she said softly.

A light smile crossed Nicola's face. "Is it presumptuous that I booked a table in—" she stopped and glanced down at her watch "—twenty minutes?"

"Highly presumptuous," Rosie said, unable to hold back the wide grin that spread across her face. "And I'm starving."

"Then I know just the place," said Nicola, her eyes twinkling with delight.

Rosie tucked the bouquet under her arm, and together they ventured out into the sunshine of the hot summer evening, hand in hand.

Nicola was excited to take Rosie to Alexi's old restaurant, the classic French bistro featuring a side patio with tables covered in white tablecloths and a lattice overhead with hanging vines and little white lights. It was busy, as it always had been, but between the tables which were spaced out just enough and the light music that wafted from overhead speakers, the space had a nice easy energy but allowed for private conversation.

Their server led them to their table, which overlooked the street and enjoyed a nice breeze.

Even though Alexi wasn't visible through the back door leading to the kitchen, sitting down at the patio and drawing in the familiar scents of garlic and parsley felt like a homecoming for Nicola.

The new owners hadn't changed much. When they learned Nicola had returned, they managed to be warm and welcoming without intruding on her and Rosie's quiet dinner.

Over the next two hours, over plates of ratatouille, moules frites and sole in lemon-butter sauce, all Alexi's old classics, Nicola told Rosie everything.

Some parts of the story elicited laughter, and others brought Nicola to tears. She shared more about the hollow ache that came with her rise to celebrity, of the people she'd allowed to get close to her only to find that they wanted only to bask in the glow of her spotlight. She spoke of the guilt over the disaster that was Alexi's restaurant and then of what happened to Alexi himself. And finally, of the heavy sense of duty she felt toward Gabriel, a weight she'd carried alone for too long.

All through this, one by one, their waiter discreetly delivered all the dishes made from recipes that Alexi had once made in the bistro's kitchen, meals he'd taught Nicola how to cook, all the same flavors that had launched her career. It made her feel like Alexi was there with them and as though in the glow of the candlelight and the scent of lemon and butter, he was watching over her. And for the first time in years, the weight of it all began to lift.

When they walked out of the restaurant together, despite how much they'd eaten, Nicola felt lighter than she'd felt in years, like the burden of what she'd been carrying was starting to evaporate through the breeze.

She and Rosie walked hand in hand down Parliament Street, then through the cobblestone paths of the Distillery District right down to the waterfront, where the ferry from the islands had just docked and happy couples and families were disembarking.

"Ice cream?" Nicola asked, nodding toward a soft-serve truck.

"I couldn't eat another thing," Rosie said. "That was incredible."

"Come on. Kids cone?"

Rosie grinned. "Fine. I guess I could manage that."

They sat together on a bench overlooking the lake, the sun just set and the water rippling with the last pink shimmer of the sky. A flock of seagulls flew overhead, cawing in the breeze.

A wave of melancholy and nostalgia washed over Nicola until she turned to Rosie and found her licking her ice-cream cone, the golden glow off the water reflecting in her smiling eyes. Then, she just felt at peace. She'd made the right choice by coming here. And there was something else she wanted to do.

Nicola turned to Rosie and laid her hand on Rosie's thigh. "I want you to write the article," she said.

Rosie shook her head and lowered her ice-cream cone. "I get it now," she said. "Why you didn't want your story spread across the world. And I feel badly that I did anything to pressure you. You don't owe anyone anything."

"Really. I want you to write it. It feels, now…important. That others understand what happened." She paused. "I owe it to Alexi, and I owe it to you. You unlocked something in me, something that's holding me down for a long time now."

Rosie's gaze softened. "But I—"

"I want the story out," Nicola said firmly, "and I don't want it told by anyone but you. You're an exceptional writer, Rosie."

Rosie's eyes welled up, and she shook her head a little.

"What? Why are you upset?"

"I'm not," she said. "It's just…hearing you say that. It means a lot."

"I mean it," Nicola said. "Your sensory descriptions, the beautiful figurative language you use to bring the area to life… It's exquisite." She waited a moment. "So what do you think? Will you do it?"

"I'll do it," Rosie said slowly. "But on one condition."

"What's that?" Nicola said.

"I get to come back and visit Sugar Maple Farms." Rosie raised an eyebrow, mock-stern. "You never did make me that pie."

Nicola frowned slightly, searching for the memory.

"Peach," Rosie said, smiling. "You offered blueberry or peach. I'll take peach."

Nicola held her gaze. "I'll make you that pie. But I get a condition too."

"Is that right?" Rosie leaned in a little. "Okay. What is it?"

Nicola hadn't been sure if they'd get to this point in the conversation. But she'd been hopeful. And in this moment, it felt so right. "If you agree to come with me to France this November. For a chef's summit I've been invited to. After the article, I think it's time you start writing your book." She watched Rosie's expression shift from playful to surprised and then delighted.

"Think about it," Nicola continued, drinking in Rosie's delight, "you'll have all day to write while I'm working. And in the evenings, we can try new restaurants or cook whatever you found in the market that day. Three weeks of French-country living. And we can visit your grandmother."

Was it manipulative? No. They were beyond that. It was a promise, the kind they'd been unable to make all those years ago even though they'd both felt that perfect inevitability, the perfect match. It just hadn't been their time.

But now, if Nicola could bottle this exact moment, Rosie grinning in the fading light, the soft scent of vanilla lingering between them, she would. Sealing it up like preserves to savor through every long winter to come.

Rosie leaned into Nicola's arms, then looked up at her, grinning. "Yes," she said, making Nicola's heart soar. "Or should I say, *oui*!"

Epilogue

"Can I bring you a taste of the mille-feuille?" Leo asked Rosie as he passed by on his way to the kitchen balancing a tray of dishes. "Just a small bite to try?"

"I'm tempted. I heard it's to die for," she said. "But I'll pass for tonight. Thank you."

It had been near to impossible to turn down the various treats and dishes that the restaurant staff had offered as Rosie had sat at the bar for the past hour, nursing a martini and waiting for the moment that Nicola hung up her apron and came to collect her. Especially when she saw the delicate morsels and perfectly plated treats they whisked by on the way to their lucky diners. Tonight's menu looked sublime. Dungeness crab with spring-pea mousse and pickled spicebush berries. Halibut with fermented peach-leaf butter, honey-thyme lacquer and summer-squash ribbons. And the mille-feuille, a stacked pile of oat and spelt with bee-pollen crème and smoked honey drizzle.

But she'd politely declined each offer.

Nicola had promised Rosie a surprise at the end of service. And that surprise, Nicola had said, involved eating. So Rosie was content to defer gratification. Because any meal involving Nicola Kim, she knew, would be one to remember.

The dining room had almost emptied, and Rosie's instructions had been to arrive now, but she'd come early to observe the diners enjoying Nicola's cooking. Impossibly, it seemed that Nicola's skills and creativity had reached a whole new level over the past year, and watching the enjoyment on the faces of her patrons was better than any front-row theatre ticket she could imagine.

Rosie opened her bag slightly, feeling around for the manila envelope that held a surprise she'd been waiting for days to share with Nicola. It had been hard to keep the secret, but she knew it would be worth it to share at the exact right time.

"I see you're wearing a new dress," a voice called from behind her.

She turned to see Nicola, already changed out of her chef's whites into a pair of black jeans and a light blue T-shirt. Her gaze flitted across Rosie's outfit, a cream-colored slip dress threaded with the lightest of gold threads, making it shimmer in the dim lighting of the restaurant. She'd bought it when Nicola had informed her that there was a "special evening" and a "surprise" coming up.

"Is it acceptable?" Rosie asked, grinning.

The way Nicola looked at her made the question redundant. "You ready?"

"I'm ready. And very curious," Rosie said.

"Let's go."

Rosie followed Nicola through the kitchen exit to where Nicola's Jeep was parked outside. "We're going off-site?" she asked. She'd pictured the kitchen having emptied out and Nicola making her something to eat in the privacy of the dining room, or maybe going back to the cottage in the woods. Both would have been great options. But it seemed an adventure was in store.

With the warm summer breeze whipping through the open roof, Nicola guided them along the dark deserted country roads. When she turned off, Rosie spotted the little barn where Nicola had taken them on her tour of the area. It glowed in the distance.

"What's happening here?" Rosie asked.

"You'll see," said Nicola.

After they parked, Nicola led Rosie to the barn's entrance and pushed the door open. In the middle of the tidy space, which had walls lined with silver vats and a number of tools organized in piles, there was a table set up for two, with a blue checkered tablecloth and an arrangement of daisies in a Coke-bottle vase.

"Sit," Nicola said, gesturing to one of the two seats. "I'll be right back."

Rosie took a seat at the table while Nicola disappeared into the back of the barn, emerging moments later with a tray of oysters and all the accoutrements. "I thought you could do the honors," she said, passing Rosie the shucker. "Now that you're a pro."

"I had a pretty fabulous teacher," Rosie said as she picked up one of the shells with a tea towel and, seconds later, popped it easily, separated the shell and laid it down on the bed of shaved ice.

"I'll leave you to it," Nicola said. Nodding with approval. "I've got one more thing to prepare."

Rosie continued to work on the oysters, listening as there was some clinking in the back area. Nicola returned holding a bottle and two flutes, which she deposited on the table.

"This," she said proudly, "is the very first uncorking of my Pétillant Rosé. I wanted to wait for you to try it." She pushed it toward Rosie. "And I wanted you to see the label."

Rosie put the tea towel and shucker down and picked up the perspiring bottle, examining the label, a simple and elegant design with what looked like a hand-painted pink alabaster rose next to gold lettering. She squinted, then laughed as she read the text, looking up at Nicola, eyes wide. "La Vie en *Rosie*?" she exclaimed. "You named this after me?"

"Sure did," Nicola said. She took the bottle from Rosie's hands and pulled the metallic closure from the top, then twisted the cork until the pop sound reverberated through the space.

She tipped the bottle into two delicate crystal flutes. The wine was a soft pink, with delicate bubbles and a fizz that settled quickly. Nicola passed Rosie a glass, then held up her own. "To the woman who made my life...well...*rosy* again."

Rosie clinked her glass against Nicola's and held her gaze as she took in a short draw, taking in the scent of wild strawberry, watermelon rind and a hint of honeysuckle and wet stone. "Mmm," she said, closing her eyes lightly. "It's perfect." She took another sip and let the flavors fizz and dance on her tongue for a moment before she swallowed.

Nicola tasted from her glass and then nodded. "I'm glad you think so. Because I have almost three hundred cases. We'll use most of them in the restaurant, but I want to make sure we put a few aside. For our own celebrations." Hearing Nicola say it was magic.

The last year had been perfection. The trip to France was something out of a dreamscape—a haze of cobblestone streets, church bells, buzz of mopeds, local wines served in pot Lyonnais, sugar-coated almonds and cheese and crusty baguettes. Rosie had filled several notebooks with notes during the day, and at night, after meeting her grandmother for a walk through the town square, she and Nicola had luxuriated in the glow of the setting sun.

When they'd returned, it had only been a few months of back-and-forth from the city to Sunset County before they'd decided that where they both wanted to be was the little cottage at the edge of the inn's property. Both had wondered if it would feel cramped and they'd be eager to move, but so far, with the hours Nicola kept, it didn't feel small. They liked being close. Rosie was working remotely for *Savorist,* whose readership had grown enough since her article's publication to keep publishing for the time being. Jeremy planned to retire soon, and they'd come to an agreement that if Rosie wanted to take the helm, she could, or they would celebrate with a final issue that they would all feel good about.

"Have an oyster," Nicola said, nudging the metal platter toward her.

Rosie picked one up and spooned a small clump of

horseradish and added a small dash of hot sauce before tilting it back into her mouth. "Perfection," she said after swallowing, then took another sip of her drink. "I have a surprise for you too," she said. She pulled the envelope out of her bag and passed it to Nicola.

"What's this?" Nicola said, raising an eyebrow.

Rosie grinned. "Open it," she said.

Nicola slid a piece of paper from the envelope, and Rosie watched in anticipation as Nicola scanned the document, then looked up at her, eyes wide. "Is this what I think it is?" she exclaimed.

"Yup," Rosie said. "A deal memo for my first book. It'll be on shelves this time next year."

After her article had been published, Rosie had spent the next several months in between her *Savorist* assignments working on her book, a fictional account of her grandmother's life set in the sun-soaked fields of France. She'd shopped it around to a few agents who specialized in similar books and signed quickly with a woman named Adelaide Moore, who'd called Rosie's writing "delectable."

And only three days earlier, she'd opened her inbox to find an email from Adelaide, with details of an offer from Wooden Table Books, an offshoot of a Big Five publisher.

The advance wasn't going to make her rich, but it was enough to signal to Rosie that the publisher would ensure her book saw the light of day.

Nicola let out a whoop, put the paper down on the table, then tugged Rosie up out of her chair and wrapped her in a tight squeeze. She stood on her tiptoes and kissed Rosie on the top of her head. "I'm so proud of you," she whispered softly into her ear. "I knew it was only a matter of time."

The warmth of Nicola's breath on her neck and her validation of Rosie's talent made her shiver. It might be just one book contract—and it wasn't like she hadn't been published before, with *Savorist*—but in that moment, she felt like she'd conquered the world, and as happy as she'd been when she'd gotten the news from Adelaide, now everything felt perfect.

"So wait," Nicola said as she tipped some more bubbly into Rosie's drink. "Does this mean you're going to be famous or something?"

Rosie grinned. The old her would have said forget it. The book would do okay, if she was lucky. But the new Rosie was dreaming big. "*NYT* bestseller or bust," she said, laughing. Although the truth was she didn't need the validation anymore. Life was feeling...complete.

"And will there be a book two?"

"Fingers crossed," said Rosie. "I just need to come up with a new premise. And a new location."

"Well, funny thing is..." Nicola said, her eyes dancing in delight. "Gabriel just let us know that Sugar Maple Farms will close for the month of November. They have a few upgrades to the property planned, so after the peak of fall colors and before people start traveling for the holidays, it seemed like the best time to close. So I happen to find myself with some time on my hands..."

"And a willingness to travel?" Rosie asked, grinning. Her mind raced with possibilities. There were, of course, other locations in France they could explore. Provence, Alsace, the Loire Valley. But beyond, San Sebastián, Kyoto, Oaxaca, Marrakech, Kerala…the possibilities were limitless.

Rosie breathed in deeply, picturing the next few months before they embarked on their adventure, and even staying put felt like the vacation of her dreams. Long days in the cabin with her laptop, dreaming up her next story. Taking breaks to walk in the woods or swim in the cool waters of Lake Shaughnessy. Greeting Nicola at the end of her long shifts. Life with the woman of her dreams.

"Yes," Rosie said, with utter confidence. "Yes to all of it."

"Wait here," said Nicola. She got up from her seat and disappeared again into the back area. Moments later, she reappeared with a cart that clattered with silver-topped dishes as it moved across the floor, her eyes alight with pleasure. "Now. Let's eat."

* * * * *